MADE IMMORTAL

THE BLOOD REGENT 2

MARISSA ALLEN

Made Immortal: The Blood Regent 2

Copyright © 2023 by Marissa Allen

All rights reserved.

This is a work of fiction. Names, characters, places, and events are used fictitiously and any resemblance to actual events, locales, or persons is entirely coincidental.

This book or any portion thereof may not be reproduced or used in any manner whatsoever without the express written permission of the publisher except for the use of brief quotations in a book review.

Edited by Cait Marie

DEDICATION

It took me some time to be able to finish this book, but I made it. I want to thank my husband for always being my cheerleader. This is also for all of my readers.

Just remember you can do anything you put your mind to. Remember that if you have a dark day that tomorrow is another chance for the sun to shine. Don't be afraid to reach out to the people who love you.

The world is better with you in it.

1

The door opened and shut quietly, followed by a soft rustling. Slowly I closed my laptop and looked over from my place on the couch. Gwen was making her way to the kitchen awkwardly with the groceries. Uncrossing my legs, I shot up to grab one of the bags from her as it slipped out of her grasp, managing to catch it before it hit the ground.

"I'm never going to get used to the smog here," Gwen said as she shook out her hair after dropping the other bags.

I had to agree with her, my dad had sent us to Neria over a month ago to get ready for this mission and the sky still seemed unnatural. "Well, hopefully, we won't have to deal with it much longer." Although, I had a gut feeling that wasn't going to be the case.

Neria was the neighboring kingdom, and the feud between our ruling families went back hundreds of years. We thought it was over after my mother died and my father had to re-marry. My stepmother comes from here, you see. Her father, King Edgar Ravensbone, was still the ruling monarch here in Neria. The wedding was supposed to be a truce, but my father had been naïve in that thought. What we didn't know was that she was planning a coup to take power. Which involved getting my father to fake his death by holding me hostage for leverage and convincing the people I was sick and couldn't come into public any longer.

What really happened was she had locked me away to be experimented on and tortured for six years. Some might have described it as a lab, but I saw it for what it was: a prison. I was twelve when she took me. When I should have been growing and finding out who I was, instead, I lost all of that time to terror and pain. Now, at the age of twenty, I was trying to figure out who I was.

I'd been with Chase and the team since I was rescued two years ago. Since then, I'd gotten used to my role, and the team had gotten used to working together. We were now a well-oiled machine. We'd been sent on all kinds of crazy missions in those years. We'd even been here once already, almost a year ago.

This place was so strange compared to home. There was no nature anywhere. Everything was paved over, metal, glass, or plastic. The buildings speared into the sky, and if you caught the sun at just the wrong time it could blind you. I missed the forests and farms of home.

While we were in Neria, on top of our mission, we also hoped to cause some trouble for my dear old step-grandfather. The fact of the matter was, if we kept the Nerians busy, they wouldn't be able to keep sending Esmerelda help to fight us back home. This would help us strike a blow for the Kabrian people without even being within our borders.

I looked up as there was a clamor of feet making their way to the kitchen. Benson, David, and Atty came busting into the room with the smiles of jackals. David went straight to one of the bags to start searching through it.

Made Immortal

"Hi, Gwen. Thanks for doing the shopping." David looked up to give her a quick peck on the cheek and squeezed her shoulder. Atty leaned back against a wall of the kitchen, and Gwen's gaze landed on him a bit longer than necessary. Atty returned the look from under the hair hanging in his face, and Gwen's cheeks turned just the lightest shade of pink.

"Yum, what did you bring us?" Benson asked, chuckling. "I've been craving those peppers."

"Don't worry there are some in there," she said, then she tapped David on the shoulder and handed over a jar of peanut butter that had been in a different bag, as if knowing exactly what he was searching for. He grinned and hugged her quickly before running back to his room. He had been tinkering on something in there for hours.

I was leaning against the island when there was a slight pressure against my arm. A hand ran its way to my shoulder as someone came up behind me. I knew it was Chase. I could tell when he entered a space; his aura seemed to be on its own frequency just for me. I leaned back into his firm embrace, and he kissed the top of my head. As always, the softest of his touches sent shivers through me as he pulled my hair over one shoulder, kissing along my neck like a butterfly brushing me with its wings. I could feel the collective eye roll from everyone in the kitchen.

"Hey, how was it out there?" Chase asked Gwen, his breath skimming across the tender skin of my neck. Electricity sparked as his fingers trailed so lightly from behind my ear, down my neck, and kept slipping lower. I felt the rumble of his chuckle vibrating into me as he wrapped me tight within his arms.

Gwen leaned back against the sink and crossed her arms. "It's getting worse. The tighter a grip they try to keep

3

on people, the more chaos it causes. People are starving, being kidnapped, and the young are starting to fight back. They're going to cut the rations to the edges of the city again." She chewed on her lip.

I could tell she was worried. She had such a big heart, and I couldn't help but fee it too. These people needed help just as badly as ours did back in Kabria. We had heard rumblings of a movement against what they were starting to call *a military occupation of the city.*

Chase nodded, and I could feel part of him tense as he no doubt started to calculate that into how to proceed. The fact that Neria was at a boiling point something we always had to keep in mind, as any movement could change the plan. We all had been taking shifts, making sure to keep up to date on the news cycle, as well as any resistance chatter. We hoped nothing too explosive would happen until after we were able to make our move.

Benson clapped his hands and broke the spell we all had seemed to fall under, then he gestured for Gwen to get out of the way. "All right, out, all of you; I have work to do. Dinner will be ready shortly."

We all made our way to the other areas of the house. Atty and Gwen headed toward David's room. Chase took my hand, and we walked into the living room that was set up with a massive computer array that tracked multiple cameras throughout the city. He tugged and twirled me into a quick dance, his hands pulling me close and swaying. I leaned my head against his chest, feeling his heartbeat and his deep, even breathing.

As much as I loved this feeling being held, the need to get back to work was tugging at me. I leaned up and kissed him softly, before pulling away, going to sit chair in front of the screen, and started to cycle through the live feed of the

Made Immortal

city. An algorithm was using facial recognition to try and find certain targets we were looking for.

Hiding in the chaos of the summit, there would be a black-market sale of a weapon of mass destruction. Stopping the sale was the mission, by whatever means necessary. Scientific curiosity to make the world a better place was often the basis for some of the deadliest technology in history. The recent development up for auction was nanobots that could release any type of pathogen. Something that could be used for healing, but instead, it would no doubt be used for death and to spread terror.

I held out a badge to Chase with the name Charles printed on it under a small photo of him. He took it from me nodding. It was for his first day of work the next day.

We had been getting most of the team jobs over the last few weeks. We made friends at some companies that would be helpful and nudged the team's resumes to the top of the lists. Chase was starting with a security firm tomorrow that, among other things, was hired for the Neria Tech Summit.

David was the first one we placed. He'd been working as an entry-level assistant with one of the companies premiering a new product at the summit. He'd already hacked into their security system and would get us cleared that day.

Chase would have access to the security team's communications, so he would be able let us know what's going on and lead anyone off our trail if we need to make a quick exit.

And if that swift exit became necessary, Atty's new work in maintenance would help. He would be setting up those escape routes, as well as ways to trap pursuers.

Gwen had started working with a catering company as a waiter for the many parties of the wealthy. She had been gathering intel at a surprising rate, as there seemed to be parties or celebrations for any occasion and "the help" to these people were of absolutely no consequence. At the summit, she would sneak in weapons with the catering and then stash them for us.

And finally, I would be going as an angel investor, or someone who gives money to companies who they believe in, with Benson acting as my guard. That would allow us to move about the summit freely and gather intel. The goal was to get entry to the big sale, so we'd been putting out rumors to build the reputation of my shell company since we arrived a few weeks ago. If we pulled this off, we could possibly set the tech and weapons companies of Neria back months or maybe even years.

While we waited and prepped for the summit the experience of living in Neria was soul crushing. People in the outer city were disappearing in droves, and so far, we hadn't been able to find where they were being taken. I knew why, though; I had seen it before. It was the best way to get test subjects that would likely die in the process without any unnecessary questions.

When it came to the missing, I was obsessed. When I wasn't working on getting ready for the summit, I was searching. I knew I worried Chase and the others. They helped me track down leads and went with me as I searched the city as often as they could, but they knew I wouldn't be free from this burden as long as the missing were out there. I felt this connection to every one of them and every family who didn't know what had happened to their loved ones. They were experiencing the pain and the fear I had spent six years enduring. The despair that they would die there, and no one was coming to save them. They needed me, and so far, I had failed them. I wouldn't stop until they were all safe.

Made Immortal

While we searched, we saw the conditions the others were living in. It was inhumane. They were barely able to provide food for their families, even while working in the factories that were making them sick. Medicine was nowhere to be found, and when you could it was too high a price to obtain. Some housing had no heat, no insulation, sometimes no running water.

To make it worse the rich acted as if the country had never been more prosperous, touting that it was shining with all of the technological advancements.

After being here in Neria and seeing where Esmerelda came from, understanding her culture, she was even more terrifying. They were ruthless, sharp like the scalpels she used against her test subjects. The last time Esmerelda and I crossed paths, she snapped my wrists like twigs with her bionic arms. She possibly had other upgrades; I wouldn't have been surprised if she did.

We'd seen so many strange body augments in our short time here. The rich get bionic upgrades for fun. Whereas, for the poor, sometimes it was their only option for health care. They were given faulty units that were infected with malware. The prosthetics didn't fit. Parts that shouldn't rust have rusted. The gap between those with means and those without was mind blowing.

I went back to scanning the computer fees, seeing if there were any new leads on the missing. As I started to dive into the dark web, Chase set down the badge next to his keys and spun me in the chair toward him.

"Vi, look at me." His firm tone had me gazing up at him. He took my hands in his and pulled me up into a hug. "You are doing as much as you can." He held me tighter. My tense muscles started to relax. He had been giving me this reminder often. He knew I wasn't taking it well that we had no leads on where the missing had gone and that I blamed myself. He'd started this mantra as a way to get me out of my head.

I hugged him back, burying my face into his shoulder.

"I will find them," I said firmly, and he nodded, his chin finding a place to rest on top of my head. After another moment, we pulled apart and went to sit on the couch. My stomach grumbled, the smells wafting from the kitchen reminding me how hungry I was. He grabbed one of my hands and started to massage my palm and arm, then he moved to my other hand.

I had spent so many hours and days diving into the dark web to get leads on the missing Nerians. Then, when I had a lead, I was rushing off to find out what I could. Too many of them brought me to dead ends. My muscles were tense all the time, and I always felt on edge. I missed the fields and trees from home. I hated being surrounded by the metal, glass, and smog of Neria

"Dinner will be ready in five," Benson called from the kitchen. Chase and I headed in there to set the table.

"Benson, you are a culinary genius, and I can't wait to dig in," Chase said.

With his hands in oven mitts and his *Kiss the Cook* apron on, Benson brought over the mashed potatoes and rosemary chicken. It looked amazing and smelled better.

But the hair on the back of my neck stood up as the others came into the room. I turned to find David rubbing his face and the other two looking shock.

2.

"What happened?" Chase asked, shoving his chair back as he stood.

I, on the other hand, sat hard into my chair.

"Joseph called," David said after taking a deep breath.

"And?" Chase asked.

"Attikus is set to be executed tomorrow." The air seemed to still as we processed what David just said.

The mission we had been sent on to Neria last year was to rescue the doctor Joseph Acron out of Neria after his cover helping the rebels had been exposed. Attikus Star had been there when we rescued Joseph. The duo originally started helping the rebels when they had learned what Joseph's scientific breakthroughs had been used for. Joseph's research was the basis for the experimentation on myself and others.

Attikus was part of a rich and powerful family and had been helping the resistance from his place of power with information. We had offered to take him to Soland with Joseph, but he had decided to stay to help in the way he could. They had also been the ones to provide the information about weapon that was being sold at the summit. Attikus had been instrumental in us even being here right now.

"We have to get him," Gwen said, looking at Chase.

"Of course we do. Do we have a location?" Chase asked, and David nodded.

"Turin Square," Atty said, which made Chase, Benson, and I gasp.

"The square? It's public?" Absentmindedly my hand reached for my throat, then dropped to my chest. Like the pressure could calm my racing heart, which it didn't.

"They are going to do hooded hangings as a deterrent against traitors," David said.

"It's barbaric." Gwen's lip curled and her nose wrinkled. Her disgust was clear on her face.

"Let's pull up what we can and make a plan," Chase said, and he and David wandered off with their heads together.

I stared at the food in front of us, knowing none of us were hungry any longer.

"We'll get him," Benson said firmly, but I couldn't shake the terrible feeling that came over me. I schooled my features not to convey my feelings to the others.

"I can't believe we didn't hear anything about them even being on to Attikus," I muttered.

"Vi, we can't see and hear everything. Now, we know, and we'll go get him." Gwen patted my hand. "Something must have just happened and they are rushing to cut off all loose ends. We still have time to save him."

I was too anxious to keep sitting around. I stood quickly. "I'm going to get changed."

Everyone else agreed, and we all headed off to our rooms. Chase grabbed my arm as I passed through the living room. David turned to look at the screen Chase was pointing at.

"Here, look. They're setting up in the square; everyone is there for treason, so all five of them will have their faces covered. They'll have to bring them out with guards, and because it's public, we'll be able to get closer. We're going to have you be a diversion since your persona non grata there already," he said, looking to me. "The rest of us will be able to get closer to the guard, attack all at once, and in the commotion, get out. We'll have Gwen in a sniper nest. It starts at sunrise. If we leave in the next hour, we'll get there a few hours early to get set up."

"Sounds good. I'll make sure I wear my suit." My chest tightened as I saw the tiniest flinch from Chase. I knew he hated when I used myself as bait, but it had come in useful more than once. I was the one best equipped and most capable of protecting myself.

The first thing Chase, David, and I worked on almost two years ago was a specialty suit for me. In the versions since David had come up with a stronger material and slim armor sections that wouldn't impede my movement. Its color could also shift and blend into the dark, and it was skin-tight. At least if I was ever caught, I looked fabulous in it. My arms and legs were reinforced to take high-impact assaults and give some protection against bullets if they weren't direct hits. There was a mask made of nanomaterials that would build up from the neck to cover my head. My favorite parts were the soles that muffled my steps.

David had also just finished the prototype of nanoweapons that would swell from the wristbands, which I could control with the tiniest movements they picked up from the muscles in my hands and arms. I could create any type of hand-combat weapon or shield with small movements. I hadn't used them in an actual fight yet, but tonight was as good of a test as any.

Chase nodded to David, and he gave us both a wave. David sat back down to look into more details on the data Joseph had sent over as I turned away to head back to our room.

Anger boiled up within me. When Chase and David had first rescued me, I had been terrified and angry over my own trauma. As the months dragged on, the more missions we went on and the more I saw of the world, an underlying rage built inside me. How had the ruling elite let this happen to their people? How could anyone see the amount of pain and do nothing, or even make it worse? How could they not see the worth of those lives? The more I saw, the more it hurt and the angrier it made me.

Chase and I were both quiet as we changed and gathered our weapons. David had built the suit to respond to certain touches, making it knit together on command instead of having to zip anything. It was like a second skin, and a wave of calm washed over me as it slid closed. Since being rescued by the rebels, I had very quickly grown comfortable with fighting.

The experiments the queen put me through had succeeded. I healed quickly, I was strong, I was fast, I could hear more sharply, and I could see more clearly. I was always hungry now because of the changes, but other than that, I was *more* now than I had been.

While most of the time these days I felt like I was crawling out of my skin with my anxiety, when I put on the suit, a strange calm fell over me. Fighting was what I was good at; this was what I knew I could do. I shook out my shoulders and bounced on the balls of my feet a few times. Turning, I caught Chase chewing his lip as he watched me.

12

Made Immortal

"Please be careful," he said quietly.

"I'm always careful." I walked to him and wrapped my arms around his neck. I wanted him to feel the same confidence I did. How I felt almost invincible. I pressed my body to his and kissed him.

"You are never careful," he mumbled in a grumpy tone, pulling back to look into my eyes.

I could see his concern for me. I could feel it, but I was scared that the rest of them would be hurt. The same attack would harm them more than myself. Keeping them safe was my top priority. We did not agree on the level of risk that was acceptable to do so, and we probably never would.

"I always come home," I said, smiling softly at him.

"But one day, you won't if you keep going like this." His features hardened at the thought, and he pulled away to go back to the others.

I stood there for a moment, biting my lip. I didn't like worrying him, but he wasn't going to stop me from protecting the people I loved, even if it meant putting myself in a dangerous situation. I was built for this. At times, I wondered if I might not be able to do anything else, and I couldn't lie to myself about the fact that I enjoyed the fight; I enjoyed the risk. It cleared my head like nothing else could.

I grabbed his hand and pulled it to my lips for a kiss. We shared a look and I saw him soften. His stupid smirk spread across his face, and he grabbed me quick for a kiss before pulling me out into the hallway. The tension was gone, we had work to do.

When I made it into the living room, I noticed how pale David was. He looked sick. The fear for Attikus and what this outcome would mean for Joseph as well was clear. David had become close with Joseph since we got him out of Neria. They were collaborating constantly via vid screens and sharing their work on reverse engineering the work the queen had done to me, seeing if it might be possible to save any of the other people we might find. Joseph was the only doctor I trusted. The only one I would let near myself or my blood needed for the research.

I walked up behind David and set a calming hand on his shoulder. He reached up to cover it with his own.

"While you guys head there, I'll be working on hacking into the city systems in the area to give you as much help that way as I can," David said quietly. "I'll keep Joseph updated with the progress too." He nodded at the screen, and I saw he was connected with Joseph on a video call.

"We'll get him," I said firmly to Joseph. He gave a stiff nod, but it was obvious to see how upset he was.

"Thank you, Vi. It means the world to me that you'll help," he replied.

"Always. Anything," I said and gave David another quick squeeze before I pulled away to go stand with the others.

"Benson, I've sent the directions to your comm," David called out, turning his chair to us as everyone else started grabbing their gear.

We nodded and went to follow Benson as he grabbed the keys to the van.

3

In the short distance to the square there were fires, streets blocked off, and military and police throughout the city that we had to try to avoid. We did have to go through one checkpoint, but we were all wearing a type of uniform and kept our heads down. We got a nod at our papers that David had made for us.

Gwen made her way out first, heading for a rooftop that would suit her needs. The rest of us hung tight where we'd stopped in a parking building near the square. As the first light of the sun emerged, people started to sprinkle into the square—tired but still buzzing with anticipation for the upcoming deaths of the 'traitors'. We blended in and made our way to different areas of the stage. I held my hood close to hide my face; I wouldn't be needed until the event was starting.

The others checked in as they made it to their positions. I weaved my way through the crowd, working my way to a relatively easy-to-climb building.

As the guards moved into position the crowd started to cheer and howl. A man in a fine-looking uniform came to the top of the stage. The PA system picked up his voice, but not before a terrible sound from feedback made everyone flinch.

"Good morning, citizens of Cinder City," he said, throwing his arms wide. The crowd lurched and yelled, whipping themselves into a frenzy like sharks after chum. "We have for you today, justice against these traitors to your country! To your king!"

More cheers from the crowd.

"Bring the prisoners," the man called.

I unzipped my jacket and dropped it. My hair fell around my shoulders as I climbed up the ladder to the fire escape. I saw a few people watch me, pointing and gasping. Slowly, more and more looked my way as they noticed the others.

I touched my neck, and my own voice started to echo through the crowd. The suit locked onto the soundwaves and took over the PA system. "*You* are the traitors to your country."

My voice seemed to shock the rest of the crowd. All eyes turned my way. The guards were halfway to the stage with the prisoners when they all came to a stop as confusion appeared to sweep over everyone.

I stood on the edge of the fire escape. My arm kept me locked in place but leaning over the people below me. A small streak of sunlight landed on me, breaking through the buildings around us.

Even though he wasn't linked to the PA system anymore, I could hear the man on stage and the radios to the others.

"Get her! That's Genevieve Astor; they want her dead or alive!" Almost all of the guards pointed their weapons toward me. Bullets rang out, and the crowd screamed and started to scatter out of the square. With the sheer number of people pushing their way into alleys, I saw some who fell get trampled by the panicked others. I flinched, adding their lives to my ledger.

I launched off the fire escape, flipping through the air and aiming for the stage. The guns trained toward the sky and then, before they could think about it, at each other as I landed. I knew the others were here working to get the prisoners out, but I couldn't see any of them. My focus was on the guards, trying to keep everyone's attention on the stage and letting the mobs dissipate.

With a flick, a nanoweapon dagger was in my hand. As hard as steel but completely under my control if I need an edited form. I slashed at the men closest to me and saw the man in charge trying to flee. I threw the dagger. It stayed in its form, locked to its last instruction, and slammed into his back, making him topple forward.

"I've got one prisoner," Chase said into our comms.

"I have two," from Benson.

"I have another," Atty said. "Who has the last one?"

"They're by the stairs. I think they're hit," Gwen called from her perch into her own comm. I heard the thunk of her bullet sinking into someone's chest, then another and another. She didn't let up.

Spinning, a shield came into existence on my arm. Lurching forward I hit a guard running my way— tossing them back. A volley of bullets came from my right, and I made another shield appear. Not being quite fast enough some slipped past and hit my suit, but most were knocked away. Pushing toward the stairs; I grabbed a gun off one of the guards and sprayed at their knees as I slid off the edge of the stage.

I threw two daggers, and the nearest guards went down.

Scrambling as quickly as I could. I made it to the person on the stairs, their simple frock covered in blood. As I pulled off the hood I activated a force shield to block both of us from the guns firing behind us.

Attikus's eyes were full of fear; he was clearly having a hard time breathing. Blood poured from a gash under his hands. My heart stopped, and grief washed over me. I could tell there were only moments left.

"I'm so sorry." My voice, barely as whisper, caught in my throat and tears welled in my eyes. "We tried."

His eyes closed, and I felt his presence fade.

Still linked to the PA system, my scream of grief echoed in the square. I gave myself a moment, then two, but then it was time to get back to work. I looked up and locked eyes on one of the security cameras. They would know who had been here.

"Go. Everyone out," I growled into my comm. I reached down and grabbed Attikus. All of the guards were down and groaning, or not moving at all. Chase ran to me. He took Attikus and headed to one of the escape cars we had left in different routes. As soon as Chase put him down and climbed in I turned to face the square once more. I heard him pull the door closed and they sped away.

Looking around, I waited for the right moment— the Nerian reinforcements were coming into the square. Once they were close enough, I turned and ran. Grabbing a nearby hoverbike and I sped down an alleyway. A large portion of the new wave followed me in a completely different direction from my friends.

They chased me through most of the city, but I lost them by jumping off under a bridge and moving to a hover-board. Heaviness hit me seeing people huddled around trash cans filled with items on fire for warmth.

Made Immortal

My route took me across the city, back tracking, crossing my paths in different directions, leaving hints of my route as I did. If the people chasing me did find them, it would take them on even more of a wild goose chase.

The longer I was gone, the stiffer and sorer I got. As the adrenaline faded, I realized how many hits had gotten past my shields. By the time I had made it to the house, I was limping. Stiffly, I pushed through the front door. Chase's head snapped up, and he rushed over.

While the suit regenerated when it was slashed or punched through, the wounds under it didn't. The way Chase put a hand to the side of my face, I knew I must have been bleeding.

"Gods, Vi," he whispered.

"I always come home."

He furrowed his brow at my repeated words but helped me farther into the apartment. He got us to the couch, and we both dropped down. Everyone was quiet.

Chase seemed to sense the question on my mind. "David let Joseph know what happened."

I nodded and glanced at David, who looked terrible. He just shook his head, got up, squeezed my shoulder, and then walked to his room.

"Who was everyone else?" I asked, searching around. None of them seemed to be here.

"It was Attikus's driver, cook, assistant, and his contact with the rebels. The contact had a safe house they could take everyone to, getting them out of the city and protected. They'll contact us if they need any assistance. They took

Attikus with them, and they'll get him back to his family," Chase said.

Chase and I exchanged a glance. He looked like he wanted me to himself, and I needed to be alone with him. It was getting difficult to keep myself together. The shaking was starting, my breathing quick and shallow. He took my hands and pulled up to take me back to our room, as if reading my mind. I would check in with the others when I managed to pull myself together. I didn't want them to see me crack. He closed the door with a soft click behind us. Then, he turned to me, and his hands lightly ran over me, seeing where I flinched.

My lip quivered, and I threw my arms around him. Chase held me close as I broke into sobs.

I failed. Again. Another friend dead. I couldn't breathe. I could feel myself slipping. I wanted to scream.

We slid to the ground, and Chase held me as I rocked and shook, crying softly.

Slowly, my breaths came more evenly. Slowly, I ran out of tears. I was so tired. My entire body was heavy, and I felt like I was in a fog. Chase tapped my shoulders and released the edges of the suit so he could start checking my shoulders and neck for injuries.

My mind wandered to the sight of Attikus, terrified and knowing he was dying. I couldn't save him. Joseph was going through this loss, and it was my fault. The tower of names of people I couldn't save was so tall it was leaning, ready to topple and bury me.

Chase must have felt me tense up because he kissed me firmly and gave me the look. The look I got when I was too far into my head. He pulled at my suit, and I slipped the rest of the way out. I laid back on the bed, flinching as I did, finding new wounds. Chase shook his head and walked to

Made Immortal

the nightstand to grab the medical kit. It was always within reach these days.

As I laid back against the pillows, I felt relief wash over me. I sunk into the bed, and it couldn't have been more than moments before darkness engulfed me.

4

I groaned as I touched my hand to my forehead. My entire body ached. I threw my arm back down on Chase's side of the bed, but he wasn't there. Flinching, I pushed myself up on my elbows as our door opened. Chase came in with juice in one hand and a bowl of fruit in the other for breakfast.

"Morning," I muttered.

Chase smiled as he sat down next to me, handing over the fruit and setting the juice on the nightstand. Far away enough that I knew it would smart something fierce to reach for it, which may or may not have been on purpose. His smirk gave me my answer.

"Afternoon." He chuckled and ran his finger down my cheek.

"Gods, please tell me it's only tomorrow," I said, taking a bite out of a strawberry.

He nodded then took a deep breath before diving in. "Vi, you have to stop taking so many chances."

"I'm fine." I couldn't help throwing myself back on the pillows. "It's my job to keep all of you safe. Even with the

Made Immortal

risks, it wasn't enough to save him," I snapped, and he arched his brow in frustration at me, and I deflated quickly and sighed. "This is the best way to keep all of you safe. Even with my risks it wasn't enough. I won't be able to live with myself if anything happens to any of you. I know the risks I take. You can't just tell me to stay home."

"I'm not telling you to stay home. I'm just asking if you could not act as a human shield all the time. The suit isn't completely impenetrable," he said, pointing at my almost healed cuts and bruises. "Your luck isn't going to hold out forever."

"You can't hold me to the standards of the rest of you," I muttered. "I'm not like you. I can expose myself to a larger amount of danger and not be at any more at risk than the rest of you behind me."

Chase huffed and crossed his arms but didn't press it further. This was not the first argument about this, and I knew it wasn't going to be the last. David creating more safety gadgets for the team was our compromise. After testing my suit a few weeks ago, David had almost finished the ones for the rest of the team. Apparently, next up was a more compact suit that could be summoned at will—like my mask—out of a belt or bracelet. The replicating nanobots were the same reason the suit seamed itself and created my unlimited projectiles and weapons.

"I have to get ready; I have my first shift in about an hour." Chase gestured toward the living room. "David and Atty are back, and Gwen already headed out. I think Benson is still sleeping too."

I nodded and flinched as I shifted my position, but the ache was easing. "Have a good day. Be safe," I said as he pulled off his t-shirt and grabbed his work shirt. I bit my lips, watching him, his body intoxicating to me, but then I

23

noticed the bruises on his back. "What happened? Are you okay?"

I tried to get up, but he gently pushed me back.

"A few guards got in some good shots with batons when the chaos started. It's nothing." He shot a stern look my way.

"Hypocrite," I huffed." Just be careful."

I couldn't help but smile as he walked toward me tucking in his shirt. He gave me a quick kiss on the forehead and tapped my nose. I leaned back against the headboard, rested my wrist on my knee, and bit into another strawberry. A drop dripped down my chin, and I swiped at it.

He had a longing look in his eyes, but he shook his head, smirking before he slipped out the door.

Eventually, I got out of bed and started to stretch my sore muscles. I went through a round of a yoga flow, some push-ups, and lunges. Feeling more back to normal as I got up to grab a sweatshirt. I stopped in front of the mirror and ran my hands over my scars on my shoulders. It was a habit every day. Just a reminder that I was strong enough to do anything. Nothing could break me. Turning, and tugging my sweatshirt over my head I padded on bare feet out to the living room, quiet as a mouse.

Atty jumped when he saw me.

"You need to wear a bell, dude," he grumbled, but then smiled at me. He had been curled up, reading another book. His books had far more romance in them than he would ever admit. I took one from his room to read once, enjoyed it, and slipped it back without a word. It was adorable, but I knew he'd be defensive, so I never said anything.

David started laughing louder than was necessary for the comment, and I shot him a glare. He quirked an eyebrow, and then he had the same look he got when he was going to possibly get in trouble for something but was

Made Immortal

excited to do it anyway. He glanced at Atty with a smug smirk. "You should have seen her when she was a kid. Clumsiest person I ever met." He turned back to me. "Remember the time we were chasing that stray dog on the grounds?"

I narrowed my eyes at him; I did indeed remember that day. "No," I started, but I was too late.

"She went skidding on a pile of wet grass—it had just been raining—and went face first into this giant muddy puddle, feet sticking straight up and wiggling, trying to get herself out." He pointed his fingers toward the ceiling to demonstrate.

Groaning I wiped my hand down my face as Atty crackled in laughter. "It could have happened to anyone," I muttered.

"It didn't happen to us," David countered, crossing his arms, clearly feeling quite proud of himself, before we were all laughing together.

I dropped down heavily next to Atty, bouncing him up and down on the cushion, and he didn't even flinch. Already back to reading his book. Something caught David's attention though. I just leaned my head back and closed my eyes; he'd tell us if it was anything important. That was one of my favorite parts of living together in Neria. There were times when we just sat in silence and enjoyed each others company. It was incredibly relaxing. I felt even tighter bonds with the entire team in the month we'd been here. They were my family. We had become a well-oiled machine after so many missions together. Especially when we went out hunting, searching for the lost Nerians.

Sometime later, Atty nudged my boot with his. Blinking my eyes open I looked over. He was a quiet person overall, but I had really gotten to know him. He was incredibly funny when he grew comfortable with you. He had been the one to make me laugh on some dark nights.

"You good?" he asked, knocking his arm into mine.

I nodded. "Yeah, I'm fine. I'll be right as rain by tonight."

David stood up quickly and headed for his room, his comm chiming. I raised an eyebrow, but I had a feeling it might have been Joseph. The two had become close over the last few months. At least they could be a small comfort to each other during this time.

I pulled my feet down from the coffee table and slapped my thighs, groaning as I pushed myself up from the couch. I took David's spot at the computer and started my checks. Our search had flagged a few messages. I clicked on one and read it once, then again.

"Atty," I called over my shoulder. He ignored me. "Atty," I snapped again.

He looked up surprised at my tone.

"Nathan is going to be there."

He didn't seem to grasp who I was talking about. "Who is going to be where?"

Chase and David would have known right away, but Atty hadn't grown up with us. I'd have to grab David as soon as he came back out. "Nathan Ketler is going to the summit."

Slowly, he appeared to understand what I meant. "The King of Soland is going to be there, and you're on a first name basis with him?"

I nodded laughing. "We've known each other since we were kids." They had actually met briefly when we saved Joseph. We had been able to get Joseph to Soland, the neighboring kingdom, where he could live in relative safety.

Made Immortal

Nathan had given us a safe space to cross the border and helped settle Joseph in and even provided him with a lab.

"Why?" Atty asked, his hand on the back of my chair as he leaned over my shoulder.

"Because our father's new each other." I said like it was obvious.

Atty just sighed and shook his head. "No, why is he going to be at the summit?"

As if on cue, the news sites started to ping with notifications. I opened a clip from the National Nerian News, where Wendy Watson was reporting. She was the most trusted woman in Neria besides their king and princess—his daughter, my stepmother and the current Queen of Kabira. Wendy had an incredibly striking appearance, with cheeks that could slice if someone came in close enough, and her hair was braided wires that flickered with lights and waved ever so slightly around her shoulders.

Nerians believed nothing was as beautiful as technology. Cybernetic enhancement was what made Neria most of its money. The black market in the bowels of Neria boomed with people wanting affordable upgrades. Yet, those were known to run off of virus-infected equipment, faulty pieces, which caused death more often than not. Almost as deadly as the diseases many used them to fight, since they couldn't afford the actual medicine. When we had run into Queen Esmerelda while rescuing Chase's sister, and where we lost his mother, we realized she had upgrades just like everyone else in Neria. Her metal hands and arms strong enough to snap my wrists without flinching.

I refocused on the news clip as Wendy went on. Atty had gotten up and was watching over my shoulder.

"Today, in a show of friendship, King Edgar Ravensbone of Neria extended an offer for King Nathan Ketler to attend the Neria Tech Summit. King Ketler was happy to accept. Soland, known for their artists and free spirits, may finally be looking to learn from Neria and the power of our technological advancements," Wendy said. "Here's to hope for a strong peace and support from our neighbor Soland, especially during these trying times as our dear once princess, Queen Esmerelda of Kabria is forced to deal with slander from the radicals in Kabria over this silly *resistance*. It seems they have decided to come over the border and cause trouble here as well, but have no fear the king will flush them out in short order." She made a show of slamming her hand on the table for emphasis, and Atty made a noise of disgust in my ear.

I closed out the video. Atty started to stalk back and forth in the living room.

"The summit is in just a couple of days. What if this changes the security protocols?" he muttered to himself as he rubbed at his chin.

David came out of his room, his head peeking around the corner. I raised my eyebrows in question.

"So, that was Joseph... and Nathan," David said, and I had a guess what was coming.

"And?" I asked, gesturing at his face showing up on the newsfeeds.

"Uh, Nathan decided he was coming and told Edgar that he couldn't do anything about it. So, this was Edgar's spin on everything," David said.

I wished I could have seen the King of Neria's face as Nathan told him. I giggled at the thought.

"Nathan is furious about what happened to Attikus and the others. He may not be able to join us officially due to his

Made Immortal

council, but he has decided to put some pressure on from the media instead," David finished.

"He's going to get himself killed." I couldn't help but be worried for my friend.

"Yes, well, that kind of applies to all of us, so we can't throw stones. He's not even the only royal who does it." He gave me a pointed look. "But he needs to discuss something with you privately. He's going to arrange time for you two to have a chat during the summit. Joseph and I are going to connect later, and we'll update the plans. I'll grab Chase and let him know when he's home."

I shrugged, but my thoughts were already swirling, feeling like a storm overcoming me. I got up and watched David's eyes follow me.

"Vi." He lightly grabbed my wrist as I passed him. I looked him straight in the eye and saw that he knew. "Be safe."

I nodded, and I felt Atty watching me too as I headed back to my room. I started to rotate my arms and stretch some more and then threw the suit back on, with street clothes over it. When I stepped out of my room and grabbed my sling bag and my keys, I jumped at finding Atty leaning against the hallway outside my room with his arms crossed and a scowl on his face.

"You aren't even totally healed yet," he scolded me.

"It'll be fine. I'm just listening," I said, smiling, but he shook his head.

"I'm coming; give me two minutes." He turned back into his room, and I heard his closet door fling open and him shuffling in there.

David just shrugged and smiled at me as he walked by with a bowl of cereal and a spoon halfway to his mouth. I knew he was smugly thinking this was my own fault. He sat down at the computer, looking through data and only half paying attention to his spoon.

I huffed and leaned against the wall, waiting for Atty now. True to his word, he was ready in no time. He had the ridiculous beanie he wore all the time. It looked horrible, but Gwen had gotten it for him, so he wore it everywhere. He pulled it on proudly as he came out of his room, and then he punched me in the shoulder and walked out before me.

"Get home before Chase. Be safe," he said again.

I closed the door behind us slowly and took a deep breath.

"So, where are we headed, boss?" Atty asked.

"The Bored Bear," I said, pulling my hair up and back, raising my hood to hide myself.

Atty stopped short and glared at me. "Your plan is to go hang out at the bar in Turin Square, which still has the stage from the execution. The execution that you messed up, yesterday, and ended with your face plastered all over from the security footage? That bar?"

I shrugged and started walking again, and he jogged after me.

"You know this is why he gets so mad," Atty said. "You do stupid stuff like this all the time."

I just kept walking.

"He's terrified. All the time. But he can't say anything because you *are* stronger. You aren't invincible though. Every time you do this, you hurt him, and he feels like he doesn't have the right to be upset. He's always afraid he's going to lose you," he continued while keeping pace beside me.

My chest tightened. I knew this. I knew it hurt him, but I didn't have a choice. It was my duty. We had no time to

Made Immortal

waste. For now, there was too much at stake. It wasn't just my life; it was all of their lives, the ones who hadn't been rescued, my friends, everyone.

Atty was quick and surprisingly good at blending in, even if that meant being seen. He could flick a switch and become someone else. As we walked into the bar, I shrunk into my hood, but Atty walked in standing up straight, exuding confidence. He grabbed a seat at the bar and slapped the counter. "Gimme a Jones," he told the bartender. Jones was a local drink known for being incredibly intoxicating, and the favorite of alcoholics.

The regulars were already in for the day, with a few scattered around the room. I sat at the darkened edge of the bar that was hidden from the doorway. The bartender looked my way.

"Just a pint," I said quietly, adding a rasp to my voice, trying to keep myself as boring and forgettable as possible. Atty was grabbing most of the attention anyways. He had started to loudly spin a tale of some ridiculous adventure that was actually partly true. The other patrons groaned over this new blow-hard disturbing their peace.

I could tell the bartender had already lost interest in me and was keeping her eyes on Atty. No one liked loud strangers here.

The closest table had two younger men, who looked to be the stock of soldiers or guards. They shook their heads and leaned in close together to talk low. I adjusted my hearing to focus on their conversation.

"I haven't seen most of the guys that were on shift yesterday," one said.

The other nodded. "Even if they're still alive, we probably won't," he said in a harsh, angry tone.

31

"What do you think they do with them?" The first one gulped. "You know, the ones we won't see again."

"Nothing good. Keep your nose out of it." He set down his cup with a force that sent it sloshing onto the table.

"But they work for the government. They have to have some record," the other went on.

"Either they are punished for failure, or they are found useful in other ways." He was glaring at the man who kept asking questions.

"Like they transfer them to another station?"

"How new are you?" Growling, the angry man pushed his face toward the curious one. "They fill you with drugs and diseases and see what happens."

The curious man sat up straighter, clamping his mouth shut and looking down to his drink. I tried to keep my face hidden and my excitement under control. I grasped onto my cup to give my hands something to do.

Someone stood up quickly and aggressively headed toward Atty. I looked back to the men, trying not to miss if they said more, but knowing I might have to help Atty.

The door of the bar burst open.

Benson stalked into the room, his red messy hair looking like flames backlit from the sun outside, and I relaxed. He was close to a head taller than anyone here, an imposing figure. He had the stature of a professional athlete or maybe more like a bear—cuddly either way in reality. His muscles had muscles. All eyes went from Atty to Benson. As he came into the dark bar, he flashed a bright smile and slapped Atty on the back.

"I see we're starting early, my friend," Benson said, and the man who had been advancing on Atty returned to his seat as the two started to make a show of old friends catching up.

32

Made Immortal

The two men I'd been listening to also seemed to settle back down after the excitement.

"What do you mean?" the first one asked in a frightened whisper.

"Some guys said they've seen people get ordered over to the doc over in Ponics Sector, and no one ever sees them again. They say the queen did it to that Amazon—the princess. Now, they're doing it to hundreds. All I know is, I'm not going to do *anything* to get their attention. So, I'd keep my mouth shut if I were you; just do your job." He had a worried look as he stared off, his view not focused on anything really.

I got up quickly and headed out. Atty threw down enough to cover our drinks as he and Benson made up some story about having an appointment to get to. I walked down the road, and they followed as I ducked off a side street.

"Ponics Sector," I said excitedly. "They bring people there, and no one sees them again. They're sending guards to a doctor in the Ponics Sector."

"Okay, let's get back, tell David, and we'll start planning," Benson said, throwing a thumb toward home.

"What, no," I stammered. "We're like two sectors over. We can just run over there really quick and get a lay of the land." I pointed the other way.

"Why do you need to go right now? Let's see what we can find out first," Benson said. "Do you know why I'm here? Because I had a feeling you'd take a crazy risk." He looked at Atty. "You... just..." Benson put his hand to his temple and sighed. "Well, I'm glad you didn't get punched before I got there."

"Why can't we just go now and check it out?" I argued.

Atty turned us both to face forward and pushed us down the street.

"Because you won't just look. You're going to charge in there before we know what is going on or how best to handle it," Benson countered.

"Did Chase tell you to keep an eye on me too?" I huffed.

"No, you know he didn't, because he's just as stubborn as you. We're all worried, not just him. You can't keep up this pace, Vi. Let's go back, get more intel on this place, and then we'll check it out after the summit," Benson pleaded.

I stopped short. "You know as well as I do that there is no hanging out here after the summit. My face is going to be plastered everywhere, more than it already is. I have to do this now before I can't. I'm the face of their..." I hesitated. "My—our war, but this is my purpose." I was pleading now. "I have to protect them. They have no voice, they are afraid, and they don't deserve this. None of them."

I pointed the way to the Ponics Sector again. I had to try. I had to see what I could find out. Two days and they might be gone, and I might never get a chance like this again.

"Fine, but you're filling in David while we head that way. No risks, just to look," Benson said firmly.

I nodded and linked my comm to David to fill him in.

5

"I'll patch you over a map and everything I have on the area," David said once I had filled him in. "At least they're with you. Link me in when you get there; I'll patch into the city video feeds."

"You are the best," I sang. I had almost a skip in my step. I couldn't believe the luck. Something was going to come from this. I could feel it.

"You're welcome," he replied.

"Thanks," I said in a softer voice.

"Mmhmm, yeah, I know." He laughed. "Okay, I sent you everything."

Our comms chimed, and Benson was able to expand a holomap of the sector.

"There are a few different doctors they could be referring to, but they all work within a few blocks of each other in the medical suites," David told us.

Shining on the map were red four lights hovering in the outlines of different buildings. I let my eyes glide over the map, focusing, making sure to memorize the streets and anything that could block a quick exit.

The Ponics Sector was for those in the city who were wealthy. None of the citizens we had seen recently could afford any of this type of care; they wouldn't even be allowed on these streets. I shrugged and dropped my hood back, took out a pair of sunglasses, and wrapped my hair in a scarf to fit in more easily with the boys and this part of town.

The sun seemed on the attack as beams blasted back at us from the steel and glass buildings rising before us. Shaking my head from the blinding light, I headed toward the first of four offices. Not many people were on the street. Most had drivers just bring them into the area. No one really walked.

Looking around, Atty quickly walked toward a hovercar resting in a parking spot. "David, get the cameras," he said, then he pulled out a slim device that popped the locked doors open.

"Got it. You're good," David told us. We all slipped in, and within moments Atty had the hovercar overridden and we were slowly heading down the street.

We set the auto-drive to take us in leisurely loops of the area. David had set our program to dig through the city's security coverage of this area. He was reviewing sections flagged by the computer while we gathered what we could. These car's were so advanced David was also able to walk us through being able to hack the car's software to turn it into an audio receiver for the area as we made our sweep.

I kept my focus on trying to hear anything that might help as the guys kept an eye out. I heard a lot of normal conversations between people who worked in the area and their clients, but then I heard shuffling. Definitely lots of metal being pushed and banged around. I tapped Benson on the shoulder, and we had the car slow and then park.

Made Immortal

We were right next to one of the doctor's offices on the map.

"All right, this is the last of them. We'll be completely out of here in thirty," someone inside said and I gave a pointed look to the others.

"Something is being moved. It sounds like chains. They won't be here if we come back later. This is our only chance to get any information," I pleaded.

Grudgingly, they nodded. I jumped out of the car and raced toward the office.

"David, lock it down," I called, hearing the boys running behind me. I pulled off the scarf and glasses and activated the mask of my suit while pulling daggers into my hands.

"Okay, the power is cut." As David said it, all the lights of the street shut down and the buzz of the area quieted.

I looked behind me and saw both David and Benson pull out their guns.

"Stay back," I told them.

They both hit their necks, and their entire suit started to spread from a slim necklace I hadn't noticed them wearing.

"David finished our suits," Atty said with the most genuine smile. "He said yours is almost done."

I said a prayer to the gods under my breath for us to make it through this without any harm coming to my friends. We could take all the help we could get. Then, I kicked in the front door of the building to the screams of the receptionist as she saw our weapons.

"Get down," I roared.

The girl covered her head with shaking hands as she dropped behind her desk. As we passed her into the hall-way, I heard a gun cock behind us. I pointing down, and the boys both automatically ducked. I turned and threw a dagger, and it slammed into the woman, who was about to pull the trigger on her automatic weapon. The bullets went spraying into the ceiling.

Atty and Benson both headed farther into the building and I turned back to follow them. They crouched as they threw doors open to search the next rooms. I left them to do the sweep and went toward the sounds deeper into the buildling.

"You should have been out already. Now, we have to deal with this," one person yelled.

"Who even knew where we were? What is this?" another yelled back.

I could hear people readying their weapons and their running steps.

"It's her," someone said in a tone of defeat. "You saw the video; she's here. She's coming for us."

"Don't be stupid. It's not her," someone snapped back.

I could tell they were past the next door, which by the echoing of their voices sounded like it must have been a large garage for deliveries.

"Let me," Atty said, smirking, having caught up with me. We walked up to the doors, and he grabbed something out of his pocket. He handed it to me and then mimed throwing it. I cracked the door open, pressed the button on the device, and tossed it into the room beyond, slipping to the side of the door as I closed it again.

We stood on either side the door as the device beepned inside. When the beeping stopped the door exploded into the hallway flying past us. Atty let out a giddy laugh as I pushed into the room. There was a group of men on the ground, coughing and holding their heads. One caught sight of us, and I saw the fear in his eyes as he scrambled away.

Atty and Benson fired some warning shots before the

Made Immortal

guard got his feet back under him. I walked straight to him, bent down, and pulled him up by his collar to the point his toes barely skimmed the floor. My mask slid back so he could see my face as my hair started to fall around my shoulders.

"It's you," he stammered.

I looked around to find only one covered truck in the garage, but there was evidence that many more had been here. There were only guards here now— no prisoners. Glaring at him, I made sure we were eye to eye.

"Where did they go? Why did you move them?" I growled.

"I don't know. They didn't tell me." He flinched as I pulled his face even closer to mine.

My rage boiled to the surface. "Why did you move them?" I screamed.

"Be—be..." he stuttered. "Because of you. We got word after the attack yesterday to obtain the remaining guards and move the entire stock we had."

Terror filled his eyes as I realized what he was saying and punched the column of brick next to him, cratering it beneath my fist. "Stock?" I growled. "Stock? They are human beings." I shook my head.

"If—if you let me live, I'll find out. I'll find out where they went," he said quickly, holding his hands up in peace.

Before I could even think through his offer, his head snapped to the side. I looked over and found one of the guards had shot him before he could say more. Screaming, I summoned a dagger and threw it as I raced after him. He spun and kept spraying bullets behind him as he ran. It didn't take long to reach him. I tackled him to the ground, threw him on his back, and pulled off his helmet and goggles.

39

"Tell me!" I screamed.

He just smiled.

"Long live the queen," he said before smacking his teeth together. He started to convulse and foam at the mouth. I dropped him and turned as I stood. The rest of the soldiers were down or had fled. Benson and Atty seemed to be fine. I grabbed a barrel that had been knocked over in the rush and threw it as hard as I could. It smashed into the remaining truck, which made the covering flutter and I saw part of a label on the truck.

I headed toward the truck and pulled back more of the cover. Nixan Corp was painted on the side. Nixan was one of the top government contractors for Neria. It was one of the companies that would be at the summit. I was going to have to make sure I had full access to that presentation, no matter what.

I heard sirens coming our way and glanced at the boys.

"Let's go," I said, taking one last look at the downed guards scattered across the garage. I squared my shoulders and ducked through the partly opened gate, the boys following me. We made our way out of the area before disappearing into the streets and headed back home.

I could feel Benson and Atty hanging back, but I couldn't summon the ability to talk and ease their minds. I just shoved my hands into my pockets, kept my head down, and let my emotions swirl under my skin.

It was something. I finally had something. I hoped it was enough.

6

I unlocked the door, and the three of us made our way inside. Swiveling his chair toward us, David gave a relieved smile that we were okay.

"Welcome back," he said. "I've been looking into Nixan."

I had heard Benson and Atty filling him in as we approached the appartment. He gestured for us to come over to the computer, and my pulse quickened. Hope swirled through my chest. It fought for dominance as terror clung to me at the thought of this being yet another dead end.

"Nothing incredibly helpful, but I'll keep digging." His gaze softened as he saw me deflate.

Atty put a hand on my shoulder and squeezed it tightly. "We'll all look."

I smiled as best I could, but I was so exhausted that it barely registered. I ran my hands over my face and rubbed at my temples.

"Thanks. I'll be back in a few." I turned and headed for one of the bathrooms. Softly closing the door, I turned the water in the shower on to scalding. As I waited for it to heat, I set my hands on the countertop of the sink and stared at my reflection.

The cuts were gone; so were the bruises. I looked much better than I felt. But even with all of my healing, the scars from the prison still crossed my skin. Inflictions from before the serum worked on me; it only stopped new scars from forming. They served as my reminders that Esmerelda hadn't broken me, at least not completely. My soul was healing, albeit slowly, with the help of the people who loved me. I lightly traced one down my neck and over my shoulder. Tears threatened to fall, and my breath caught in my throat. Memories of what they had done to me flashed through my mind, my hands balling into fists. I flinched at the recollection of the pain and fear.

A hole opened up inside me as I thought of all the people meeting that fate right at this very moment.

I got into the shower, hoping the water would burn the memories out of me. I wrapped my hands behind my neck, turned my face up toward the stream of scalding water, and just let it wash over me.

You are death. It follows you, and you are too weak to save them, said the voices. *Everyone you love will die, and it will be your fault.*

I crumbled and sank down, curling around my knees. The water flowed over my back and down my face and shoulders. Quietly, I let it out, silently sobbing, my tears mixing with the water.

The thoughts had plagued me since Alice's death, Chase's mother. With each report of deaths from the rebels, of each person I couldn't save on a mission, the thoughts drowned out everything else.

Made Immortal

I couldn't fail again. Who would die next because of my inability to save them?

Slowly, I was able to gain control of myself again. I stepped out to dry off. As I did every time, in the mirror, I took a long look at the scars across my back. Focusing on my determination to keep going. I was stronger than I thought. Thinking back to the person I was in the prison to who I am now, I had come a long way. I wasn't that defenseless, scared little girl anymore.

Pulling myself together I quickly got ready to head back out and help the guys. Walking out, I rubbed my hair between a towel. David hovered behind Benson and Atty, who were on their laptops on the couch. He had a small device he was using to poke the neck releases of their suits and looked at the readouts.

"Well, the new upgrades seem to have worked as expected. I should be able to finish the upgrades on your new one by tomorrow, Vi," David said, not looking up from what he was doing.

Looking over his shoulder to me, Benson said, "So, Nixan has been buying up tons of smaller tech firms to monopolize their designs. I'm sure they have to be the company behind the nanotech."

I walked into the living room, grabbed my own laptop, and dropped into a seat next to the couch. I opened it, and the screen whirled to life. Instantly, it chimed with links the guys were sending over. I took my headphones off the table next to me and popped them on.

The music put me in the zone to start digging through the data. I started with everything they had sent over. Each new piece of the puzzle gave me new avenues to explore in the dark web. Before I knew it, I saw movement out of the corner of my eye as the door opened, glancing up I realized the sun had set.

Chase and Gwen walked in together. After stretching out my stiff muscles I pulled down my headphones. We hadn't said a word the entire time; all of us lost in our own research.

Chase came my way and kissed me on the cheek.

"How was your first day?" I asked him.

"Informative," he said, moving behind me to wrap his arms around my waist and set his chin on my shoulder. He nuzzled my ear, which always made me giggle.

"Stop, that tickles." I laughed.

"I had a meeting with Jared, Nathan's head of security today," Chase said. "We have the full schematics and positions of all security, their shift changes, and the blind spots."

"My company is going to be in the convention center tomorrow to start setting up," Gwen chimed in.

Something caught my attention on the television. We always left the news station on, although we normally left it on mute. The others had noticed as well. Atty grabbed the control and turned the sound on.

On the news, covering half the screen, was a photo of me.

"... recent attacks are perpetrated by none other than the rogue princess of Kabria," Wendy Watson went on. "As we have reported before, our beloved Queen Esmerelda of Kabria, has been under heinous attacks by her estranged stepdaughter. These rebels," the anchor spat, "have no honor, no sense of patriotism. Now, these criminals have crossed the border and are attacking our citizens. The government has set up this line." A number flashed on the screen. "If you see this woman, report it."

Atty muted the program, but it showed a video of us at

44

Made Immortal

the execution. My stomach tightened, thinking of Attikus. More video was shown of us at the doctor's office. Chase squeezed me tightly as he saw the video from earlier today. I could feel a low rumble from his chest.

Guilt flash over David's face as Chase must have looked over at him. I slipped out of Chase's grip and grabbed his hand to tug him to our room.

As we slipped inside and the door clipped shut, a chime came from my comm. It was a message from my dad. I pulled it up.

Saw the news, good job. Keep it up.

I closed the message and turned toward Chase. The look on his face was heartbreaking.

"What was that?" he asked.

"Dad," I said, giving my attention back to him.

"Not that, you took Atty and Benson into a firefight!" he barked. "What were you thinking? The summit is tomorrow." He was yelling now. "What is wrong with you? Why do you keep doing this?" His hands balled into fists.

I pulled back, surprised. "I'm doing my job." I glared at him.

"That isn't your job." He pointed his arm toward the living room. "*That* is your obsession, which is going to get someone hurt. You could have put the mission in jeopardy. Not to mention, what if Benson or Atty got hurt?"

"I didn't want them to be there; they came on their own," I said, starting to pace on my side of the room.

"Yeah, because someone needs to keep an eye on you. What are we supposed to do if you get hurt or, gods forbid, you're killed? What would happen to that weapon if we aren't there to stop the sale? All because you can't keep your mind on the mission, we could have lost our chance to stop

45

it." His turned away from me, I could see him trying to calm himself.

I couldn't help but feel my own anger rise. Why didn't he understand. "How many people are hurt or dying that are being captured? We found something." My voice raised to match his. "We found one of the depots, and we were so close. It's Nixan. They look to be involved with nanotech too. We wouldn't have found anything if we waited."

He turned back to me, but his face was twisted in pain.

"These people need us too. It's happening here just like at home. I can't stop now." I sat down on the bed, and Chase joined me. He picked up one of my hands and held it in both of his.

"I can't lose you," He said quietly.

"I always come home. Everyone is fine, and we found a new lead. It's a win," I said, placing my other hand against his cheek. He leaned into it.

"It's going to be harder now that your face is everywhere." He sighed.

"It's been planned for," I said, and Chase squinted at me, seeming confused. "Dad wanted to make sure Neria knew I was here."

"Why didn't I know?" he asked.

I gave him an exasperated look. "I didn't need you to be worried. Plus, it's my dad. Are you surprised?"

He gave a small shake of his head. "You should have told me. Nolan should have told me."

"Well, now you know. The summit is tomorrow, so all's well that ends well. Don't jump down my throat please," I squeezed his hands tightly. "It was dad. I didn't have much of a say." I tried to pout the best I could.

Chase sighed and pulled me back on the bed, and I curled into his side, my head on his shoulder. With that, the

Made Immortal

argument was over. For now anyway. The conversation moved to how his day was, and he filled me in on some of the blind spots he found and how Jared seemed to be a good guy. I then told him about the things I had found out about Nixan and the new questions they had brought up.

Nixan was the largest tech company in the country and had offices, substations, and personnel not only all over Neria but the whole continent. If they were involved, taking them down was going to be much harder than we had originally thought. The idea of Esmerelda having some control over the largest company in the continent was more than we might be able to fight. What made it worse was Nixan's had companies of all types—bio-upgrades, tech, weapons, vehicles, even food and cosmetics.

Benson called out to everyone that dinner was done. Chase and I pulled ourselves out of bed and headed into the kitchen. It smelled amazing as always. I grabbed a bowl with salad and a casserole filled with mashed potatoes and took them to the table.

As Gwen set a cup at one of the place settings where Atty was putting a plate down, they quickly came face to face and stood there for just a moment longer than necessary. Both of their cheeks turned the slightest shade of pink. Internally, I couldn't help but giggle. I tried my best to keep a straight face. It reminded me of Chase and myself after I had been rescued.

"Vi, they sent over your itinerary for the summit," David said, and my comm pinged with the data.

. . .

47

As we sat down, I pulled up the calendar. I scanned the information, running through the day, trying to figure out when exactly the auction would be. My best guess was it would be after the presentations.

My stomach growled loudly, and everyone laughed.

"I guess it's time to dig in," Benson called and we all started filling our plates.

I still had to eat more than average to compensate for how quickly my body burnt through calories. Benson always made sure to cook extra food so I could eat as much as I needed. Although, Benson ate as much as I did, but it wasn't surprising with how enormous of stature he was, so that probably had something to do with it too. I could only wonder how his parents must have felt feeding him through his growth spurts as a kid.

"So, we'll have multiple exit routes ready, and we've left vehicles at each one. I'll be hooked into the security system for the convention center and the local city controls during the entire event from the booth," David said, twirling his fork in the air.

"People have been asking about this mysterious Isabella who will be there." Gwen looked my way.

"Good. Because I still haven't actually been invited to the sale." I chewed on my lip. In the event that I did not end up getting the invite, the others would be on the lookout and we'd go in with force if necessary.

"We've planted plenty of rumors; they'll want your money. It will be fine," Chase said in such a tone that I believed him. Everyone nodded, but I couldn't help but notice how tightly he clutched his fork.

They discussed more of the plan for the umpteenth time. The gravity of the mission weighed on all of us. After

Made Immortal

we were finished, Atty got up and started collecting the plates. I stood to help, but Gwen tugged me down.

"I got it. You guys go on." She made a gesture for me to get out of the way.

I smiled and nodded, wanting to give them time together. Gwen went over to help him with the dishes.

"Benson, will you come with me? I need help testing something," David said. Benson nodded, and they headed off for David's room.

Chase tugged me into the living room and set the speakers to play our favorite song. He held out his hand, and I took it. He spun me around the living room, catching me, swaying with me. The music wrapped around us. As he looked down at me, we were chest to chest, and the rest of the world fell away. Leaning down, his lips caught mine. He pulled me closer, one hand slipping through my hair. My fingers dug into his shoulders in response. I would never be able to get enough of this man.

Eventually, we broke apart, and he kissed my forehead. He looked into my eyes, and the love I saw there was all-consuming. Heat flooded my body as the depth of his feelings washed over me in that one look.

"I will always want to protect you, no matter how much you can protect yourself. I don't know what I would do without you." His voice caught in his throat.

"I know," I said, brushing a lock of hair back from his face. "I will always come home to you. Whatever it takes, but you know this is who I am. It's not something I think I'll ever be able to change." I settled against his chest, and we continued swaying to the music.

He nodded. Although, I knew his worry would never fade, and I understood that was something he would never be able to change as well.

49

David and Benson came back out, and David was holding a few devices.

"Okay so," he threw me a headband, "this is for your hair."

"No duh, genius," I said.

"Just put it on," he said, rolling his eyes.

I put it on and heard a small gasp from Chase. I walked to the mirror hanging on the wall. My hair had begun turning black, the color flowing down to the tips. David then handed over a small case that held contact lenses. I cracked it open and put them in. I jumped at the virtual notifications that popped up around the room.

"It'll take a bit to get used to, but these will also give you infrared and night vision. They have facial recognition, which should be helpful at the summit. They also hide your eye color."

I walked to a mirror and pulled my hair back to mimic a bun. These few changes were already surprising. Add some makeup and glasses and I would be unrecognizable. I took everything off and set them down. I gave David a quick hug.

"Thank you. That will be perfect," I told him.

We all found seats in the living room, Gwen and Atty joining us after a while, holding hands no less. Benson brought out a board game, and we spent the last night we'd all be together before the summit laughing and making unforgettable memories. Just like before every big mission, we decided to spend time while we could, knowing it could be the last time we'd all be together.

7

Chase tightened his arms around me as my alarm started to go off. He nuzzled my neck, and I couldn't help but moan at the feeling.

"We could just stay in bed," he mumbled softly.

I twisted in his arms to face him. I ran my fingers across his cheeks, and I could see the worry in his eyes.

"It will just be for a day, maybe two," I said, giving a soft laugh and shrugging.

"Don't joke," his tone was serious.

"I'm sorry." I poked the end of his nose. "It's just going to be business as usual."

"It hasn't been, not for you, not since we got here." One of his hands twisted in my hair, the other pulling me closer by my waist.

"I know. I just can't turn a blind eye when I know what they are being subjected to." I brought his face to mine. "But I will see you when this is all over, and you can yell at me then." I kissed him deeply, trying to help him feel at ease. "For now, I have to go be nice." I groaned and threw my legs over the side of the bed to get up and get ready.

I grabbed an oversized sweater and pulled it on as I padded around the room in the moonlight. Benson and I had to run into town early to make my presence known. They expected my flight to land at four in the morning, so we planned to arrive shortly after and run into some of the summit speakers during breakfast in the hotel. There were two men I was interested in getting to know, and they both stuck to their routines. Marco Diaz and Gregory Getry were two legends in Neria. Diaz was the creator of some of the first biotech now used all over the country, and Getry was the mind behind the Nerian Censored Digital Content, the sole media outlet in the country. They only distributed information that was deemed acceptable by the king, pushing his propaganda to all of Neria.

Chase rolled his eyes at me. As he got out of the bed, the sheet slid off him, and I couldn't help but bite my lip. I shook my head and tried to get my mind back on track. A few of the things I needed were strewn about the bedroom, and he started to pick them up for me. I slipped into our compromise outfit. Gwen hated it, but I refused to wear heels for any part of this mission. So, the outfit was a combination of a rising tech leader and a slam poetry artist—all black turtleneck, pants with pockets, and high top sneakers.

As I put the headband on, Chase wrapped his arms around my waist and kissed my shoulder lightly. When he looked back up, my golden curls were a shimmering black. I pulled my hair into a tight bun. Chase went and dropped back down onto the bed as I finished my makeup, then I took a deep breath and put the contact lenses in.

Grunting I couldn't keep from swaying slightly as they booted up over my vision. Chase looked over, chuckling under his breath. A box zoomed around his face, and his name came up next to him. Details of his record scrolled

Made Immortal

across the screen. I shook my head and blinked a few times to steady myself. They would take some getting used to, that was for sure.

"What do you think? How do I look?" I asked, gesturing at my outfit as I spun in front of him.

It was his turn to bite his lip. He stood, crossed to me in seconds, and crushed me to the wall. We crashed together, and for a few moments, neither of us held anything back. Soon, much too soon for my taste, Chase broke the kiss and stepped back. I wiped at my lipstick and gazed at him, unable to believe I got so lucky to have him in my life like this. He winked, grabbed me by the hand, and pulled me out of our room toward the others.

Everyone was already in the kitchen when we stumbled in. Gwen handed me a cup of steaming coffee, and I couldn't help but moan as I took it. I couldn't function without a good cup of coffee. Everyone chatted away as I sat back. Internalizing this moment, this last month where we got to just live and be slightly normal. As normal as soldiers or spies or whatever people might call us could be. We'd always have this to remember. Plus, it didn't matter where we were; if we were together, we were home. All of us.

My comm unit started to buzz. Benson looked at his own, and David got up and headed for the computer.

"Time to go," Benson said, patting Atty on the shoulder as he headed for the door.

Gwen gave me a quick hug. Chase was standing with David as I headed over to them.

"Arm," David said, and without hesitation I gave it to him.

He clasped a beautiful bracelet on my wrist, and as he did it netted itself together. It was a mix of black, silver and gold metals, and I could tell it was nanobots right away.

53

"It's beautiful." I whispered.

"It's your suit new suit," he said. From the look on his face I could tell he was proud, and I was too.

"This is incredible." I said, waving my arm around. It was so light, I couldn't believe an entire suit could come from it. This had to have been the next step from the prototype of the others' suits he had been working on. I wrapped him into a bear hug. "I love you so much." Then gave him a kiss on the cheek.

He laughed and squeezed me tightly. "Yeah, yeah. Just try to bring some of the gadgets back this time."

I shrugged. "I make no promises."

As I started to turn away he pulled me back and hugged me again. "I love you too."

I cupped his cheek and we shared a look that crossed time. All of our years together wrapped up in that moment.

Chase gave us the moment, and when it had passed he grabbed my hand, and we walked towards the front door. "I'll see you soon. Don't do anything I wouldn't do."

We shared a brief kiss, and he pinched my cheek before I followed Benson out to the car. It was sleek with tinted windows, the kind of thing the elite would be driven around in here in Neria.

As I hopped into the back and Benson started the car, I looked around, catching one last glimpse of the apartment.

It had started. There was no going back now.

"So, breakfast, huh?" Benson asked.

"I know. I'm so hungry," I said, and we laughed.

"Do we have a budget for this?" Benson asked, as we were both notoriously the two who were always hungry.

I held a card between my fingers. "David managed to get into some police accounts, and borrowed just a *little* bit."

That got a chortle out of him.

Made Immortal

We pulled up, and the sun was just starting to rise. One valet ran over to open my door, and the other got the keys from Benson. They bowed and thanked us for staying. As they grabbed the rest of the bags, one of them asked for the one I was carrying. I turned on a charming smile and held on to it firmly. "Oh, no, I have this one. Thank you." I didn't trust they weren't going to search everything. Which is why I moved everything sensitive into this one bag.

They smiled politely and nodded before we were motioned to the front desk.

"Checking in?" the woman at the desk asked. As I came around, I noticed that her arm was bionic and her eyes shone neon teal and had to be cybernetic.

"Yes," Benson said, pulling our documents out of his jacket pocket. The woman made quick work of getting us our keys and advising us that everything would be taken to our room for us if we wanted breakfast, as that had just opened.

I watched, admiring this woman, tech and all. When I first learned of the upgrades people got for themselves, I just didn't understood why anyone would want to do that. Yet, living here, I saw the beauty of the under streets. I saw how these upgrades saved lives, helping the poor when they couldn't see an actual doctor, going to the black market instead. As well as how this helped people express their true self. How this made them feel whole. Exactly how they wanted to be seen and how they saw themselves.

Early when we arrived, one night we had gone to an underground club, and the energy of that place had been infectious. We danced, we laughed, we learned the stories of the people here. Families destroyed, people missing, rampant disease, attacks from police, food and power shortages. Some loved harder, some fought harder, some hated more, but everyone had been impacted. Many were chosing to do something. Small things, big things, it didn't matter it made an impact.

Benson turned back and handed me a key. He nodded toward the elevator and then followed me as I set off. Benson went into my room first and did a quick check, and I followed in once he gave the okay. He went through our adjoining door to his room. We ran scans for bugs in both rooms but didn't find anything out of the ordinary, thankfully

Turning to Benson "Let's go. I'm starving,"

He grabbed the door and pulling it open. "Lead the way."

8

I made my way into the dining room with Benson a few paces behind me. It had just opened and was empty save for two old men and a waiter, who seemed to have a keen eye for the men's every whim.

The men both sat with papers open, blocking their view of the other. Benson caught the waiter's eye, and he waved to show we could pick where to sit. I maneuvered us a few tables away with my back to the two. Benson sitting across from me could keep an inconspicuous eye on the two of them. I could hear one of them take a sip of their coffee and the other change pages in his paper. The waiter met us at the table as we sat down.

"What can I get you?" he asked quietly.

Not wanting to be disruptive, I matched his volume.

"Two coffee's. I'll have the capital breakfast." That happened to be one of the largest breakfasts that came with everything.

The waiter looked at Benson.

"Yeah, I'll have that too," he said.

The waiter nodded, noting that into his tablet. He gave a quick bow and excused himself.

I rubbed at my eyes then my temples. The lenses were giving me a headache. I looked straight at the white linen tablecloth—a nicer fabric than I had felt in quite some time. I was used to the simple tables at the mess hall back home in the rebel camps.

The waiter came back and poured us both cups of coffee, leaving cream and sugar at our table.

"Thank you," I said with a smile. I seemed to have caught him off guard as he did a double take when he walked away. He shook his head as he made his way back out of sight.

I pulled out my cell phone—one of the burners we had obtained. I opened the National Nerian News, the main channel of the NCDC and Gregory Getry's pride and joy. Getry and his news conglomerate had complete control of what the people of Neria consumed. It was mostly all propaganda.

The world-famous Nerian Tech Summit kicks off today!

The headline caught my attention as I started scrolling. I kept searching and finally, I found a small article that mentioned large numbers of people in the city becoming ill, blaming the poor in the area for unsanitary habits. Another said radicals were the reason for the disappearances of citizens, stating that young people were leaving to join the rebels and how they were traitors against their country.

Flashes of people huddling around fires in trash cans raced through my mind. They'd resorted to finding scraps to eat in the dumpsters, then they were attacked by the businesses in the area. My blood pounded through my veins, the

Made Immortal

underlying beat to the rage that I found harder and harder to contain. The intensity doubled knowing this culture was the birthplace of the woman who would do the same to my country.

Neria needed to burn, and her citizens were almost ready to light the fuse. All they needed was a spark. From the ashes, maybe something better could grow.

The waiter brought out our meals. My stomach was growling, and Benson and I both dove into breakfast.

"Good to see the young enjoying themselves. I never would have been able to handle all that before a day like today," one of the men said as he folded his paper and set it on his table. "Are you the Miss Isabella Contra we've heard so much about?"

I turned slightly in my chair to get a better view of him. "Sounds about right. In regards to my eating habits not that it's any of your business, but it seems like you wouldn't understand the hunger after a hard days work." I paused and made eye contact with the man who was scowling at me now. "It's a pleasure to meet you, Mr Getry."

"Quite snappy this one," the other said, looking from Getry to me over the rim of his coffee cup as he sipped with a mischievous smile on his face. "The young need that fire, or else they'd never make these new advancements, would they? Us old timers are stuck in the past and the history we made."

I smiled. They were exactly where I expected, true to their routines. The two men I wanted to have eyes on and get a feel for.

Mr. Getry huffed at that. The other man, who I already knew due to our research, was Marco Diaz. Diaz had created some of the first implants. His company created the chips that allowed communication between the implants and the implantee. As well as powered certain mods that required more than bio-electricity provided by the body. The two of them were the bedrock of what Neria had built their wealth upon.

"Pleasure to make your acquaintance. You can call me Marco. I was hoping to find out more about you and your company."

"Nice to meet you, Mr. Diaz, but I do lean toward keeping myself and my company more of a mystery." I waved my hand dismissively.

"I don't think I even know what your company does," Mr. Getry said with an air of superiority, looking at me like I was nothing but a bug, easy enough to squash if he wanted to.

"Nanotech. It's all proprietary, so we don't say much outside of that. We're here looking for ideas we might be able to enhance." Arching an eyebrow I leveled my gaze at Mr. Getry.

He glowered back at me.

"From where we started, the size of technology these days is incredibly impressive," Mr. Diaz said in a calming manner, as if trying to settle the buzzing energy between us.

Turning my gaze to him instead. "Mr. Diaz, I was actually hoping to meet with you today to discuss our technology to fight disease that could be combined with many of your implant designs."

As he watched me, I couldn't tell what he was thinking, but he did seem to be sizing me up. I had a sliver of worry he had some idea of who I really was.

"I'd be happy to. We'll have our people set something up." He settled his coffee cup down and picked up his paper again.

Made Immortal

I laughed a bit, knowing I had no people, and that most definitely wouldn't be happening.

"Of course. Well, enjoy your breakfast." I nodded to both of them and turned back around to give Benson a silly smile. I could feel Getry's glare boring into my back. The goal was accomplished; I wanted to make my presence known to these two. They held more power than most of the government officials in Neria. So far, so good. Now, I just had to make it through an entire day.

We settled into relative silence as we finished our breakfast. Except for Mr. Diaz sipping his coffee loudly every once in a while, which only made Mr. Getry grumble in annoyance. As we got up from the table, the waiter came over to grab our dishes.

"Have a great day," he said in a manner seemed like a force of habit more than anything else.

I smirked and nodded. Before walking out, I tapped my comm unit to his, and there was a small chime as I transferred some credits to him. I could tell that while this was one of the nicest hotels in the city, it didn't mean the workers weren't struggling like the rest of the lower class in Neria.

"Oh, no, that's not necessary," he said, preparing to send it back to me.

"It most definitely is. Have a good day." I winked, and with that, I turned on my heels and headed out. I didn't glance at the two men as we left the dining room. I could feel their eyes following me as I did though.

9

A group of security met Benson and me as we reached the back entrance to the convention center. They enveloped us in a circle, and the man in charge went over the plans with Benson again. I didn't pay much attention to what they said and instead spent my time memorizing the view as we moved around the room. The people manning the booths had also just started to trickle in.

I saw David plugging in some cords at his booth when we went by. I caught his eye for just a moment, but otherwise we didn't acknowledge each other; we knew all the security cameras were being monitored. We wouldn't even attempt comms until we knew David was also in the security system. Which, if everything went according to plan, should be in the next twenty minutes.

"Ma'am, it's time for your first meeting. Please follow us," someone said, and Benson followed two of the men as I trailed behind him. Two more followed behind me. They brought us to an unassuming door that looked just like all the others.

They held it open, and when I walked through, no one

62

Made Immortal

followed. Benson closed the door behind me, standing outside with the rest of the security.

I turned to survey the room and saw an imposing man with shocking red hair and freckles standing in the center. He extended a hand to shake mine. I grabbed it and squeezed tightly.

"Miss Contra," he said. Since we were in the room alone, I tapped a button at my wrist. There was a low tone before a small pop and a hush fell over the room. We had to act for the cameras, but no one would be able to hear us.

"Oh, Nathan, it's so nice to see you." I leaned against one of the desks in the room, crossing my arms across my chest.

"I wish I could give you a hug, but next time. Anyway, about why I'm here..." He changed the topic by clapping his hands together.

"You shouldn't be here," I said, raising an eyebrow at him.

"Yes, as everyone has said." He rolled his eyes. "I knew you'd be here though, and while I don't need to piss off my nobles, something has to be done. I want to help."

"Nathan, you've been helping. You've given refugees places to stay; you've given us intel. That is enough. We don't need your country in a civil war also. Then, the entire continent would tear itself apart. It isn't safe here. The thing we're after is dangerous."

"My reason for being here is not completely selfless. I have a request," he said with a look from long ago that told me he was showing composure but was worried underneath. The look he had when our fathers had caught us doing something we weren't supposed to and gave us a lecture.

63

"What do you need?" I asked, quirking an eyebrow at him.

"I want to invite David to come to Soland and help Joseph on his projects. Joseph said that while they can get quite a bit done as is, they could get their research done faster if they were in the same place. Speed is the name of the game at the moment," Nathan said, looking up from under his lashes, as if unsure of himself. He seemed to feel incredibly uneasy with the request.

I held still for a moment, caught off guard and processing. While my gut reaction was to tell him no, emphatically, the request made plenty of sense.

I paused another moment, wondering out loud, "Did you ask him already?"

"No, no!" Nathan held up his hands in a placating gesture. "I wanted to see if it might even be an option before offering it. I know how close you are, and I know he's a big help to Kabria. And you are kind of the boss now."

"I'm not even close to being the boss," I scoffed. "Go ahead and ask David; it's his decision. We'll support whatever he decides. It's not a bad idea."

Nathan nodded, looking relieved, like a weight had been lifted off his shoulders. "Thank you. After all of this hullabaloo, I'll ask him."

"Hullabaloo, as in the imminent sale of a possible lethal weapon of mass destruction to those intent to cause harm?" I said, waving my hand around lazily.

"Yes, that." Nathan chuckled.

"I still can't believe you actually convinced people to let you come here." I was impressed, actually. It must have been quite the feat.

"I am incredibly charming and convincing, and did I mention charming?" He tipped an imaginary hat.

Made Immortal

"Please get out of here as fast as you can. Who knows what we're going to come up against today." I was worried for him. I hoped today would go well, but how often did things go as planned?

"Oh, that's right!" Nathan slapped his hands together. "I almost forgot. I've got gifts! Secret gifts." He put a finger to his mouth and gave a wicked smile. "Joseph got in contact with the rebels he used to work with. He got them to agree to meet all of you, and I've agreed to send them some supplies and whatever I can manage without anyone knowing."

"Oh, Nathan, thank you. Thank your people for us. They need so much help here. I wish I could give you a hug too." I straightened up and clapped his shoulder quickly.

"Next time, dear." He put his hand on top of mine for just a moment. "I just figured, why stop at only helping the ones who get across the border? The volunteers are all here of their own free will, just wanting to help people in need."

A soft knock came from the door. I turned off the device that had been muffling our conversation. Nathan straightened his tie, and we turned and headed back into the fray. We gave each other a last quick glance and tapped our foreheads with a tiny salute before walking in different directions.

"So, what did he have to say?" Benson asked under his breath.

I held off on saying anything until we passed a particular loud area. "He smuggled in some volunteers to help the citizens. He arranged a meeting for us with the rebels, and he wants David to move out there to work with Joseph."

Benson cocked an eyebrow at that but otherwise didn't react. I shrugged then quickly let the mask of a CEO take over. We made rounds; I smiled, shook hands, and listened and nodded to explanations of projects. While some of the technology could really improve the way of life, on the flip side, many could also be used for harm. It was a chilling thing to see firsthand. Yet, in the back of my mind, I logged them all to see if we could get them to help us instead of Neria.

We came around to the booth David was helping with right on time. He gave a small nod as we walked up, which was the signal that he was into the security system. I turned toward the speaker of the booth and gave them my attention as they started their presentation. In my peripheral, I saw David drop a card, then Benson picked it up and handed it back. What anyone watching wouldn't realize was Benson gave back a different card. The one David passed him was programmed to get us through any door in the building.

We moved on, making our way down more of the aisles of booths for the next few hours. Nothing out of the ordinary happened until an aide came running up to our group.

"Hello, Ms. Contra. Sorry to interrupt, but a meeting had to be moved. Can you meet with the other leaders now before the panel?" She looked stressed and overwhelmed.

"Hi. What's your name?" I asked her.

Letting out a large breath, she smiled meekly. "Sarah."

"Well, thank you for letting me know, Sarah. That's perfectly fine. Can you show us the way?"

"Oh, yes, ma'am!" She clutched her clipboard tightly to her chest and perked up.

I smiled and nodded and followed her as she rushed away. Benson caught my eyes, looking worried, knowing what this change of schedule probably meant. I knew the feeling; I was all too aware of the collateral damage here if things went wrong. Sarah led us through the convention center to a set of doors that opened to a lavish dining room.

As I scanned the room, I wasn't surprised to see I was the only woman here. Many of the men were laughing and clapping each other on the shoulders. All of their eyes devoured me as I entered. I watched them back, looking as aloof as I could manage. I went to the bar they had on the far end of the room, grabbing a bottle and pouring myself a drink. One of the men came up next to me and was about to speak when Marco Diaz came over, stepping between us. He stopped for a moment, staring at the other man. The young man, obviously intimated, backed away quietly.

"You look quite calm in a room full of snakes," Mr. Diaz said, taking the bottle from me and pouring himself a glass as well.

"I'm a snake charmer in my spare time," I said, turning to view the room, leaning my back against the bar.

Mr. Diaz chuckled at that. "I have no doubts. Just keep your eyes open. They can strike without warning."

With that, he walked back toward the center of the room again and started talking to one of the men. I listened to the room, giving each group a few moments to see if anything of interest was being said. Sipping my drinking slowly, I saw some glance my way a few times, but no one else came toward me. I could hear them whispering about how there was no way I had done anything to merit being here with the likes of them.

The doors on the other end of the room opened, and a man flanked by two huge bodyguards came striding in. A chill ran through me as I realized one of them was Jasper, Queen Esmerelda's other lab rat. One of the others the serum had worked on. One of the only ones to survive like

Marissa Allen

myself. He was a hulking man, making everyone else in the room look like children. I had met him briefly the last time I was in the palace, when the queen broke my wrists.

Everyone's attention turned toward the man in the front as he smiled and opened his arms in a welcoming gesture.

"Well, here we are, then! Who's ready to be on the cutting edge of technology?" he asked, clapping his hands together.

10

"Thank you, everyone, for being able to make it. Although," he paused for effect, "we all know this is the event everyone came here for. So, let's not waste any time."

There was a small chuckle from the group.

A screen behind him flared to life, and he grabbed a remote as a presentation came on the screen. "This auction is for the planned objective payload pathogen yield, or P.O.P.P.Y as we call it. A mist form of nanotechnology, where the tech can be programmed like a virus. Please watch."

A video started to play of a gas being released into a room with glass walls and people within. They looked confused and then afraid as the mist covered them and they began to cough.

"Depending on the programming, the effects can be immediate or take hours to show in the subject."

Within a minute or two we could see their veins become more pronounced and their skin seemed pale. The veins turned blue then black, the people starting to appear almost like cracked marble. They stumbled to their knees before collapsing and not moving.

"Now, one of the most exciting things about this product is it can also be targeted. If the DNA of the subject is provided, the mist can affect one person in a crowd of thousands."

I schooled my features so they wouldn't see the terror I had of this weapon falling into anyone's hands. Benson shifted from foot to foot as he watched. Greed filled all of the others' eyes. They were almost frothing at the mouth, no doubt thinking of the plans they had for this technology.

"Don't you own a nanotech company? What are you doing here?" one snapped, looking down his nose at me.

"This is a game of chess, and I'm just here to make sure you're so far behind us you can never catch up." I didn't look his way, but was internally smirking. I had made up a reason, hoping to unsettle him— just because I could. A girl had to find amusement where should could.

Others must have heard, as some of them made incredulous noises and rolled their eyes. Some were sizing me up, actually looking at me as a competitor for once, not just some girl in the room.

The auctioneer clapped regaining everyone's attention. "Now, shall we start the bidding at twenty million?"

One of the younger men was the first to raise his hand.

The bidding went on to ridiculous numbers as Mr. Diaz and Mr. Getry stood there appearing almost bored. I followed their lead, not bidding myself, yet I kept my eyes on them. Mr, Diaz caught my attention; he was glancing around the room, seemingly assessing those putting in the bids. As it started to slow, Mr. Getry put in a bid and Mr. Diaz glared at him. The auctioneer asked if there were any last bids, and I put my hand up, staring at Mr. Getry. We

70

Made Immortal

bid back and forth, but eventually, I saw him flinch, and he didn't raise his hand again.

"Going once, going twice, sold to Ms. Contra," the auctioneer called. I had no idea what the bid had come to—we didn't have the money anyway. He grabbed a device from Jasper. My jaw clentched as our eyes met, but he didn't seem to recognize me.

I felt Benson readying himself as the moment we'd been waiting for approached. I wasn't sure if he recognized who Jasper was though.

"Now, please just enter your bank account information, and once the transfer is complete," the auctioneer held up a flash drive, "this will be all yours, including the encryption code."

"Of course." I took the device. "Time to pay the piper."

That was the signal. It was time.

The lights went out, and a few yelled in surprise. My lenses automatically switched to night vision, and I saw others pull weapons from within their jackets.

I grabbed the flash drive from the auctioneer and turned to bolt, but before I could, Jasper grabbed me and threw me backward. I slammed into the auctioneer, and we both went crashing to the ground. The flash drive had been knocked out of my hand when I landed. I looked for it, trying to scramble away from Jasper.

From the way he moved, it seemed like he was just seeing slightly better than normal in the dark and not using any type of night vision. His movements were close but not focused exactly where I was. I used that to my advantage. Seeing the flash drive, I moved quickly to grab it without breaking my stride and raced for the doorway.

I pulled the headband off. The goal once we got out was to make sure I was seen... again. The video of me from the execution had been making the rounds and making noise among those who Neria had failed. We had heard that the local rebels had many new recruits showing up over the last few weeks. As much discord we could sow the better. The more Neria had to focus on at home, the less help they'd be able to provide Esmerelda.

"Guys, Jasper is here," I said breathlessly into my earpiece.

Benson shouldered his way through the doors, and I was hot on his heels. We hadn't made it more than a few feet out of the room before something grabbed my ankle and I went slamming face first into the floor.

"Benson, the drive!" I screamed.

He spun, catching sight of me tossing it his way. He grabbed it out of the air, turned, and booked it out of the room. Getting this data out of here was the most important thing. I would be able to take care of myself.

I focused back on Jasper, who had my ankle in his huge, meaty fist. Giving a mighty push, I slammed my other foot into his face, rocking him backward. As I got pulled with him I used the momentum to latch on to him, my elbow pounded into the side of his face multiple times.

One of his hands wrapped around my throat, and with his larger size, he tossed my like a rag doll into the wall. My nose cracked as he followed up with a right hook. Blood dripped down my lips. I kicked out with all of my strength, and he dropped me as he stumbled back.

I straightened up, wiping at the blood with the back of my hand. I smiled before charging at him. We crashed together, and I slugged him while he got a shot to my ribs. We exchanged a few more blows before I grabbed his arm, using all my strength I tugged and jutted out my hip to send him flying over me through another set of doors into what might have been a training room. I stalked after him, tapping my bracelet, and my suit came sliding out along my body. As I crossed the threshold, he swung part of a desk straight at my head. I ducked with just enough time for it to go sailing inches from my face.

"Chase, I'm headed your way," Benson said on the comms.

Jasper ran for me and managed to grab my upper arm and hurl me into more of the desks in the room. I crashed through a few of them before smacking into the wall. I forgot how strong he was, and he was so much faster than he should have been for as big as he was. Not as fast as me though. I stood up, trying to catch my breath, having to lean over my knees for a second, as he came walking toward me in no hurry. With a single thought, throwing knives materialized in my hand, and I threw them, each thunking solidly into his chest. He swiped at them, knocking the connections apart, but the blades would still be in the wound, slowly dissolving. Not deadly, but it would hurt.

He roared, and I pulled another dagger into my hand and slashed out, cutting his face. My ribs were on fire; I think some were broken. I limped back, putting more room between the two of us. Some light shone into the room behind me from a window. I glanced up, saw the look on his face, and knew this wasn't going to end well.

"The trashcans straight ahead, Benson," Gwen called, telling him where to find the closest stash of weapons.

I could hear gunfire over the comm. In the second I was distracted, Jasper was there, slamming into me, breaking through the window, the glass cutting deep into my flesh as we plummeted from the thirteenth story of the building. The weightlessness caused my stomach to do flips.

Jasper tried to keep a hold of me as we fell, while he

snapped out what looked to be a small compact grappling device. He fired it toward the building, and it snagged on a balcony we soared past. It stopped us sharply. His grip wasn't enough as he jerked to a stop, and I was ripped from his grasp, continuing to fall.

Out of instinct, I grabbed at one of the next passing balconies. It felt like my shoulders were ripped apart before my fingers slipped and I dropped again. I caught on a few each time, slowing my fall but it didn't stop me from crashing through the canopy above the entrance, the landing knocking me out as I hit the pavement.

I came to slowly, my head spinning, I hurt everywhere. I heard Gwen on the comms.

"Benson, Chase, and I are on the way to you, Atty."

I shook my head, trying to clear the fog in my mind. I held my temple and noticed a giant ring of bystanders recording me on their vidscreens. I heard Jasper coughing as I tried to take a deep breath but was unable to. He was on the ground as well and looked like he must have still fallen some of the way.

Pushing myself to one knee as soon as I could, I looked to Jasper through the hair falling in my face. There was a crowd of people around us, looking terrified but morbidly curious. Especially as we got up, both of us obviously injured but alive.

"Atty, we're through. Blow it," Chase called. They had made it to the service entrance, where Atty had planted some explosives to take down that section behind them. "Vi, you almost here?"

I could hear the worry in Chase's voice.

"I'm going to have to catch up to you later. Go. I got this," My voice was quiet as I still hadn't caught my breath.

"Where are you?" Gwen asked. "We'll come to you."

Made Immortal

"Vi, we're coming," David said. "Guys, she's out front."

"I need you to leave. That's an order. I got this," It wasn't a request. As I stood, holding my ribs, I saw a couple of men with guns coming out of the building and heading toward us.

One of the men threw a canister at my feet, and it started to release a mist. Terror gripped me, knowing exactly what this was, worried not just for myself but the bystanders around us. My eyes began to water, then I felt like I was spinning. I dropped to a knee again. Looking up, I found Jasper towering over me with a vicious smile on his face. Yet, no one else seemed to be affected by the mist.

"How?" I managed to ask.

"Targeted to your DNA," he said, victory in his voice as I lost consciousness.

11

The world slowly came into focus. Metal gleamed above me. I groaned as my entire body ached. The awareness that I was in an ambulance gave me a jolt.

"Glad you're up. I wanted to make sure you knew the rules before we got to where we're going," Jasper said gleefully.

"And where would that be?" I asked, trying to pull up my arms and realizing they were clasped in the same restraints from the prison.

I could see he got enjoyment in my slow understanding of what was happening.

"We're taking you home, and when we get there, you are going to be punished like you deserve," he said.

"Everything there is punishment," I snapped.

"No, that comes later. Once you've paid your penance, then we'll get to work on you being of service to the queen. We have to see what makes you tick, you know. You were so much more than the doctors expected. That's why they continued their work on me, honing me and my skills until you looked like a teddy bear. I will always beat you,

Made Immortal

Princess. For some reason, they won't let me kill you." His face twisted in anger as he said it. "They want to see what happened to you after you left. They had only been able to test you while weakened before, but they have a new lab, where they can see what you can really do."

I knew the bloodlust I felt in a fight. Who knew what went through *his* head.

"Once we get you to the depot at the docks, you and all the others will be shipped off to black sites never to be seen again. Without you to motivate the people, they'll be easier to bring to heel." He crossed his arms across his chest and settled back against the wall.

A shiver ran through me as I thought about what I had endured over the years. How it was probably nothing compared to what they were planning to do to me now. I couldn't go back. I would *not* go back. Hate radiated through me as I stared at Jasper. Yet, if I waited to get out of here, at least there would be a clue to finding the missing people. We needed to search those docks.

I knew from before that the cuffs they had me in were electronically controlled. The guard sitting next to Jasper held a taser tipped baton.

"I will kill you if it's the last thing I do," I growled.

"You aren't going to be killing anyone, you stupid girl," he spat.

I waited for the right moment, and when the ambulance jumped after hitting a bump, I twisted as much as I could and jerked my knee up, hitting the guard. It was enough to bounce him backward into the wall. His body involuntarily ricocheted from the sheer force of the impact. As he fell forward, the movement triggered the baton, and it landed on my cuffs, shorting them out.

When the cuffs opened, I grabbed the baton and

stabbed it into Jasper's neck, in the moment's he was paralized I managed to swing the baton into his cheek. I launched myself through the gap to the driver. I grabbed the wheel, turning it sharply to the right. The seat jabbed into my side as the Ambulance started to flip. Everything in the ambulance that wasn't screwed down started to tumble through the air as we went end over end into the ditch.

I awoke again, feet from the ambulance, thrown through the windshield. I hoped my healing could handle the beating I was taking today. I drug myself along, unable to stand yet, trying to get more space between myself and Jasper. I could hear groaning from the wreck and could tell it was him. I wasn't sure if the ambulance crew could have survived that or not, but he would have.

I heard the banging before I saw Jasper kick the back door off it's hinges. His face was covered in blood, and he was holding his shoulder and limping. At least I wasn't the only one reaching my limits.

My breathing came out short and ragged, and I tried to crawl farther. I only had one good arm to drag myself away, and my vision was still spinning.

This can't be it, was all I could think as I knew my attempts of escaping would be useless.

"We... com... " Static filled my comm, like my friends were finally just coming into range.

"We're almost there. Can you hear us?"

I couldn't help but smile at the sound of Chase's voice. No matter what happened, at least I heard him one last time.

Jasper made it to me. He grabbed me by my arm and pulled me up, but I could barely stand. He started to drag me back toward the ambulance.

"Down!" came Gwen's order over the comms.

Made Immortal

I used everything I had to dive toward the ground, breaking from Jasper's grasp. Shots fired, and multiple rounds slammed into Jasper, knocking him back and toppling him to the ground. A van came screeching to a halt near me, the door flying open and Chase sprinting the distance to me. He grabbed me; there was no time to worry for my injuries. He drug me to the van, closing the door as soon as I pulled my legs in. The van screeched, tires spinning as we raced back into town.

I just laid on Chase's lap, staring at the ceiling as it came in and out of focus. Some breaths caught in my throat. The sounds of my coughing rattled as I heard and felt liquid where it shouldn't have been.

I felt Chase's hand caressing my face and the blur above me must have been him. We pulled into a garage. Pain laced through me as they grabbed me to switch to another car. Before we made our way out and down a maze of alleyways toward our next safe house.

I saw David's face in a moment of clarity as he was kneeling next to me. I felt pain as he pressed down on my side. Looking down and just saw blood pouring from under his fingers. Fire and lightning were flowing through me, burning me from the inside. My vision blurred again, my head spinning.

"Why isn't it stopping?" I heard David mutter, but I couldn't pick up my head.

"What is happening with her skin?" Gwen asked.

"It's P.O.P.P.Y. They just showed us this at the auction," Benson said, worry thick in his voice.

Floating in and out of consciousness, I heard Chase ask, "Why isn't she getting better?"

I don't know how much time had passed before I heard Gwen's voice. Light, barely audible. "You can do it Vi. Please."

That was all I heard before I slipped away once more, back to where I couldn't feel, where I didn't have to worry or hurt. I found myself thinking I wouldn't mind staying here forever. I was so tired.

Pain flared in my veins again.

"There was something in that mist. She isn't healing like she should. We're going to need blood. We need an operating room." David's voice was there. It reminded me of something, some reason to try to pull myself from the dark, but I didn't have the strength and returned to nothingness.

I groaned as I opened my eyes to bright white light above me. Terror gripped me. I knew those lights; pain came with those lights. I screamed and went to pull against my restraints but ended up throwing myself toward the end of the bed. I was breathing heavily, slowly realizing I wasn't back in the prison. There were no restraints.

"Where am I?" I asked, looking around wildly, trying to reorient myself. A woman in scrubs and a mask held out her hands to show she wasn't a threat.

"It's okay, you are safe." She looked behind her and nodded to someone in the doorway. The person nodded back and turned to leave. I saw a tray of tools and grasped for it, falling out of the bed as I tried to take a step. The tray crashed to the ground. I grabbed the first thing I could and waved a pair of clamps at her.

80

Made Immortal

"Where are the others?" I growled.

She crouched near me, still holding her hands up. "Just outside, my friend is getting them."

I heard steps coming closer, running down the corridor outside, and then the group all arrived at the door. Chase pushed his way in, followed by the others.

"Everything is fine," he said.

I took a deep breath and dropped the clamps. I wrapped my arms around my ribs groaning and toppled onto the bed.

Every motion sent jolts of pain through my body. The woman came over and helped hook me back up to some type of bag with fluid in it. I had pulled myself free in my fear. She ran a light across my eyes, took my pulse, and jotted some things down. I just stared at her, still trying to reorient myself.

"Where are we?" I asked.

"I'm a doctor that helps the Nerian rebels. We've been attempting to stabilize you. You lost a lot of blood, had multiple broken bones, torn ligaments, and you weren't healing there for quite some time. We weren't sure you were going to make it. It seems as if the mist they gassed you with bonded with you on a molecular level and was pumping some type of toxin into your body."

"Um, thanks, I guess," I said, sitting back and flinching. "Did you fix me?"

"It will take more sessions to completely heal you, but yes, you are recovering." She threw a thumb over her shoulder at David. "Your friend here broke the encryption on the flash drive you all managed to obtain. We were able to reverse engineer the technology to get you an antidote. It's slowly clearing the toxin from your system."

"They can do this to anyone." I shivered. The implications were terrifying.

81

"Yes. It looks that way." Chase walked over to grab my hand, looking me over with worry. I assumed I didn't look great.

"The docks." I gasped. "The people, they are taking them to the docks; they're moving them. We have to go," I said, trying to get up, only to be pushed down by the woman.

"You are not going anywhere," she said sternly. I had to agree I wasn't going to get anywhere like this. "If you promise to keep an eye on her, I'll leave you."

She gave the others a steely look, and they all nodded before she left and closed the door behind her.

They all hovered around the bed, worried looks on their faces.

"Thanks for picking me up," I said, laughing and then gasping at the pain.

"Always." Chase ran a hand over my cheek, leaving his thumb there for a moment. I knew he would never say *I told you so*, but this time, he had been right. I was not invincible. I was just happy we'd all made it out of there alive.

A wave of exhaustion swept over me. I felt a little nauseous as it hit me.

Chase kissed the top of my head then leaned down to kiss my nose next. "Sleep. We'll be here when you wake."

"The docks, someone needs to go." I whispered before I dropped into the void again.

12

I wasn't sure how long I had been out. It seemed late, and Chase was the only person awake who I could see in the infirmary. He leaned over and grabbed my hand. There were dark bags under his eyes, and his jaw had stubble showing at least a few days of not shaving. I wondered how long I had been here.

Relief and warmth enveloped me seeing him here. Remembering where I was I looked to him. "Do you trust them?" I asked quietly as I peered around to see if anyone might be listening.

"These are some of the same people Joseph was helping before he left. They're good people. They're basically us but in Neria. The rebellion has been growing, especially recently," he said. "We've actually been in touch with him; he's been working with David to create the serum for you."

Well, at least we finally managed to get in touch with the rebels. "Is Jasper dead?"

"No, we just put him down for a bit," he said, shaking his head.

"I'm sorry," I said softly.

83

"You came home." He shrugged, but how exhausted he looked twisted a knife of guilt in my heart. "Good thing David put a tracker in your suit."

I raised an eyebrow but then laughed, which morphed into a groan.

I stretched my hand out, and he took it gingerly. "You can say it."

"I'm just happy you're okay." He looked shy, unsure of what touch might hurt me. He ended up just intertwining his fingers with mine. "That mist... It turns out they've been using this for assassinations of some Nerian dissenters. So, the people here have already been working on a counter agent for some time. With David's and Joseph's help, they were able to crack it. Luckily, they had research already started. They weren't sure if they would be able to figure it out fast enough." He sighed, his breath wavering. "I thought I was going to lose you." He wiped his hand over his face, as if trying to get rid of the echoes of grief now that I was safe.

I reached up and cupped his chin in my palm. He leaned into the touch. "We need to stay," I said firmly.

"I know." He nodded. "We're all in agreement about helping. We're going to get those people back to their families. And we'll cause some trouble while we're at it."

He leaned over and grabbed a tablet that he had leaned against the chair. The screen flared to life, and he typed in something. Videos started to flip across the screen—news reports. My face was everywhere. Video of me over the last few days. The videos of Jasper and I crashing to the ground and me getting gassed. Then, videos of fires and explosions in certain areas of the city. In the poorer parts, riots were clashing with the military that had been called in.

"Revolution is nigh," Chase said. "They're calling your name in the streets. You aren't just a face of our resistance;

Made Immortal

Neria's rebels are following you too. The first steps to try to take back the city have started."

"Death follows me," I grumbled.

"Hope follows you. You make people believe in their right to freedom," he said firmly. "You've always been a leader. I know you never wanted it, but you are a symbol of so much more now. The people believe in you and your cause; they're tired of being trampled and are taking back their rights. What I've always seen, who you could be... this is in your soul."

"Thank you," I said, meaning it. "How long before I can get out of here? We need to get to the docks right away, before they move all the prisoners again. We need to get the missing people back."

"You need to rest. Let us figure out everything else for now." He got up and kissed my forehead. "Try to get some sleep," he said.

While I wanted to argue, I could tell I was fading quickly. Maybe a nap wouldn't be so bad.

The next time I woke, I went to sit up and felt slightly better than before. The infirmary was mostly empty at this point. I cautiously shifted to try to get my legs over the edge of the bed. I grabbed the bar that held the bag of liquid pumping into my arm. It had wheels, and I drug it closer to myself. I hung on to it, trying to steady myself and get my feet under me.

A few moments and a couple of shaking steps later, I felt like I was getting the hang of it. I just needed to move very slowly. I was in luck as the door was already open. I looked around after making my way into the hallway. The it was dark, but I could see some dim light coming from down the hallway to the right. I started my sluggish trek down the hallway.

As I made my way to an open room, I saw midday light streaming in from the cracks in the newspaper covering the windows. As I kept moving it turned out the light I had seen was coming from computer screens. It looked like many of our own safe houses. There were a few people watching the news and scouring parts of the Nerian net. A woman looked over, and her eye shone electric blue in the dark, and a large scar crossed her face and eye. The other people didn't move from looking at their screens. The woman looked surprised and headed over to me. Before she said anything, she led me toward the couch in the room to sit.

As she stood back I got a view of her and she was an imposing woman. Now I saw she had more scars down her neck as well. Her hair was shaved on one side, with the other short and braided back out of her face. She looked like she could give me a run for my money. "Hi there. My name is Naya."

"I'm Vi," I said.

She laughed at that. "I know. You've actually been here for a while. Plus, everyone in Neria know's about you now." She pointed towards one of the news outlets flashing my face across a screen.

I nodded at that. "I guess you're right." I laughed. "Well, it's nice to meet you, Naya."

"Nice to finally meet you, Vi," she said, shaking my hand firmly.

"So, what do you do here?" I asked her.

"A little bit of everything." She chuckled. I heard familiar steps coming down the hallway.

Made Immortal

"She's being modest," Benson said, coming around the corner. "She runs things here."

In the look he gave Naya, I instantly felt something between the two of them, some kind of electricity in the air. I would have to ask Benson about that later. What had everyone gotten up to while I had been out?

"We'd been watching you for a while before you came here. The way you united the voices of the Kabira people, made Nerians see they weren't alone. We saw that something could be done. We've had a lot of people come to us because of your courage," she said.

I still wasn't used to the idea of having so many people taking action because of my decisions. A small voice inside reminded me that anything that happened to them would be on me. Revolution was bloody, and I was already drenched in crimson.

"Well, I'm here to help," I said, just hoping I could do some good. "Benson," I looked at him, "is Nathan okay?" I was so selfish for not thinking to ask until now.

"Yeah, his security had him out of there and headed for the border as soon as the lights went out." Benson sat in a chair nearby, and Naya sat on the coffee table near him.

"At least there's that. Did he talk to David?" I asked, thinking of the offer Nathan had proposed when we met. Before everything went haywire.

"Yeah, Joseph did. David didn't want to make any decisions until we got you on your feet though," Benson said, and I nodded. I knew David would be laser focused. He would obsess over it, not sleeping, not taking care of himself until he solved the puzzle. As if reading my mind, Benson added, "He's finally sleeping."

"That's good. Everyone else?" I asked, thankful that they all seemed okay.

"Everyone is fine. We've just been here praying you would be too," Benson said, reaching out to squeeze one of my hands.

"Naya." A young girl came running into the room, and we all looked over. "He's here," she said quickly, breathing sharply.

"Perfect, can you bring him in here?" Naya asked, and the girl nodded and took off again.

"We have a lot of kids who lost their parents," she said in a sad tone, looking after the girl. "They like to help in the little ways they can. Bunny came to us almost a year ago. She's always had excess energy and loves passing messages along."

I thought of the many people showing up at the rebel outposts throughout Kabria, heading for the hope the rebels gave that they had heard of in whispers. These kids had parents that had been killed or were missing, leaving them alone to fend for themselves. I remembered one boy, who had made it to our headquarters, took pride in making sure every officer had shoes polished to perfection. I nodded, understanding far too well. Bunny came bouncing back in with a man following her. I raised an eyebrow as Marco Diaz walked into the room.

"You've looked better," he said, glancing me over before going to give Naya a kiss on the top of her head, he looked to be of an age where he could have been her father. The move was caring, protective, it reminded me of myself and my friend's.

Narrowing my eye's I looked him over. His grey hair more disheveled then when I last saw him. I had no idea what he was doing here, but Naya didn't seem in the least bit perturbed about his arrival. Apparently, at least with the way Bunny and Naya acted, it seemed like this might be a

Made Immortal

common occurrence. "I've felt better," I muttered, furrowing my brow, still not trusting this situation.

He laughed and sat on an overturned bucket, seeming completely comfortable in the dim, dingy, dated base. I never would have pictured him in a place like this.

"That was quite the show you put on. It's all over the news cycles." He pointed at one of the computer screens. There was a caption of *Terrorist Strikes Again* underneath the video from the summit. "They've got quite the bounty out on you: two million."

"I'm insulted. I'm worth so much more." I rolled my eyes.

"That you are, indeed," he said, steepling his fingers.

"How, or why, I guess, are you here?" I asked him.

"How do you think this is funded?" He gestured to the building. "Not all of it, but I was the first investor years ago. Around the same time the government perverted my work," he said, hate filling his voice.

He had created the very first implants and the chips that helped control them. The basis of the tech industry in Neria. He was basically the grandfather of the most profitable and widely used technology that was now the backbone of the county. I had heard that he was wealthier than the king. I saw now the hate and anger he had for what they had done to his precious creations. Apparently, he was ready for change like the rest of us. More so, maybe.

"So, you're undermining Neria?" Still unsure of his motivations.

"Yes." He nodded.

"Why were you at the auction?" I ran through everything he had done on that day, and I started to see it all in a different light.

"Same reason as you. I couldn't let any of them get their

hands on it. Only," he paused, giving me a playful look, "I planned to actually pay for it, but I thought I'd see what you were up to once I saw you there."

I mulled that over. During the breakfast he had seemed to enjoy goading Mr. Getry. He had been watching the others in the auction closely, just as I had. He had been sizing up the enemy. I could see how the rebels here in Neria could benefit from an inside agent, especially one as rich as he was.

"I see, well glad I saved you some money Mr. Diaz." That had him cracking a huge smile as he leaned closer to me.

"Call me Marco."

I couldn't help but smile back. As wary as I should have felt, I couldn't help but feel like I was really going to like him. "Nice to truely meet you Marco."

13

Under Naya's direction one of the children ran off to find and bring the team to this room. They managed to hide their shock as they came in to find Marco sitting with me. Chase looked from Marco to me and I gave him a slight nod— letting him know everything seemed to be fine.

"Mr. Diaz, pleasure to officially meet you," Chase said, holding out his hand to shake.

Marco grasped his hand and shook it vigorously. "Call me Marco and It's my pleasure. You all are quite the talk of the underground. And overground too, I guess." He laughed.

Marco's attitude seemed infectious, and with Naya, Benson and myself not being on the defensive everyone else seemed to relax.

"So, what brings you here?" Gwen said, crossing her arms, not letting her guard all the way down.

"We were hoping you might stay for a while." He looked to Naya who nodded. "We have some things you all could really help us out with."

Atty scoffed. "You know everyone wants us dead, right?"

"You aren't alone there," Naya spoke up. She was right; I was sure wanted the rebels dead too. They'd been a thorn in King Edgar's side here in Neria longer than we had.

"What can we do?" Turning slightly, so I could get a good view of Marco and Naya at the same tine, but my ribs flared at the movement. I did my best to ignore it.

"After we go to evacuate the docks, we're hoping to make a stand in one of the most impacted areas of the city," Naya said. "It's going to take a lot. The king's forces are attacking the hospitals, the community centers, and the temples. The people are ready, but they need muscle. They need hope too."

I ground my teeth but nodded. As much as I hated it, the truth kept slapping me in the face. If I could help these people, I had to.

"When is the mission to the docks?" I asked, flinching again as I tried to sit up straighter.

"Tonight," Naya said.

"Okay, bring me up to speed," I said, but David plopped down on the couch next to me, the bounce making me gasp.

"You aren't going anywhere," he said firmly, patting the back of my hand. He stared me down until I nodded.

I wasn't going to be of any help, not by tonight. *Tomorrow maybe,* I laughed to myself. It probably wouldn't be safe for me to try to get out of town, even if I wanted to. I would have to see how I could make myself useful here instead, and then I would just try to get back on my feet as soon as I could.

Chase crossed his arms, quiet, calculating, planning. I caught his eye, and I got his little smile, the one just for me, before his attention drifted away again.

Made Immortal

"Then, I'll do what I can to help from here," I said determined.

David nodded. "I always need a hand." He wrapped his arm around me and I snugged into his side.

"And after the mission, we have some people we'd like you to meet in the infirmary," Marco said.

"Yes, of course," I said, happy to try to help where I could. Anywhere I could. I wanted to be of use in a way other than brute force.

"Well, I'll leave you for now." Marco got up with a flourish that seemed more energetic than I expected from a man his age. "I don't want to wear you out. I'll be in touch soon."

With that, he was gone.

"Can someone tell me the plan at least?" I asked the group. They all clattered into the nearby seats.

"How are you feeling?" Gwen asked.

"Why are you out of bed?" Benson followed. They were all talking over each other.

I gestured for them to be quiet. "Youre giving me a headache."

The group hushed, looking ashamed.

"So sorry. Is this better?" David asked in a soft voice as he looked me over.

I slapped him away. "It was a joke."

We laughed, and I saw Naya standing alone outside of our little circle.

Benson threw a smile her way. "Naya, you can probably explain better than we can," he said, like he was hoping she'd get more comfortable with us.

"So, we've been going over the blueprints and information from our contacts about the docks," she said, her leadership coming to the forefront. She was clearly used to

93

preparing people for things like this. "We've reviewed the security footage we could get our hands on, and we've been able to map the route of the security officers. There are three main buildings where they could be hiding everyone. We're going to have a team go to all three locations and breach at the same time. We have boats in the basin ready for evac as soon as we move."

"Benson, Atty, and I are going to be on the breach teams, and Gwen will be set up to provide cover," Chase said, leaning back in his chair.

"You get to be the man in the chair with me," David said, which made me smile.

"What time are you leaving?" I asked.

"We still have a few hours left. We're going to set up at dusk," Naya said.

"Naya!" someone called from down the hallway.

"It's good to see you up, Vi. If you'll excuse me." She nodded to us and then went into the hallway and headed toward the call.

I raised an eyebrow at Benson as soon as she was out of view. He blushed but said nothing. I smiled and shook my head, happy for him.

"Vi, seriously, how are you?" Gwen grabbed my hand.

"I'm fine. I promise. It's just going to take a bit longer to heal up this time." I smiled, but I was starting to feel the exhaustion slip over me again. "So, what exactly was the deal? I know the mist targeted me directly by DNA. I just don't understand what happened. Why didn't I heal like normal?"

"It was designed to destroy tissue. Anyone other than you wouldn't have made it past a few minutes. They had been expecting you; it was tailored for your genes specifically," David said, rubbing the back of his neck. "Somehow,

94

Made Immortal

they found a compound that would replicate with your body's healing process, destroying the tissue as it tried to regenerate. The wounds kept reopening, and the damage was extensive. It was really close, Vi. We have to take this seriously." He had a grave look on his face.

"So, I'm just as vulnerable as everyone else in this room right now." I waived my arm around. I felt a tear at my shoulder but ignored it. "This doesn't change anything. I'll heal up, and once I do, I can go back to work. You did it, you fixed me. I'm getting better."

"You need to be careful—more than you normally are. No human shield. No bulldozer. You need to call us in if Jasper shows up," Chase said firmly.

I nodded. His point had been made. "I promise. Cross my heart. I'll be more careful." I flinched as I drew a cross on my chest. My side flared with pain as I did it.

There was a collective sigh from the group. It reminded me how much I was loved. How much I had to live and fight for.

"Good!" Gwen clapped and pulled her chair next to the couch. She grabbed a tablet and shoved it in my face. "So, you also went viral... again. Look." She flipped through, and video after video popped up, some with animation, music, or strange quotes plastered across the screen.

Aghast, I looked at her in terror. "What is that?"

Everyone started to laugh.

"Oh, and this one," David said, pulling out his vidscreen to show me different ones.

"You are the voice of a generation." Gwen beamed. "They're being posted and shared so often that the NCDC can't keep it off the web. It's been going strong for days now."

"Your name is whispered all over the city. It's painted in

some places too." Atty chortled and shared a look with Gwen, which made her giggle.

"Something big is happening here," Chase said, nodding. "It's good we're staying. I think, I hope, we can help. At least a little bit. Not to mention, strategically, the king can't send troops to Kabria if he's busy at home."

"If by some chance, the rebels manage to oust the old man, we might even have some friends ready to step in and help," David said, and we all agreed.

"Wouldn't that be something," Benson said, leaning against the back of the chair.

We all sat with that idea for a while, hoping. Could we call it hoping? Wishing? We would try our best to make even the smallest part of it come true. Anything we could do to help the people here.

Anything.

The others started to chat among themselves. My eyes fluttered closed. I was happy to hear their voices in a chorus again, all talking over each other. I felt the warmth of having my family there, surrounding me, making me feel safe. I slowly slipped back into the void.

14

I startled awake as someone shook my shoulder. On instinct, I went to protect myself, but the movement had my body flaring with pain. Snapping my eyes open, I saw Chase leaning over me, and I took a deep breath and relaxed.

He gave me an amused smile. "We're heading out shortly. I just wanted to see you before we left."

Groggily, I glanced around and I was still on the couch. I wiped at my face and tried to shimmy into a more comfortable position.

"Just relax. We'll see you after we get back." Chase kissed me quickly before pulling back.

Over his shoulder I saw the others behind him. The group looked out of place in their stealth gear while making silly faces at me.

"We'll see you soon," Came the chorus from them.

"We've got your back," David said, sitting next to me and handing me a tablet as he opened his own laptop.

"Okay, be careful," I said, watching them leave.

"Always." Chase laughed and kissed me quickly, and

then he gave David a quick squeeze of his shoulder before joining the others.

"They'll be okay," Naya said, walking up and pulling on her gloves. "We'll get everyone home." She said it with such a passion that I knew she was thinking of all the Nerians that had been kidnapped, the ones this mission was going to rescue.

"Thank you." I nodded to her. She gave me a quick salute before she followed out the door that my friends had just gone through.

David and I had spent some time chatting, trying to keep my mind off everything about to happen. It hadn't been working well. I felt so anxious thinking of my friends, the kidnapped, the rebels. Hoping everything would be okay.

I stretched a bit, testing out my muscles. I was already feeling better now than I had a few hours ago. I curled up more comfortably on the couch.

"How are you?" David asked, surveying me.

"Like I got run over by a bus, then chewed up by a bear, and then thrown down a ravine." I was trying my best to not laugh. I tapped at the tablet, bringing the screen to life.

David did laugh. "That's probably not far off. Just take it easy. It's going to take a while to heal from this one. Here." He tapped on his computer, and screens popped open on my tablet.

I started to flip through a few different security cameras, some blueprints, and a write up from someone who must have been scouting the location. Through the security cameras, I could see it was almost dusk. Almost time.

David pointed to the computer screens along the wall. There were feeds popping up from body cams. I could see the team as they came into view of the other's cameras. One

98

Made Immortal

of the people working the rebel computers looked over her shoulder at us.

"Sir, they'll be in position shortly," she said.

David nodded. "Thanks, Silvie."

She smiled and turned back to her computer, fingers flying across the keys. She was breaking into the security system of the docks.

"Okay, everyone, get in position," I heard Naya say through the comms.

"I'm all set for cover," came Gwen's reply.

"Entry point alpha ready," a man said, whose voice I didn't recognize.

"Entry point beta ready," said another. More started to sound off. There were a total of six teams.

I started to grab the video feeds of Chase, Atty, Benson, and Gwen on my tablet while everyone started to fall into place.

David leaned over and put his hand over mine. "Everything is going to be fine."

"I'm just sitting here helpless. I feel useless," My anxiety was making me feel uncomfortable in my own skin.

"You can't control everything. This is going to be a good lesson for you. Our friends are the best there is; they know how to protect themselves. They'll get themselves and all of those people home." He gave a strong decisive nod.

Biting my lip between my teeth, they were dry and chapped, and I grimaced as one broke open. I ran my tongue over it, wincing at the pain.

"Breach in three, two, one, all go," Naya called.

As we watched, the people at the computers tapped a few keys and the entire security grid went green. Doors popped open for all of the teams as they made their way inside of the multiple buildings.

99

Just as we always had, these teams moved as one. Each made their entries, and I could see them sighting down their weapons. Some cleared rooms while others moved at a face pace into the belly of the buildings.

Then, the comms were live with noise as they started to encounter the guards. Multiple explosions set off gas throughout the buildings. Luckily, our teams were equipped with night vision and gas masks.

There were volleys of gunfire. Men yelled—mostly the guards trying to figure out what was going on, calling for help. Our teams were well oiled machines, ready for everything, while the guards were caught unaware and unprepared. I grabbed David's hand again and tried my best not to crush it.

"We found some of the prisoners," came a report from one team. I looked to that camera view and saw dozens of people huddled toward the backs of gated cells, cowering, holding their arms over their heads, unsure what was going on.

"Close your eyes," one of ours said to the people. He set something into the lock of the door, and with a small burst of light and a puff of smoke, it swung open. "Let's go. Everyone out now. Follow them!" he said, pointing to the others, who were waving their arms motioning the way for them to go. "Extraction alpha is a go."

We had gathered quite a crowd to watch what was happening. Some were holding on to each other, breathless, waiting to see if everything ended up okay. Who knew how many might be hoping for a glimpse of their loved ones.

"Beta needs cover!" one of men shouted, sounding out of breath. More gunfire rang out around them.

"Maneuver them to the windows," Gwen called, followed by the sound of her racking her rifle. Once in view,

100

Made Immortal

she laid down fire, the windows smashing, and I could see the guards through the security camera jerk and fall as her bullets found their mark.

"Pull up the bus!" Naya called, and a bus came crashing through a security gate on the edge of the docks. The first group of prisoners poured out of the building and went racing toward it. The doors flew open, and they piled inside.

I looked back to the group that included Chase. They were making their way through the part of the dock with the shipping containers. I saw Chase put his arm up to stop the others as they came up just out of sight of a group of men.

They were moving prisoners into a container that was about to be loaded onto a ship. The guards looked around, hearing the gunfire and the explosions around the docks. They shoved the rest of the people in and slammed the doors to the container.

Chase curled a finger, and Atty came up next to him. I could see Atty grinning from Chase's camera. In tandem, Chase laid down fire while Atty threw flat disks with blinking lights toward the guards. Benson ran toward the container and the prisoners.

The disks, lights flashing faster, exploded at the feet of the confused guards, who had been shooting randomly, clearly unsure where the bullets were coming from yet. Gunfire rained down on the container, but the steel held, keeping the prisoners safe.

"Follow me," Benson yelled, pulling the doors open. He led them toward the water. "Delta incoming; boats ready." A boat came sliding up to the edge of the dock. Benson held out a hand and started helping the prisoners drop down into it.

Atty ran around the perimeter of the area, slapping more devices on crates and what looked to be a guard outpost as the others helped Benson get the prisoners into the boat. Before Atty arrived last and jumped down, he grinned as he pressed the button on a trigger and the explosions ripped through the compound. The guard post creaked before the supports started to crumble, and the entire building came down, dust billowing everywhere.

Alarms, at this point, were blaring. Giant lights flared to life as the guards tried to scramble to see what was going on.

"Beta's on bus two!" someone called, and I saw another bus had been brought in and loaded up for another group of prisoners that had been found. The sound of a chopper sounded, and the spotlight headed toward the docks from the city.

"Everyone out now," Naya called. I saw her laying down fire against some guards while she ran toward a bus just as it was starting to make its way toward the gates. The back door swung open, and one of the prisoners held out a hand to grab her and pull her in. "Evac procedures, get yourself lost before moving to rendezvous point."

Through the security cameras, I could see the docks were in shambles. Buildings were caving in; fires were growing from some of the explosions still.

David let out a breath beside me, and he squeezed my hand. I turned to him, emotionally exhausted, and wrapped my arms around him, and he hugged me back tightly. Even though all together the extraction had been quick, it had been incredibly well planned and executed.

"We've got your six. We'll meet you back at the rendezvous point," Gwen said, and I saw her still firing as the buses and boats made their way out. The bullets raining down were more than she was shooting so apparently, she wasn't the only sniper there. She'd be getting out with them it seemed.

102

Made Immortal

A cheer went up from the people surrounding us, and they started to give each other high fives as the teams made their way out. Everyone was giddy, and the feeling was infectious.

I leaned back against the couch.

"They won't make their way here until early in the morning. You know they still have a few anti-tracking measures to take. So, why don't we get you to bed, and we'll see them in the morning?" David said, holding out a hand to help me get up. He moved the pole holding my IV bag, I had forgotten about, in front of me and I grabbed onto it to help me keep my balance. Someone must have changed it when I was sleeping because it was almost full again.

"Um, Miss Astor." A little girl came running up to me.

I hoped I wasn't scary to the kids, covered in cuts and bruises. "Uh, hi. You can just call me Vi."

"Um, Vi." She nodded as gravely as a small child could. "We just..." She was looking down and rubbing her hands shyly. "We just wanted to thank you for coming to help us. We've seen how brave you are, and I hope I can be as brave as you some day."

My heart swelled but also broke. "You've already been just as brave as me. I wanted to thank you and your friends for taking care of me. I hope I can return the favor."

She beamed and went running off to some of her friends, whispering to them as they all giggled and looked my way.

David just smirked. "You've done way more than you ever meant to." He laughed, grabbed my arm, and helped me limp down the hall. He took me back to the infirmary, and I collapsed onto the bed.

"Wake me as soon as soon as they get back," I told him firmly, but I was already fading. The hours since I left the

103

Marissa Allen

infmirary had exhausted me, even with a nap included. I hated feeling this weak.

"I promise. Sleep well." David turned and headed for the door. Looking back and smiling once more, he flipped off the lights in the otherwise empty infirmary and closed the door quietly behind him.

15

There was a clatter and a chorus of noises and voices as people started to fill into the infirmary. I looked around and realized they might need more beds than they had. I grabbed the pole next to me, the bag it held almost empty, and rolled myself out of bed.

As people caught sight of me, some of them gasped, but I looked toward the doctors. I limped away from the bed, tapping one on the shoulder. All I had to do was point to the bed and they nodded, taking the person they were holding up to it.

"Can I help?" I asked the next person I got to.

They looked me up and down. "You can help by making room."

I nodded and started trying to do just that. Yet, as I passed, some of them held their hands out toward me. I moved closer and grasped their outstretched hands. One of them held their shoulder as blood seeped through; another had a rough bandage around their head and eye. I didn't know what to do, but just seeing them, letting them touch me, seemed to be enough for now. As I walked through the room, I heard my name whispered from person to person, until I finally reached the hallway and shut the door behind me.

I leaned against the wall, resting my head back, and stared at the fluorescent lighting. I was still able to hear them, but at least they couldn't stare at me anymore. I felt weak, and I wasn't sure if it was because of my injuries or that whole situation being a little too much to handle. Taking a deep breath, I tried to calm myself and my racing heart.

"Vi!" came Gwen's voice, and I heard her race down the hallway.

I was so relieved to see her as she slid towards me. I reached out and hugged her close. "Oh, thank the gods. Is everyone else back? Is everyone okay?"

She nodded. "Naya hurt her shoulder. Atty, that stupid boy, got hit by some of his own shrapnel, but it's superficial. Otherwise, everyone is fine." She returned the hug gently. It still hurt, but it was so worth it to have her arms around me again. "No actual losses, but as you can see, quite a few people needed to be looked at. Mostly though, they just need some water, food, and a good night's sleep." She took my arm, she helped me back to the great room.

"Is there a count of how many people you got back?" I asked.

"They're still working on it and getting names so we can start contacting families, but Vi, it was a lot," she said, tugging on my sleeve and smiling up at me. "The next task is finding them safe passage to Soland to get them and their families to safety." She patted my hand.

"We should contact Nathan," I thought out loud.

"Oh, don't worry about that, David's already talking

Made Immortal

with Joseph, and Nathan's aware." She was beaming. "We did it, Vi. We did a really good thing."

"You did," I said, smiling back.

"*We* did it," she said again. "As much as I hated you being hurt by the mist this never would have been possible if Jasper hadn't monologued when he had you."

"Always here to help." I laughed, and winced again as I did.

"Vi!" Chase called and came running up as we made it to the main room. Gwen held out my hand so he could take it from her and help hold me steady. He wrapped his other arm around me, his grip soft but firm.

I grabbed his shirt and tugged him sharply down to my lips, kissing him with a type of desperation I didn't feel very often. I had been so worried he would be hurt, or worse. All of them. I didn't know what I was going to do if something had happened to them.

Chase returned the kiss roughly, forgetting my wounds for a moment. I held in any grimace or gasp, not wanting him to stop because I knew he would if he thought he hurt me. We broke apart, both breathing raggedly, and I blushed as I noticed how many people were there.

He led me to the couch, where the others were huddled around. Gwen had gone to Atty, who had gauze wrapped around his calf. Apparently, they had already gotten the shrapnel out.

"I am so happy to see you all," I said. Naya was there too, batting away the people trying to look at her shoulder. She caught my eye, and we exchanged a strained but happy look. "It's good to see you," I told her.

She nodded quickly but then turned back to the people next to her. She pointed down the hallway, giving orders to those closest to her. They all bustled off to their tasks. Then she turned back to us. "We owe you all a debt of gratitude," she told us, they way she held her shoulder gave away the pain she was in.

"Nonsense," Chase said. "We're happy to be of help. I wish we could do more."

"More will come. For now, we'll enjoy the win," she said, smiling. "Well, I have plenty to do to get this all under control. Let my people know if you need anything." With that, she headed down the hallway.

David was heavy in conversation with his tablet, and I scooted closer to poke my head over his shoulder. Joseph was on the screen. He beamed when he saw me.

"Hi, Joseph," I said.

"So good to see you, Vi," he replied.

David tapped his temple to mine. "Joseph, I'll call you later, but for now, get those transports ready, and we'll let you know the location shortly."

"Sure thing, talk to you later," he said with something in his voice I couldn't quite place. I was happy they had become closer. Joseph was amazing, and I couldn't think of anyone better for David to finally have in his life.

"David," I said, taking his hand, trying to convey I wanted to talk about something serious. "We haven't had a chance to talk about Nathan's offer."

Chase came up next to us, seeming to hear what I had asked him. The rest of the group was close but not necessarily in ear shot. It had been a while since the trio had time to be together, just us.

"Yeah, bud. What are you thinking?" Chase asked.

"I don't know." He shook his head. "I can't just leave you guys," he said, looking back and forth between us.

"We have no bearing on this decision. If you leave, we will be just fine. It's not like we'll never see you again. You

108

Made Immortal

will still be talking to us all the time, and you can still make us all the coolest gadgets. What do *you* want to do?" Chase asked, emphasizing that it was David's decision.

"We just want you to be happy," I said as I laid my cheek against his shoulder.

"Joseph and I could get our research done much faster if we were in the same place," he said, shrugging, clearly lost in thought. "I don't want to leave you, but I can't stop thinking of everything I could do if I went."

"You know we'll always support you. We want what is best for you, forever and always," Chase said, and I nodded.

"I love you guys." David grabbed us both and pulled us in for a bear hug.

"We love you too," Chase and I both said, and we all broke into laughter. The others started to pull their chairs in closer.

"Benson, Atty, I'm so happy to see you." I reached out my hand and squeezed theirs as they each grabbed mine.

Gwen was curled up on the arm of Atty's chair and had her arms around his shoulders. He had a hand rubbing her thigh lightly, not even really seeming to notice.

"Does anyone know what's we're going to be up to next?" Atty asked.

"Over the next few days, we'll be getting as many as we can to safety and connect them with their families. I've been talking with Naya, and she's hoping that once we're all healed up a bit, we can start making the rounds to get Vi's face out there," Benson said before looking my way. "If that's okay with you, anyway."

I nodded. "Yeah, why not? Sounds good to me."

"We also want to do some reconnaissance. We need to find out more about the military, their plans, the nanotech, and how they plan to use it. How we can counter that mist," Chase said, his mind already in strategy mode.

"Hopefully, all this will cause enough of a disruption to stop the Nerian transfers to Kabria too," David chimed in.

"Whatever we do, I need to look as normal as I can as quickly as I can. I need them to think I'm healed enough to be a problem." I twisted a bit back and forth, feeling the pain lessening. It was still enough to knock me down, but I should be able to walk on my own without wincing within the next few days. I hoped.

"Joseph had some ideas on that," David said glancing at my IV bag but then held up his tablet. "He has some new serums to combine with the current treatment to help speed up the process. I need to run some more tests, but hopefully we can have something to try tomorrow."

"I'm ready whenever you are," I said, grimacing as I twisted something while just trying to shift my weight.

David got up from the couch and kissed the top of my head. "I'm going to go start on this. I'll see you all tomorrow."

"Let us know if you need anything," I told him.

He nodded and then slipped away.

Gwen stretched while yawning. Atty looked up at her.

"I don't know about you, but I'm ready for a nap." He stood up and wrapped an arm over her shoulder. She nodded, put a hand to her lips, and blew us a kiss before they headed toward wherever they had us sleeping.

Chase held out a hand to me and helped pull me up. Benson got up at the same time. He came over, and I leaned up to plant a kiss on his cheek.

"I'll see you guys later." He smiled, but instead of following Atty and Gwen, he went the way Naya had gone.

"Wanna get out of here?" Chase asked, and I nodded.

Made Immortal

"Well then, let me show you to our suite." He bowed, putting one arm out to show the way before grabbing my arm again to help me limp back out of the room.

We made our way down a few different hallways. We came to a room similar to the infirmary. Basically one big empty room filled with whatever they needed. This one filled with multi-tier bunks instead single beds. Most had blankets hanging around them for some semblance of privacy. I saw as Atty and Gwen slipped under one farther into the room. Chase took me to one of the corners of the room. Since it had the full ninety degrees the blanketed area was a bit larger than a single bunk provided. The area had plans and folders spread out around on the floor. He set me down gingerly before he went to work picking them up and putting them on the top bunk. There was a little battery powered lamp lighting up the small area.

"Go ahead and lie down, I'm gonna take the floor." He pulled my pole around and straightened my fluid bag. "I should get you a replacement," he muttered.

I grabbed his arm, and with a sharp tug, pulled him to the bed. "Leave it. The people you rescued might need the meds more. We can figure it out tomorrow. For now, come here and cuddle with me, you big lug."

He curled himself into my side and drew his finger along the scars up my arm to the ones on my shoulder and up my neck. His lips followed so light that goosebumps rippled along my skin.

"I've been so worried about you," he whispered as he pulled away.

I ran my fingers from his temple to his cheek, the hair in his face slipping back under my touch. His hand came up to grasp mine. I could feel the tension leaving his body. He

Marissa Allen

had been on a razor's edge for days, I assumed. Now, here he was, slowly relaxing into my touch.

"We're here; we're okay. Today was a good day. We did good. You did good," I told him softly.

He nodded before reaching up and grabbing the lamp to turn it off. We curled into each other, and before I knew it, we were both deep asleep. Finally feeling safe for the first time since before the summit.

16

I stretched out testing what flared with pain and what didn't. It was better than yesterday, but I still was healing much too slowly for my taste. Chase smiled against my neck as he nuzzled me. His lips grazed my skin and left goosebumps in their wake.

"Morning," he murmured.

I kissed his forehead as we started to untangle from each other. He grabbed my arm and helped pull me to sit upright. His hand went to the fluid bag, and I noticed it was completely empty now.

"Let me go get you a replacement. I'll grab some breakfast," he said, getting up from the cot and pushing the blanket wall out of his way.

I propped my back up against the concrete wall the bunk was lined against and started to test out my range of movement. As I rubbed at my sore muscles, they made me wince, but I kept at it, knowing that in the end, I would feel better.

It wasn't terribly long before Chase returned, but when

he did, he wasn't alone. Naya pushed her way through the blanket divider behind him.

I went to stand up, but Chase put a firm hand on my shoulder and urged me to sit back again.

"Don't get up," Naya said, crossing her arms over her chest and sighed deeply.

I looked between them as Chase replaced the bag of IV fluid. When he was done, he sat next to me, wrapped his arms around me, and pulled me close.

"Everyone wants to thank you," Naya started. "They're starting to hope again. I can see it in their faces."

"We don't need any thanks, and I had nothing to do with last night," I said, and I felt Chase chuckle lightly beside me.

"That's not true. The people in the infirmary, their entire demeanor changed once they saw you. The children are laughing and playing; they were even telling stories last night over dinner." She paused for a moment, and I felt Chase tense just slightly. "We need some of that badly, especially for those from some of the areas hit hardest. We want to get moving to another base closer to the edge of the city. That's where the worst of it is. It would be best if they could see you as soon as possible."

"Of course," I said, nodding, but Chase's arms tightened around me just ever so slightly.

"She means today." His voice was clipped.

I swiveled to try and catch his gaze. When I did, I was shocked at how tired he looked. "I'm already feeling much better. It's really not a problem," I said, nuzzling the bottom of his jaw.

"You need to rest." He seemed so stressed. Then, catching my eyes, he let out a deep breath. "Couldn't you just wait a day or two?"

114

Made Immortal

I turned back to Naya. "Is a day or two going to lose the war?"

"Will you be here in a few days?" she asked, giving me a leveled look.

"I will be here as long as I'm needed. I'm not going anywhere." My voice was firm, and I held her gaze.

She nodded, pushing her hair back, running her fingers through it jaggedly. "I'm going to trust you."

Though the words seemed sincere, the tone was clear. She worried it would be a mistake. It wasn't easy to trust when you were in her position.

I grabbed at her hand as she headed out. "I will do everything I can for you and your people."

I squeezed, and she looked down her arm toward me. I let her hand drop. She paused for another moment, and I could see her thinking.

"Benson said you were good people," she said with a nod and turned away.

I curled into Chase. His arms gathered me close before sliding me back to the wall. I pouted as he got off the bunk, but as soon as he threw me a ration pack, my mouth watered. I tore into the bag and started to wolf down the food. Once I was finally able to put my hands down and take a deep breath—I had been starving—Chase handed me a glass of water. Using both hands, I raised it to my mouth, drinking greedily.

"Better?" He laughed and threw me another ration pack. I saw he had grabbed quite a few. "I got you plenty." He leaned over and kissed my forehead. "I'm so happy to see you." His voice wavered.

"I'm really sorry," I said quietly, feeling self-conscious. He deserved to say, *I told you so.* He sighed and got back on the bed then pulled me close.

115

"You can't apologize for being yourself." He mindlessly played with my hair. The feeling was intoxicating I didn't want him to stop.

"You were right; I have been taking risks," I said, but he put his finger over my lips to quiet me.

"Do you remember when we were kids and you were always convincing us to sneak out of the palace at night to go run in the forests under the moon. The wolves didn't scare you, bandits didn't scare you, rules didn't scare you. You wanted to see something beautiful, risks be damned, and when we got caught, you tried to take all the blame. That is just who you are. You will protect everyone, no matter what happens to you in the process." He shuddered but he brought my face to his, eye to eye. "I love you, and all that entails. I never expect you to be anything other than yourself."

I pressed my lips to his. We spent the rest of the day alone, enjoying this time to rest and just be together.

***

"Sir," a voice said from the other side of the curtain.

"Yeah, come on in." Chase smiled at a young boy who slipped in. "What can I do for you?"

"David wanted me to let you know Joseph is here. The shipment from Soland came in, and he came with it." With that he nodded and took off back into the building.

I looked to Chase, confused. "Joseph came here?"

"Oh, um, yeah," he said appearing guilty.

I poked him in the ribs. "What?"

"So, David and Joseph are both going to work from here for a bit," he said, rubbing the back of his head, smiling mischievously.

Made Immortal

"Well, that's cool, but what prompted him to come here?" Joseph was from here; these were his people. I guessed it made sense.

"Joseph has some ideas, but he needs to actually be with you to work on it. We should be able to make some real progress in combating the mist for you, and maybe everyone," Chase said.

"That's good news. Let's go say hi."

Chase put out his arm and helped me off the cot. I had to tightly grasp the IV pole. It helped me stay upright. I hadn't moved much in a while, and now I was stiff and sore. One deep breath. I closed my eyes. Two deep breaths.

No pain, no gain. I steeled myself and started off down the hallway. Chase led me through the building, but kept a close eye on me. He was visibly tense and ready to jump into action if I fell. Yet, he let me walk on my own.

He held the door open, and I limped my way inside. David saw me and smiled, then Joseph turned in his chair, catching sight of us and getting up to meet us.

"Oh, Vi. Thank the gods you're okay." He held me at arm's length, his practiced eye looking me over and taking in my condition. When he was done, the corners of his eyes creased as he smiled widely. "It's good to see you."

I wrapped him in my arms and gave him a stiff hug. I hadn't seen him in person in some time but over the past year we had become close as he worked with David. Then, I pulled back and looked him straight in the eye. "I am so sorry. I should have saved Attikus." My fists clenched so tightly my nails broke the skin of my palms.

Attikus had been Joseph's long-time friend. More than that, they had been a couple too. Attikus had stayed in Neria when we managed to extract Joseph to Soland. Attikus was from a very rich family, and he had stayed to try

117

to influence the country from a place of power, until he was arrested. Tears threatened to fall, but Joseph grabbed my hand and held it tight.

"I know you did everything you could. It was a risk he knew he was taking, and he was happy to pay the price if it helped his people." He nodded, and the topic seemed to be closed. "Now, I've been looking over the data that David's been able to collect, and there was something I found interesting. May I?" he asked David, who pushed his chair back giving him space. Joseph went to his workstation and pulled up some files then opened them up as a hologram above the table.

It was a strand of DNA with some sections highlighted.

"What's that?" I asked.

"That is the instruction manual," he said, laughing when no one except David seemed to know what he meant. "That's how they managed to get the mist to only affect you. It's like a packet that tells the substance to activate when it recognizes your DNA. Think of it as a most-wanted poster." He closed that item and pulled up a few chemical formulas. "This is the payload. As soon as it found your DNA, it started to attach and replicate. Part of it would then destroy itself and the other would find another cell to latch on to. So, the cells were breaking down faster than your body could heal itself. The lifespan is incredibly long. It's still affecting you."

I jumped at that. "What do you mean? I'm getting better," I said. Yeah, there was still pain but it had been receding, no matter how slowly.

"You're cells are continuously rupturing. All we did was slow it's replication rate. Our current treatment isn't stopping it." He pulled up another hologram, which was the view of a slide of blood. In real time, we could see the cells

118

Made Immortal

bursting apart. "But now, I think I have a way to counteract it completely."

He opened another file, but I held out my hand to stop him. "I trust you." I looked at David and then back. "If you and David think it's going to work, let's do it." I smiled at them, trying my best to not think about it. They would fix me. "Can we start tonight?"

Joseph looked at David, who nodded. He clapped his hands and got up, gathering some things he would need. "All right, let's get started."

17

"Quick, everyone off!" Naya called.

The others and I dropped to the ground before the hover copter made its way back into the sky when we were all clear. David and Joseph had come with us to the edge of the city. Streets were blocked off, buildings were on fire, gunfire could be heard in the distance.

This wouldn't be seen on any news channel in Neria; this was the part of the city blocked off from the others. The people here were being blockaded, constantly attacked by the military, and had to keep moving locations to stay somewhat secure.

We headed into what was once a school. I still felt tired, but I was able to walk without any help. I refused to bring a cane like Chase had suggested. I couldn't look weak. Everyone needed to think I was back in fighting shape.

Our group was gaining in size as we walked through the hallways of the building. I saw kids start to trail our group, following in our wake and giggling.

"Vi," Naya said, pushing a door open to a huge room.

120

Made Immortal

Rows and rows of cots were full. People coughed, moaned, and cried, and the smell curled my toes as I entered. "This is the infirmary for this part of the burrow."

Stumbling, looking around me. It was so much worse than I had thought; there were so many more people here than I had expected. It felt like barbs were tearing through my lungs. I put a hand to my chest for a moment and took a deep breath. I settled myself, pulling a mask into place.

I weaved through the room, taking as much time as I needed with every person who wanted to speak to me. They grabbed my hands, grandmothers held my cheeks. They cried, and I cried with them. They told me of their homes, their pets, their hopes, their fears.

A boy pulled me down to sit with him. There was a bandage over his face, and it looked like he had probably lost his eye, judging from the blood stains.

"I want to be brave like you one day," he told me with all the passion of the young.

"You already are as brave as me," I said.

He looked incredulous. "I'm always afraid. You aren't afraid of anything."

"Can I tell you a secret?" I asked him, and his eyes opened wide. "I've always been afraid. Courage is still doing what's right, even if you are scared." I tapped his temple then pointed to my collarbone. "I look at every single one of my scars as a badge of pride. I was terrified, but guess what. I was strong enough. All of these scars give me hope, and they remind me how strong I am."

"What scar?" the boy asked.

I pointed again to the spot on my neck, but as I ran my hands over the blemish I had touched millions of times, now all I felt was smooth skin. I looked down to my arms, and

121

some of my most well-known scars on my hands and arms were missing.

I couldn't breathe. I smiled at the boy and patted his hands. "Oh, silly me, but just remember, you are stronger than you think. You are a survivor." I got up quickly, keeping my smile in place as I raced as quickly as I could to the door.

Chase followed me. I turned to him, and he seemed to see the worry on my face. "What is it, Vi?" he asked.

"My scars are gone," I whispered, I felt like I was spiraling; the air in my lungs was trapped, suffocating me. The room started to spin as I felt on the verge of a panic attack. "I need to get to a mirror."

Chase was one of the few people who knew how much my scars meant to me. When I looked at them, I saw a warrior. I saw everything I survived and how I made it out the other side. They had stayed even after I had escaped my step mother and the tourture she put me through.My body had never healed the scars I had before my powers came. New wounds would heal, but those were supposed to be mine forever.

Chase pulled me down a hallway, and we raced to the closest bathroom. We made blind turns searching for where it might be. I wasn't paying attention to where we were, I couldn't think of anything but praying I was wrong. Luckily, was Chase leading me and he tugged me towards it as he found one. I burst into the bathroom and ran to the mirrors. I pulled my hair away from my face and neck, tugging my shirt away from my shoulders. My skin was flawless, not a single scratch much less a scar to be seen. It was a striking view. I looked invincible, but I felt like I was crumbling.

I grasped the sink so hard the porcelain cracked and broke apart. I stared at myself, aghast at what I saw. I looked

Made Immortal

at Chase, tears already dripping down my cheeks. When I dropped, Chase ran to catch me and sat with me as I knelt. I clung to him and cried. The sobs wracked my body, the tears falling freely.

"Just breathe." Chase ran a hand down my back, helping me calm my breathing so I wouldn't hyperventilate.

"I don't recognize myself," I cried. To anyone else, it might have seemed silly, but I had pulled myself together staring at those scars on so many nights. They gave me a purpose, and helped me put one foot after the other on the hard days. The doctors scaples, the burns, the acid, the poision, had left their mark, and their remnants were the proof I couldn't be destroyed.

Yet, every terrible thought from those nights, crashed down on me now. If I couldn't see the wounds when I was weak, those reminders of my strength, would I understand I could keep going? It only took one night of no hope to forget that I won't feel like that forever. I was afraid. I was tired. I was guilty.

"If you ever don't recognize yourself, come to me. Come to any of us. We will remind you how remarkable you are." He had seen me on those nights, he knew what this meant. He held me tight, and I wondered if he had been waiting, maybe since they had rescued me from the prison, for this flood gate to break open so wide that I wouldn't be able to lock it down again. My gate was gone and I was going to have to figure out a way to make sure I didn't drown.

It took some time, but I was eventually able to calm myself. I stood, looking into the mirror once more. Even though I had been crying, as I wiped at my face, my skin was smooth and clear. I gathered my hair and tied it up. As I lifted my arms over my head, I realized I had barely any pain left in my ribs.

"Let's go," I said while straightening my clothes, pulling at the hem of my shirt. He hesitated, watching me, seeing if I was really okay to go back out there. I put a smile on my face, nodded fiercely and turned on my heel and left the room. I didn't have time to break down, people needed me, it was time to go back to work.

As we entered the infirmary again I saw Joseph deep in conversation with one of the people working as a doctor here.

"Everything all right?" Naya asked, but as she caught my eye, the look she gave me gave me the idea she knew something was wrong.

"Everything is fine," I said firmly, and I returned to meeting the patients. Helping people, that would keep me moving, for now. The nurses were deep into their night shifts by the time we were done. The room was quiet as most everyone had fallen asleep.

A woman entered the room as we had been getting ready to leave. She came straight for us, holding out her hand when she reached me. "My name is Jupiter, I'm in charge here. Sorry I couldn't see you until now; a lot has been going on. Follow me. We can get you something to eat you must be hungry."

We followed her to a place in the school where some of the local militia were eating around steel drums that contained fires. I heard the whispers start not long after we entered.

"Is that her?"

"That's the princess?"

"Wow, look at them. That red-haired one is huge!"

I tried to pay attention to something else so I could tune everyone out.

David looked at me and raised an eyebrow. His look

124

Made Immortal

caught Joseph's attention, who came around the outside of the circle to join me.

"Are you feeling better?" Joseph whispered, leaning in over my shoulder.

"Like nothing ever happened," I said, trying to not think about my missing scars.

"Hmm, as soon as we can, I want to run some more tests," he said before going to stand next to David again.

Jupiter started catching us up. "The military has been conducting raids in the nearby areas. We had to evacuate everyone to this location just a few weeks ago, as our last infirmary was discovered and shelled. We lost over half of our patients, and we've since filled our beds again."

"We've been trying to clear the way for our supply routes and trying to attack theirs, but their numbers are too great and our people too hungry," Naya continued before she ended up staring into the flickering flames of the closest drum.

"We can help with that." It wasn't up for debate, and the others didn't raise any issues with my statement anyways. I had known they wouldn't.

I twisted one way and then the other. Absentmindedly, I stretched out my wrists. This was what we were good at. It's what my father used us for all the time. We could attack quickly, with a level brutality not expected from such a smal group. We were the best surprise attack they could ask for. They needed muscle, and that we would provide.

"I had hoped you would say that." Naya nodded, it didn't seem like she was surprised at our offer to stay.

Before long, we were all wrapped up in the conversation of coordinating with the front lines to provide backup as they tried to fight off the military to open up their supply lines again.

18

The leader of the rebels on the front line, Jupiter Green, was a petite woman, but she seemed to have an iron will and the respect of everyone here. I watched as she discussed the situation with Chase and the others. She had led us into an office. Naya was filling in other bits and pieces of information to the team as we talked. Naya and Jupiter pointed out spots on the maps, noting where troops or traps were placed.

"We've received word that the military is making a push into our four outermost blocks. We just had to evacuate the two blocks before those as they closed in. What we're most worried about is an orphanage not too far from there. We need to get all of the kids bussed here as soon as possible," Jupiter said, tapping her finger on a building on the map.

"They've been pushing us back to open their own supply lines, it seems," Naya added. She ran her finger down a section of main streets that connected to the inner parts of the city.

"So, the plan is to cause a distraction while we evacuate

Made Immortal

the kids, and to try to disrupt this area at the same time," Jupiter finished.

"We can launch an assault on the troops while your people work on getting the kids out. If we start our attack here and move in," Chase said, pointing to a few blocks away from the orphanage, "if we make a big enough ruckus, we should also be able to pull anyone near you to us."

"We can lend a few other snipers, though I've heard you have one of your own," Jupiter said, and Gwen gave a little salute in response. "These buildings are taller than some of the others in the area. If we set all of you here." She pointed to a building on the eastern edge of the area. "Here," she continued, indicating another building on the western edge. "And another one here." She tapped a building in the north. "That should give you coverage. If the rest of the ground troops attack from the south, pushing them into range, that should flank them and cut down their numbers."

David looked over the map, and asked them, "Do you have any drones?"

"We have a few, but they're pretty old," Naya said, shrugging.

"Could you take me to them? I could probably use some of the parts to make new ones. If we get them out there soon enough, we should be able to scan the area and have a better idea of what we'll be walking into. We won't need to rely on breaking into the city's security cameras." David rubbed at his chin, where some stubble was coming in.

"Yes, that's no problem." Jupiter waved her hand toward the others. "Lilly, come here please," she said to a girl who had to be in her teens. "Can you show David here to the old drones? Let him look around at whatever we have down there."

127

The girl nodded, and David followed her out of the room.

"If you'll excuse me, I'm going to grab some grub," Naya said, nodding to the others.

"Me too, I'm starving," Benson said, and the two of them headed out as well.

Chase was still staring at the map, memorizing, looking for angles, trying to plan for surprises, no doubt. "Why don't you all get some rest," Chase said to the rest of us. "We don't know when we'll get a chance to again."

"Barracks are that way; you can grab an open cot." Jupiter pointed down the hallway in the opposite direction the others had gone.

Gwen and Atty headed out, holding hands as they did so. I couldn't keep the smile off my face. I was so happy for them.

"You should probably go too," Chase said to those remaining.

"I'm not tired," I said, which, surprisingly, was the case. The pain I had been in, the exhaustion I had felt, it was all gone.

"I'll go back to the infirmary," Joseph said. "I can be of help."

When we had first gotten Joseph out of Neria, he had been working in secret as a doctor for the rebels while still being employed by the king on Neria. The king, Esmerelda's father, had shared his work which ended up being the basis for the experiments on me. He never said it in so many words, but I felt like he was trying to make up for how they had used his research. It had worked on myself and Jasper, but so many others died because of it. It must have been something in our genetics that kept us alive when it killed everyone else

Made Immortal

"I'll go with you. I need to talk to you," I told Joseph. He nodded, and we both headed toward the infirmary.

"You okay?" Joseph asked.

"The serum you gave me," I said, pausing, "it's working too well."

Joseph chuckled lightly but stopped when he saw my face. "What's the problem?"

"My scars, they're gone. They've always been there, even when my healing kicked in after getting out of the prison. Now, they're totally healed. I've never felt as good as I do right now," I told him.

"Well, that's not necessarily a bad thing," he said.

I felt my throat tighten, and tears brimmed in my eyes. "They were important to me."

Joseph pulled me to a stop with him. "The scars being gone doesn't erase what they meant." He patted my shoulder. "I understand, I do, but remember, scars or no, you are still here. The things you lived through have made you the amazing person you are today. You care so much, you help so many, you are the strongest person I know, and not because you could throw me across a field. But let's go run some tests. I'll take some blood, and we'll see what's going on."

We passed the main room with the cots and all of the patients, then passed through a pair of doors into another hallway, past what looked like an operating room. A chill went down my spine at the sight. Memories flooding to the surface. Joseph pushed open the door to a room filled with lab equipment. He pointed toward a stool, and I took a seat. He grabbed some plastic-sealed tools and put them on a tray with some swaps and packets. He sat next to me, the tray clattering down beside him.

Taking a tourniquet, he tied it snugly around my arm.

He ripped open a plastic package and pulled out a needle, then he grabbed some collection tubes. I took a deep breath as he punctured the vein in my arm.

The blood spilled into the tube. I started to sweat but kept inhaling slowly through my nose and exhaling through my mouth. The thought of anyone doing tests on me still triggered the feeling of needing to flee and escape. Even if I knew they had my best interests in mind, flashbacks of the prison came unprompted.

"Done," he whispered as he pulled off the tourniquet. He pressed some gauze down, and I held it in place as he grabbed the tubes and headed to his equipment.

"Thanks. How long does it take?" I asked.

"If you want to hang out, I can take a look at it right now." He dropped some blood onto a slide and slid it into the microscope. He pulled up the view on a nearby computer and controlled it digitally.

The view zoomed in, and I was surprised at the activity on the screen. "What is that?"

Joseph frowned, and he played with the settings a few different times. I watched as he opened a program and started running the data through it.

"When you were first infected, nanotech was in the mist. When we gave you the serum, we basically changed its code to repair instead. So, that is what it's doing... On a level probably ten times faster than your healing before." He spun around on the stool to look at me. "I think you might be," he paused, as if trying to come up with the right word, "*more* than you were before. In theory, this could help your oxygen saturation, as well as increase your speed of recovery from injury or overexertion. I'm want to keep monitoring you for a little while."

130

Made Immortal

"I see." I sighed. "Thanks, Joseph." I stood up, but he grabbed my hand before I could head for the door.

"You are still you. I'm sorry you lost another part of yourself, but you've also gained so much." He squeezed my hand.

I squeezed it back and then headed for the door as he started logging everything. Once in the hallway, I leaned against the cold tile and closed my eyes, rubbing at my face before dragging my fingers through my hair.

"I am still me," I said quietly. Pushing away from the wall, I shook out my arms and hands. I bounced a bit on the balls of my feet. "I am still me."

This was just the next chapter in my story.

I turned and went to find my way to the track at the back of the school. I needed to get some air.

19

Our group took off as soon as the sun rose. We were heading out on foot to a location just north of the orphanage. There was a large military presence since one of their supply routes was nearby. Our job was to essentially cause a ruckus, bring as much attention to us as we could, to keep everyone ignorant of the evacuation of the children.

"Comms check," Jupiter's voice came through.

"We hear you. We'll check in when we're in position," Chase responded.

"May the gods shine upon you," Jupiter called, and with that, we were silent as we headed through the city. At the pace we were moving, it wasn't long before we burned off the chill of the morning.

It was like a ghost town. We could see the burn marks from fires that had consumed something as small as a table inside a shop to entire buildings. I couldn't speak; it just didn't feel like this place would allow it. It demanded silent reverence for what had been lost here.

We finally came to the corner a few blocks from where the military patrolled. Gwen was already pulling herself up

132

Made Immortal

a fire escape and heading for the roof. There was a grouping of buildings where she could move up and down the block as needed without having to return to the ground.

"We're getting into position," Chase said into his comm.

"Okay, I'm set," Gwen said. "All right, they are getting ready to switch shifts. You guys should be good to go in a few minutes."

"Jupiter, is everyone ready?" Chase asked.

Her voice, the signal flickering slightly with static, came through, "We're ready."

Chase looked over his shoulder to the rest of us and motioned to move out. "Go time."

The boys moved forward, and I hung back to bring up the rear. The team had spent so much time together that we seemed to be of one mind as we quickly progressed toward the guard post. A group of guards huddled together, laughing. They were chatting as they switched shifts.

Atty grabbed an explosive from his belt and threw it toward them. It clinked against a wall, the noise drawing their attention. The device blinked a few times before releasing gas. They started to cover their faces, coughing and trying to talk into their comms. Fear seemed to overcome them when they only found static. David had given us a device that would jam the communications in the area.

The men grabbed at their guns, spinning to figure out which way the threat was coming from.

The boys had moved to their spots to flank the guard post. I walked slowly into the gas, my mask up for protection, and one of them caught sight of me.

"Stay where you are. Who are you?" he called.

I touched the neck of my suit, and the nanobots pulled back, revealing my face, my hair falling around my shoulders. I waved and smiled. "Hi."

133

Bullets started to fly. My mask slipped over me once more, and I dropped while pulling a shield up around my arm and taking most of the hits as I crouched.

Some of them needed to reload; another's gun jammed.

I used that opporituniy to lunge forward, knocking into the first one and sending him flying. I spun, kicking a leg out, and another one went crashing to the ground, his feet swept out from under him. The others yelled, the gas causing confusion.

Someone managed to reload, and they just sprayed the bullets ahead of them blindly, not knowing where to aim.

I came up behind him, slamming an elbow into his neck, and grabbed his weapon as he collapsed. I gripped the barrel of the gun and squeezed, the metal crumpling like paper.

I felt like a monster in the shadows, taking out each one while the gas floated among us.

"Incoming," Gwen said, and I heard her let off a few shots. "From the north."

"We see them," Benson responded, followed by his own firing at the troops coming our way.

Eventhough their comms were out, the sound of our first assault had been loud enough to draw their reinforcements toward us.

The last of the original men at the guard post had been crawling away from me. His back bumped into the wall. He looked behind him and then his eyes returned to me full of terror.

I squatted, and my mask slid down to my neck again. I reached out and brushed some blood from his cheek. He flinched away from me.

"Please," he croaked. "Please, let me go."

"I'll think about it," I said casually.

Made Immortal

"Please, I have a family." He was shaking.

"So do the people here," I said, gesturing to the city around us.

"I'm just following orders." He was whimpering now.

"I'll let you go," I said, and the relief on his face was plain. "But you have to do something for me."

He looked over his shoulder as other men screamed. He nodded, still clearly terrified. "Yes, yes, anything."

"Tell your friends, everyone you know, to think about the orders they are following."

He nodded his head in agreement, with enthusiasm.

"Because I'm coming. For everyone. They can decide if they want to face me or do the right thing and help the people of this country. The people outnumber you, and they are ready to face you." I grabbed his hand, and he looked relieved, but I squeezed and heard the bones break under the pressure.

He screamed and pulled his arm back to cradle it close to his chest. "Yes, yes, I'll tell them."

I stood and walked away, heading toward the sounds of gunfire. I heard him scramble away and race off in the other direction.

"What is that? Gods! Where did they come from?" I heard over the comms. It was someone on the team evacuating the kids.

"Report. What's going on?" Chase responded. He grunted, and then I spotted him and Atty behind a large cement barricade firing at more troops that had arrived. Benson was on the other side of the street.

"We're taking fire." There was a commotion on the other end before the voice came back. "Run! Everyone, run; get on the bus."

Chase caught my eye and nodded.

135

I spun and raced toward the orphanage.

"I'm coming," I called to them.

"West corner," Jupiter told me. More gunfire sounded over the comms.

I ran faster than I thought I ever had before, amazed at the ease of the action, taking in everything as I ran, almost like the world moved just slightly slower than myself.

It didn't take me long to make it to the building. I raced toward the western corner, hoping to come up behind the soldiers. I saw men firing at the bus and was taken aback. What kind of person shot at children. One of them looked to have a rocket launcher, and they were aiming it right at the building.

As I headed for him, other men started to turn toward me, finally noticing my presence. I slammed my shoulder into the man, sending him and the launcher sprawling. I heard bullets start to fire, and I grabbed the man, pulling him up to be between his men and me. The firing stopped, as they tried to decide what to do.

"Let him go," one of them yelled.

"Okay." I laughed as I tossed the man I was holding into the another. They both crashed to the ground. I turned on the rest. The oldest man set his shoulders and fired straight at me. The suit blocked the some of bullets, but not all. Yet, I ignored it, the pain barely noticeable.

I stalked toward him and grabbed his weapon. I threw the gun into the wall behind me, and it stuck into the bricks.

"Get out of here," one of the others screamed, and most of the men fled.

The older man was frozen in place by fear.

"These are children." I growled, the edges of my vision turning red as I focused only on the man in front of me. He had an air about him that told me he was the commander of the group.

He didn't say anything. He just glared at me.

"Drive. We have everyone," Jupiter said over the comms. I saw the bus start to drive away.

I grabbed the man's neck and raised him enough that he couldn't touch the ground.

"Children," I screamed. "They are innocent. You are destroying their homes, their families, and trying to take their lives, and they have done nothing to you." I shook with rage and threw him to the ground, disgusted.

I started to walk away, getting ready to head after the others, when I heard metal scrape against the ground. I turned around to see the man hefting the launcher onto his shoulder. He smiled at me, blood dripping from the side of his mouth. As if in slow motion, I saw him pull the trigger and the missile release from the launcher.

I grabbed a nearby broken piece of a barricade and lobbed it into the way. The missile exploded on impact, sending the man flying backward.

I wiped at my face; now covered in dust. Some of it was in my mouth, and I stuck my tongue out at the horrible taste. I walked to the man now gasping for air on the ground. Blood pooled underneath him. He had shrapnel dug deep into his abdomen. I leaned over him, my hair falling around my face. He gasped, blood in his mouth, terror in his eyes.

"I was going to let you live. You put yourself here."

I turned around and walked away, pulling my hair up into a tie to get it out of my face. I heard his breathing stop behind me. Looking up, I saw a security camera above. I tapped my fingers to my temple in a salute in its direction with a smile and then spirited away.

20

Looking up at the night sky, the stars were barely visible because of the light from the city. I still wasn't tired, so I figured I would try and tire myself out by jogging around the track. I didn't feel any of the pain from before.

I pushed myself faster, and faster still, but didn't even get my heart rate up.

Okay, then, let's see what I can do, I thought. I ran to the edge of the sports pitch, jumped over the fence, and raced into the city. Most of the streets were empty, buildings and stores shuttered. I saw some scaffolding against a nearby church and headed for it.

I launched myself as high as I could, clearing a few levels before grabbing one of the supports. I jumped up to the roof I aimed for the spire. Using an ornamental carving as a handhold I launched myself to the peak. It had only taken me a few jumps to make it the entire way from the street to the tip of the spire. I had never been able to jump that far before.

Gripping the highest point I leaned out as far as my arm would stretch. I could see blocks in every direction. To the

Made Immortal

south was an orange glow of fires, where buildings burned. I heard no sirens, no attempts to put it out. How hard my teeth were clenching made my jaw hurt. Forcing myself to loosen them I rubbed at the joints.

Sighing, I gave one last look to the fires before I launched myself from the dome I was standing on. The arch of my jump gave me enough time to flip once, sighting the ground coming toward me as I did. As my feet met the ground the shock of the landing was barely noticeable.

I started toward the closest blockade to see if I could hear anything useful I could tell Jupiter and the others. I had only made it a block or two when I heard a struggle.

"Let go of me," came a woman's voice.

"You're out past curfew. You know that's breaking the law." a man's voice answered. I heard the dull slap of something like a baton smaking into an open hand.

I sprinted around the corner and saw the two halfway down a dark alley. The man had the woman boxed in next to a dumpster. He was in a military uniform.

Rage boiled in my veins. "Let her go."

They both looked at me. The man seemed to recognize me. The baton back in it's holster he was reaching to unzip his pants. When he saw me, he froze for a moment like he couldn't decide whether to zip his pants or go for a weapon. He didn't have time for either before I was on him.

I grabbed him and threw him into the opposite wall. He clawed at his radio, but I was on him and crushed it in my fist before he could say anything.

"Please. Please, let me go." He whimpered.

I gave him a dark smile. "I'll let you go. To deliver a message for me."

He nodded, snot running down his face as he blubbered.

139

"Listen." I grabbed his face and forced him to look me in the eye. He shook in my grasp. "You all have a chance to leave. If you don't, you will have to deal with me. I am protecting these people, and your king will regret ever crossing me."

He nodded. As soon as I let go of his chin, he scrambled away.

I turned back to the girl. She was lean and didn't look like she was far into her twenties—if she was even that old.

"You okay?" I asked her.

She nodded. "Yeah, thanks to you. You... you're that girl from the news, aren't you?"

"Yeah, I guess so. You can call me Vi." I held out my hand, but she latched onto me in a hug instead. Startled, I froze. When she let me go I noticed the backpack she had gripped tightly in her fist and the bruise on her cheek. "What were you doing out here so late and so close to the barricade?"

"Um." She seemed unsure. "Well... I... I'm searching for my sister."

My heart went out to her and I nodded. "My friends are nearby. Do you need a place to stay tonight?"

She nodded, but she barely looked up from under her bangs.

"Follow me. Want me to take that?" I asked about her bag.

She instantly pulled back, holding it tighter. I was pretty sure I knew how she was feeling. It reminded me of when I had just gotten out of the prison. The terror and the PTSD I still dealt with.

"What's your name?" I asked as we headed toward the school. I kept looking ahead but had a good feel of where she was behind me from the sounds of her footsteps.

140

Made Immortal

"Jessie." She did keep close though, just a few steps back.

"When did you see your sister last?" I took a quick look to her over my shoulder.

"We got separated last week." Tears shimmered in her eyes.

"We'll help you look for her," I said, as we hopped over a bunch of rubble.

For the rest of the walk to the school the rebels had claimed as their base of operation we fell into silence. She seemed to be lost in her own thoughts, and I left her to them. We made it to the track and then slipped through a gate and into the back of the school.

We made our way through the hallways before coming to the main room, where there was always someone checking the feeds. Jupiter was there, leaning over someone's shoulder, discussing something quietly.

"Hey, Jupiter," I said, and she looked up.

Her face was schooled not to show what she was thinking. I threw my thumb over my shoulder at the girl next to me. Yet, I could have sworn I saw her soften, just a bit, when she saw who I pointed at.

"This is Jessie. She ran into some trouble, and I told her she could crash here. She's also looking for her sister."

Jessie shifted from foot to foot, staring at the floor.

Jupiter walked over to her with a smile and put a hand out to shake Jessie's. "We're happy to have you. Are you hungry? We have food and places to sleep. You can also clean up if you want to." Jupiter straightened, and Jessie nodded. She called to one of the people at the computers. "Can you show Jessie around, and if you can get her sister's information, then we can start checking our systems."

The girl nodded and came over. Jessie smiled shyly and followed her down the hallway.

"Couldn't sleep?" Jupiter asked.

"No, I'm wired. How about you?"

"I don't sleep much these days." She shrugged and flopped onto the couch.

I gestured to see if I could sit, and she nodded. I slipped down on the other side.

"Where exactly did you find her?" She raised an eyebrow at me.

"In the city. I needed a good workout," I said, and she chuckled at that.

"Just be careful with the strays you bring home, but she seems like a good kid." She shrugged. "I guess you're just like they said."

"I'm sure I don't want to know what that is, but probably." I shrugged. "I'm no angel. I'm no hero. I'm just a weapon that gets fired in a certain direction, not someone people should look up to." I felt like I could be surprisingly honest with her. Maybe it was because I was overwhelmed about everything going on. Maybe because she too had the safety of those she protected on her shoulders. She might understand feeling like you might fail every day, and knowing the high price if you did.

"It's hard to have to do harm to do good, knowing that if we stay and fight, our people may get hurt. We make the calls and have to live with what happens. It seems like you believe in the rights of these people, even though you have no ties to them, so much that you are willing to put yourself in harm's way. From what I've heard, you came from trauma, like we all have here, but you survived, and your story has been giving hope to those with none. These people are no longer allowing themselves to be swept under the rug

142

Made Immortal

because someone finally told them they matter. They are fighting for their homes and family. Together, as a people. You brought a spark to life, and now, more and more people are willing to fight for what is right. They know the risks and are showing up anyway." She tapped my leg lightly with her boot and smiled. "We make the hard choices so they don't have to. It's a burden, but you seem to handle it pretty darn well."

"After all of this, I just want to disappear. I want people to forget me. I don't know if I can be what they want me to be. Ever since I was rescued I've just wanted to be invisible. To live a quiet life." I brushed a piece of hair behind my ear.

"I get it. I wouldn't want to be in your shoes, that's for sure." She nodded. "You'd be surprised how well the job looks on you though." With that, she got up and went back to the computer. "You've got boots on the ground tomorrow; you should try to get some sleep."

"The job looks good on you too," I replied, but she was right. I smiled and waved as I headed back toward the barracks.

The room was very similar to the sleeping arrangement at Naya's base. I listened for Chase's distinct breathing. Finding it I slipped through a blanket wall, and I found Chase knocked out on the cot, one arm thrown over his face and one leg hanging over the edge. I crept in as quietly as I could and tried to take up as little space as possible, but within moments, he had pulled me right to him. It seemed to be a reflex, as he didn't stir otherwise. A sigh of contentment escaped me, and I was quickly lulled to sleep, enveloped in his embrace.

21

Our group took off as soon as the sun rose. We were heading out on foot to a location just north of the orphanage. There was a large military presence since one of their supply routes was nearby. Our job was to essentially cause a ruckus, bring as much attention to us as we could, to keep everyone ignorant of the evacuation of the children.

"Comms check," Jupiter's voice came through.

"We hear you. We'll check in when we're in position," Chase responded.

"May the gods shine upon you," Jupiter called, and with that, we were silent as we headed through the city. At the pace we were moving, it wasn't long before we burned off the chill of the morning.

It was like a ghost town. We could see the burn marks from fires that had consumed something as small as a table inside a shop to entire buildings. I couldn't speak; it just didn't feel like this place would allow it. It demanded silent reverence for what had been lost here.

We finally came to the corner a few blocks from where the military patrolled. Gwen was already pulling herself up

144

Made Immortal

a fire escape and heading for the roof. There was a grouping of buildings where she could move up and down the block as needed without having to return to the ground.

"We're getting into position," Chase said into his comm.

"Okay, I'm set," Gwen said. "All right, they are getting ready to switch shifts. You guys should be good to go in a few minutes."

"Jupiter, is everyone ready?" Chase asked.

Her voice, the signal flickering slightly with static, came through, "We're ready."

Chase looked over his shoulder to the rest of us and motioned to move out. "Go time."

The boys moved forward, and I hung back to bring up the rear. The team had spent so much time together that we seemed to be of one mind as we quickly progressed toward the guard post. A group of guards huddled together, laughing. They were chatting as they switched shifts.

Atty grabbed an explosive from his belt and threw it toward them. It clinked against a wall, the noise drawing their attention. The device blinked a few times before releasing gas. They started to cover their faces, coughing and trying to talk into their comms. Fear seemed to overcome them when they only found static. David had given us a device that would jam the communications in the area.

The men grabbed at their guns, spinning to figure out which way the threat was coming from.

The boys had moved to their spots to flank the guard post. I walked slowly into the gas, my mask up for protection, and one of them caught sight of me.

"Stay where you are. Who are you?" he called.

I touched the neck of my suit, and the nanobots pulled back, revealing my face, my hair falling around my shoulders. I waved and smiled. "Hi."

145

Bullets started to fly. My mask slipped over me once more, and I dropped while pulling a shield up around my arm and taking most of the hits as I crouched.

Some of them needed to reload; another's gun jammed.

I used that opporituniy to lunge forward, knocking into the first one and sending him flying. I spun, kicking a leg out, and another one went crashing to the ground, his feet swept out from under him. The others yelled, the gas causing confusion.

Someone managed to reload, and they just sprayed the bullets ahead of them blindly, not knowing where to aim.

I came up behind him, slamming an elbow into his neck, and grabbed his weapon as he collapsed. I gripped the barrel of the gun and squeezed, the metal crumpling like paper.

I felt like a monster in the shadows, taking out each one while the gas floated among us.

"Incoming," Gwen said, and I heard her let off a few shots. "From the north."

"We see them," Benson responded, followed by his own firing at the troops coming our way.

Eventhough their comms were out, the sound of our first assault had been loud enough to draw their reinforcements toward us.

The last of the original men at the guard post had been crawling away from me. His back bumped into the wall. He looked behind him and then his eyes returned to me full of terror.

I squatted, and my mask slid down to my neck again. I reached out and brushed some blood from his cheek. He flinched away from me.

"Please," he croaked. "Please, let me go."

"I'll think about it," I said casually.

Made Immortal

"Please, I have a family." He was shaking.

"So do the people here," I said, gesturing to the city around us.

"I'm just following orders." He was whimpering now.

"I'll let you go," I said, and the relief on his face was plain. "But you have to do something for me."

He looked over his shoulder as other men screamed. He nodded, still clearly terrified. "Yes, yes, anything."

"Tell your friends, everyone you know, to think about the orders they are following."

He nodded his head in agreement, with enthusiasm.

"Because I'm coming. For everyone. They can decide if they want to face me or do the right thing and help the people of this country. The people outnumber you, and they are ready to face you." I grabbed his hand, and he looked relieved, but I squeezed and heard the bones break under the pressure.

He screamed and pulled his arm back to cradle it close to his chest. "Yes, yes, I'll tell them."

I stood and walked away, heading toward the sounds of gunfire. I heard him scramble away and race off in the other direction.

"What is that? Gods! Where did they come from?" I heard over the comms. It was someone on the team evacuating the kids.

"Report. What's going on?" Chase responded. He grunted, and then I spotted him and Atty behind a large cement barricade firing at more troops that had arrived. Benson was on the other side of the street.

"We're taking fire." There was a commotion on the other end before the voice came back. "Run! Everyone, run; get on the bus."

Chase caught my eye and nodded.

147

I spun and raced toward the orphanage.

"I'm coming," I called to them.

"West corner," Jupiter told me. More gunfire sounded over the comms.

I ran faster than I thought I ever had before, amazed at the ease of the action, taking in everything as I ran, almost like the world moved just slightly slower than myself.

It didn't take me long to make it to the building. I raced toward the western corner, hoping to come up behind the soldiers. I saw men firing at the bus and was taken aback. What kind of person shot at children. One of them looked to have a rocket launcher, and they were aiming it right at the building.

As I headed for him, other men started to turn toward me, finally noticing my presence. I slammed my shoulder into the man, sending him and the launcher sprawling. I heard bullets start to fire, and I grabbed the man, pulling him up to be between his men and me. The firing stopped, as they tried to decide what to do.

"Let him go," one of them yelled.

"Okay." I laughed as I tossed the man I was holding into the another. They both crashed to the ground. I turned on the rest. The oldest man set his shoulders and fired straight at me. The suit blocked the some of bullets, but not all. Yet, I ignored it, the pain barely noticeable.

I stalked toward him and grabbed his weapon. I threw the gun into the wall behind me, and it stuck into the bricks.

"Get out of here," one of the others screamed, and most of the men fled.

The older man was frozen in place by fear.

"These are children." I growled, the edges of my vision turning red as I focused only on the man in front of me. He

Made Immortal

had an air about him that told me he was the commander of the group.

He didn't say anything. He just glared at me.

"Drive. We have everyone," Jupiter said over the comms. I saw the bus start to drive away.

I grabbed the man's neck and raised him enough that he couldn't touch the ground.

"Children," I screamed. "They are innocent. You are destroying their homes, their families, and trying to take their lives, and they have done nothing to you." I shook with rage and threw him to the ground, disgusted.

I started to walk away, getting ready to head after the others, when I heard metal scrape against the ground. I turned around to see the man hefting the launcher onto his shoulder. He smiled at me, blood dripping from the side of his mouth. As if in slow motion, I saw him pull the trigger and the missile release from the launcher.

I grabbed a nearby broken piece of a barricade and lobbed it into the way. The missile exploded on impact, sending the man flying backward.

I wiped at my face; now covered in dust. Some of it was in my mouth, and I stuck my tongue out at the horrible taste. I walked to the man now gasping for air on the ground. Blood pooled underneath him. He had shrapnel dug deep into his abdomen. I leaned over him, my hair falling around my face. He gasped, blood in his mouth, terror in his eyes.

"I was going to let you live. You put yourself here."

I turned around and walked away, pulling my hair up into a tie to get it out of my face. I heard his breathing stop behind me. Looking up, I saw a security camera above. I tapped my fingers to my temple in a salute in its direction with a smile and then spirited away.

22

"The terrorist strikes again." Wendy Watson's face was front and center on the Nerian news. The video of me leaving the orphanage played on repeat behind her. I tuned out the rest of what they were saying.

I dried my hair off with a towel as I walked into the main room. We had returned not that long ago. The kids had eaten and were getting to know the children who had already been here. Jessie came running up and threw her arms around my waist. She hugged me tightly. I didn't pull away until she did with tears on her cheeks.

"Thank you," she said, grabbing my hands and shaking them. "Cecily had been at the orphanage. You said you'd find her, and you did. Thank you so much. We owe you everything." She turned around and held her arm out, and a young girl came running up to attach herself to Jessie's side.

"I'm so happy for you both." I smiled and squatted down to be on the same level as the girl. When she threw her arms around my neck, I hugged her back. "The people here will be able to help you. You'll be safe here."

As I stood, Jessie grabbed and squeezed my hand again

150

Made Immortal

before taking her sister and heading toward the other children.

I took a deep breath. I was happy for the two. They had dealt with enough, but at least they had each other again. My chest clenched as I thought about myself at Cecily's age. The queen had locked me away, telling me my father had died and that I would never see him again. The hopelessness I felt when I heard it.

My fist clenched. Flashes of my cell, of the doctors, flooded my mind, and I could feel the pain, all of the pain again. I instinctively reached for my shoulder, and my fingers passed over smooth skin. The despair engulfed me, and I felt like I might faint. I dropped heavily into a chair. I stared into the lights in the ceiling, trying to keep myself from being sick.

"The champion returns," Jupiter said, walking toward me.

Her voice snapped me out of my thoughts, but my body was still on edge.

"Hey, good to see you," I said breathlessly.

"You saved my bacon, so I just wanted to say thank you." She smiled, crossing her arms and leaning against the wall.

"I really wish people would stop thanking me," I muttered.

She smirked at that. "You are quite something to see in action."

I held my hand in front of me, opening and closing my fist a few times. "I feel different. I mean, I am different, I have been for a while, but this... this is more. It feels strange."

"Didn't you get hit close range with an exploding missile?" she asked. "You look perfectly fine."

"I mean, the cement took the brunt of it. I feel fine. Better than fine, actually." I shrugged.

"Naya told me you almost died when they brought you to her." Jupiter leaned forward slightly, inquisitive.

"Yeah, I think I almost did. I've never been hurt like that before."

She raised an eyebrow.

"And now, you're this." She waved her arm between us.

"Yep, apparently so. The guy I was fighting, who hurt me, he's like me. Anyway, they've come up with some DNA targeted weapon, and they tried it against me. I think they said you guys know something about it. They've been using it here for a while. She keeps trying to kill me, and I keep getting stronger every time she does." I laughed at the irony. "I can't wait to show her."

"Yeah, we have, but no one's ever lasted more than a few minuets." She raised an eyebrow. "That's what they used on you?"

"My enhanced healing saved me long enough to get me to your doctors." I shrugged.

"So, Esmerelda? The king's daughter? She did this to you?"

"Yeah." I sighed.

"What does she have against you?" she asked.

I chewed on my lip and shrugged. "I have no idea. I guess I'm just a threat."

"Is it true that your dad isn't dead?" She asked.

"Hmm, yeah. Apparently, he's alive," I said sarcastically. "He spent the time in hiding building a force to fight Esmerelda. That's where David and Chase had ended up eventually. When they rescued me, after six years, their base is where I healed. It's where we learned about what her experiments did to me."

152

Made Immortal

Over the past two years we had been slowly repairing our relationship. He had been using myself and the team for specialty missions they couldn't trust anyone else with. Missions so dangerous no one else had any chance of completing.

Yet, every time I thought about how he knew I was alive and didn't come get me, the hurt and anger returned. I had thought he was dead the entire time. I was alone for the six years I spent imprisoned, putting him on a pedestal in my head that entire time, only for it to crash to Earth when David and Chase rescued me.

"We've been hearing whispers of you all for years." Jupiter nodded and I could tell she was thinking over her time here. "I never thought we'd meet you, but those whispers became the start of all this. We have a lot to thank you all for. It gave us the hope of being able to stand up for ourselves too."

"I'm glad you did. No one deserves what you've lived through," I said.

Jupiter nodded. "Come with me." She got up and headed toward the stairs.

I stood and followed her into the stairwell. Our steps echoed in the chamber as we climbed.

Jupiter finally pushed through the door that led to the roof. She went to a platform and sat with her legs dangling over the edge. I joined her and looked out at the view that sprawled ahead of us. We could see for blocks; the buildings were still burning, casting an orange glow over the horizon.

"Should we call someone?" I asked about the fire.

Jupiter shook her head. "No, that block is emptied. No one is there. There isn't anything anyone could do anyway. We won't get any help here. Just best to let it burn."

The sight of the smoke billowing into the air, the eerie

153

quiet of the city, sent chills up my spine. We sat in silence for a while.

"My dad ran a repair shop just over there," Jupiter said, pointing. "I grew up learning how to fix things. How to take a bunch of pieces and put them together to make something whole. I never expected my life to bring me here. Some days, I go to the garage and work on the vehicles just to clear my head. What did you want to be when you were young?"

"Free." It slipped out before I had even recognized the thought. "I didn't have much time to grow up before Esmerelda got her hands on me." I flinched at the reminder that I'd only been twelve when I lost everything.

"Oh, I'm sorry. We heard about your father's death, and they said you were leaving the public eye due to grief. We never heard anything after that," she said. "Until recently."

"I was imprisoned for six years. She ran experiments on me, which is why I'm this now." I looked down at my hands. "All the people they are taking, that's what she's doing with them. They are testing, for what end goal, we're still not completely sure yet. But ending up like me is the end goal, we assume."

"How many people like you are out there?" she asked.

"Two of us, as far as I know. It can't be many." I closed my eyes, thinking of the quick glances of people being pulled away down the halls of the prison, who I would never see again.

"What happened to everyone else?" she asked, but I could tell she probably already knew the answer.

"No one else makes it," I whispered.

She bit at her lip and looked at me out of the corner of her eye. "We thought that might be the case."

"That's why I needed to find them. I couldn't leave knowing they're kidnapping people in droves to do that to

154

Made Immortal

them. I wouldn't wish that on anyone. Well, Esmerelda, maybe." I chuckled at that.

"I'm very sorry you had to go through that," was all she said, and it was enough.

"Thank you. I don't ever really talk about it. I try to not even think about it, but I'm not very good at that." I mindlessly picked at the stone below me.

"I understand, but as my therapist used to tell me, bottling things up can lead to explosions that do far more damage." She mimed an explosion, and we both laughed.

"You saw a therapist?"

"Everyone needs to talk to someone," she said straight faced.

I nodded. She was right.

"Do you ever feel like you're being swallowed up by a black hole?" I asked quietly, instantly regretting it.

"I do. I don't know if anyone else does, but I think I know what you're talking about. It's okay to have bad days, but I just always look ahead. Each day is a new chance for something to get better."

"Well, I guess, even if it's just us, we know we're not alone." Speaking it out loud, having it in the wind, I felt a little lighter. I wasn't alone. I just had to remember that.

"Vi, from what I can tell. You are incredibly blessed that you will never be alone. You have people so ready to be there for you. It might help you to talk to them. Tell them how you are feeling." She nudged my shoulder.

"I'm not ready." I chewed on my lip. "I have to be strong. I can't tell them how weak I feel sometimes." I couldn't even look at her.

"You don't have to do anything you aren't ready for, but you should trust that you have people to catch you if you fall." She set her hand delicately on my shoulder.

155

I took a deep breath and nodded. "I know you're right. They are really amazing people. I don't deserve them."

"The first step is to tell yourself you *do* deserve them." She started to get up. "I have some things I need to take care of, but you should stay up here for a bit if you want. I do some of my best thinking up here."

I put my arms on the bar in front of me and set my chin on them. As I looked out on the tops of the city, my vision blurred as tears built.

My mind wandered. I was looking down at my bare feet, walking through the hallways of the prison. Glancing up to catch a glimpse of myself in the reflection of the windows blocked by blinds. Skin and bones, black eyes, the red of the new scars peeking out from under my smock. My face in that reflection year after year after year as I grew. The searing pain of the drugs in my veins. Screaming until my throat bled. The itch of the wounds healing. The hunger. The hallucinations that were bred out of no human contact.

My throat caught, and I let the tears fall. Sobs came in waves as each memory flooded me with pain, terror, and hopelessness. Grief over what I'd been through and what I lost because of it. The pain of that little girl who didn't deserve any of it.

Then, even once I was free, the pain of losing Alice, Chase's mother who had also been like a mother to me, in such a horrendous way. They had a club where they had been recruiting help for the rebels. I had reconnected with her after being rescued and within an hour the raid had happened. I had her back for just moments before I lost her again. Alice had sacrificed herself so we had the ability to get her daughter, Thea, out of the cells in the palace safely.

Made Immortal

I let all of the emotions flow through me, everything I'd been holding off for so long.

Eventually, the pain ebbed. In its place was a calm that I couldn't remember the last time I'd felt. I felt empty, but I could see a small light of what might have been hope. I had survived. I was healing, I was becoming someone else. Someone that little girl deserved to become. The past would always be a part of me, but I was who I was because of it. I could close that chapter and finally try and start a new one.

The idea caused me to gasp. I had to take a few deep breaths. I stood up, looking over the city below as the sun was starting to rise.

I was ready.

I was ready for what was next, whatever that might be. I felt light, like I could take flight if I wanted, but my job was on the ground for now.

23

Chase stopped short when he saw me.

"You okay?" he asked, coming and grabbing my arms to look me over. I hadn't gone back to our bed, and everyone was getting up and ready to start the day.

"Yeah, I think I am," I said, smiling at him but wiped at my face again.

He seemed confused but wasn't going to argue. I kissed his cheek, and we headed to the main room.

Marco Diaz was there giving candy to a riot of little children. He laughed and tried to get to all of them. "Here, here, there is enough for everyone."

Once they all seemed happy, he brushed his hands together and smacked them against his pant legs.

"Okay, all of you, shoo," Jupiter said, and the children took off in the way she pointed.

I walked to one of the tables pushed against the wall and sat down on it. Everyone else had already made their way here after getting themselves cleaned up. Chase leaned into my side as he slouched against the wall.

Marco had straightened himself out and looked to us.

158

Made Immortal

"On behalf of Neria, we'd like to thank you. We've found and rescued hundreds of people since you started helping us. We'll forever be in your debt."

"We're happy to help," Chase replied.

I looked over and saw David and Joseph in the corner whispering to each other, seemingly ignoring the rest of us.

"I've never seen anything like it," Joseph told David. I didn't mean to eavesdrop, but I was having a hard time tuning them out.

"It's not surprising. This is the first time any of us have seen anything like it. We thought her changes were coming on rapidly before, but since we attacked the virus in her, it's sped up her healing, her reactions, everything." David was holding his chin in his hand in thought. "She's probably capable of much more than we ever could have expected. We need to keep it quiet until we know more."

Joseph nodded, but then looked up and saw me watching. I shrugged and he gave me a small smile.

"You've already done so much, but there is still more to be done if you'll help us," Marco said, catching my eye. "We're looking to try to take down some of the supply routes. This is the closest we've come to being able to push them back farther into the city."

"Yeah, anything you need," Benson said, nodding.

"Perfect. Jupiter, could you give them an update?" he asked, and she nodded. "Vi, can I have a moment?"

I pushed myself off the table and gave a quick wave to the others as I followed him down the hall. After we went a good distance and turned a few corners, he stopped and looked at me.

"I have some news you might find of interest," Marco said.

159

"Okay," I said quietly, not sure why I had to follow him all the way here for him to tell me.

"It's about Jasper. We've been able to locate him, and we've been tracking him. I know the two of you have a complicated history. I wasn't sure how you wanted to handle the information, so I thought I'd give it to you alone," he said.

My heart started to beat faster, thinking of the last time I saw him. Crawling away for my life. Only making it because my friends had shown up to rescue me. Sniper rounds slamming into his chest.

"He looks mostly healed now. They must have squirreled him away somewhere for the last few days, but now he's coordinating for Esmerelda and her father. They are moving more troops into the city; something big is changing. He's currently making his way to the supply route we have the intel on. I assume they have the same thought as us and are sending in the big guns." The glint in his eye had a tint of malice to it. Marco must have really hated the king. To fund, and possibly have created this rebellion, to free the people, and causing as much damage to the king's reputation as possible.

One can only assume he brought this update to me because he saw that shadow in me. The rage. The violence I could harness to change the world and destroy those who hurt me and my friends.

"Thank you, Marco," I said.

He gave me a sharp pat to the shoulder and nodded. "I trust you will use this to your advantage. Also, I brought you down here for another reason." He looked uneasy. "I just, I wanted to say I'm sorry."

"Why are you sorry?" I asked him.

"I watched that girl grow up. Esmerelda. When I was

160

young, I wasn't smart enough to stand up for what was right when things first started to go sideways. It didn't help that most of my attention was on building technology and my company, but if someone had stepped in earlier... I'm just sorry for all she's done." He seemed exhausted.

"What could you have done? I feel like that family has had generations of problems that no one was going to be able to just fix." I laughed, but his demeanor didn't thaw, which made it die in my throat.

"We were friends once, or as much as she could be friends with anyone." He didn't seem to want to say more.

I wondered if he wasn't as old as his grey hair led me to believe, or if Emerleda was older than I ever thought.

"Well, if it makes you feel any better, you are forgiven. Just like Joseph, you had no control over Esmerelda or what she was going to do. The blame falls squarely with her, but was she always like this?" I couldn't tamp down my curiosity. I couldn't believe he knew her before she was the queen.

"No, not always. She's always been brash and blunt, but something changed one day. She never told me what it was, but from that point she pulled away. She had always been hard to deal with, but it was different then. She iced me out, and my company was taking off, so I lost sight of her. She was vicious when I knew her and had a hard time when she was younger. She didn't stand a chance at having a normal life. It's a tragedy, but as much as it's your job to save your people, it's my job to save mine. I have to stop her and the culture that created her, and you are my best bet."

I stood for a moment, letting the information settle over me. I stuck out my hand, and he hesitated, looking at it like he didn't know what it was. "We have the same goal. I'd be happy to be your partner."

He chuckled quietly and grabbed my hand to shake it.

"Partners," he agreed. "You just need to be ready. Things are changing. Quickly. Keep your eyes open."

We turned to head back to the others in a comfortable silence. I watched Marco as he walked ahead and noticed his posture. He was always to the point, always in forward motion toward the next step. He reminded me a lot of David. They were like sharks; they couldn't stop moving or they wouldn't be able to catch their breath. Deadly when their focus was directed at something.

I couldn't help but feel like the world was shifting beneath my feet. Finally, it felt like we had momentum, that we weren't being dragged back by the wild current. Things were changing. We had to grab the advantage and press it, and I knew Marco—like myself—would take whatever risks were necessary.

24

I launched myself off the bed, my eyes snapping open and taking in the room around us as I tried to register my surroundings.

A red light pulsed over head, and alarms blared. Chase jumped to his feets seconds after me.

I took two steps toward him, grabbed the back of his neck, and pulled him to me. Kissing him deeply, I wasn't sure what was going on and I would never go into another situation without giving him a reminder of how much I loved him.

Quickly, I turned, snacthing my sweater off the bed, and dipped under the blanket wall. From the corner of my eye, saw Chase smile and shake his head quickly, one hand rubbing the back of his neck before following after me.

We raced to the main room and heard some of the others right behind us. As we stumbled into the room, I threw my sweater over my head, and Jupiter turned to us.

"It's an attack; the military is here," Jupiter said as two teenagers ran to her side. "Go gather up all the children. Pull everyone out through the tunnels."

The two nodded and took off.

"David, come on, we need to destroy all the hard drives," Joseph said, and the two of them ran to the labs.

"We'll hold them off while you get everyone out," I said.

Jupiter nodded and went back to working with the person at the computer to gather the entry points of everyone. "Comms up. We'll help you as much as we can."

In one motion, Chase, Benson, Atty, Gwen, and I took off to the armory. Everyone launched their suits, which started to envelope them. I tapped my own as we started to gather guns, explosives, knives, as much as we could in the few moments we had. We saw some others running in as we headed out. It was good to know there would be more help to protect the rest of the people.

"Front door breached," came Jupiter's voice. "They've got another group coming in through the gym."

"Split up." Chase said, and we all nodded. Benson, Atty, and Gwen headed for the gym while Chase and I went for the front door.

As we neared, I heard the troops spilling into the building. I made a motion for Chase to stop as we came to a corner. I nodded to him and he laid down cover for me as I sprinted down the hallway. I cursed as a gatling gun started to fire, making me have to duck and weave to stay clear of the fire. A freaking gatling gun!

I launched myself into a slide, my knives slicing at calves and tendons. Many of the men screamed while they fell. As soon as I got to my feet, I instantly ran and tackled the man with the gun. I slammed my fist into his jaw, he fell, knocked out cold beneath me. There was a huge crash, and I flinched as the door went flying past me, torn off its hinges. A shadowy figure took up the entire double doorway before the man came stalking into the hallway.

Made Immortal

Jasper.

"Vi," Chase called, but I was alreay throwing a shock grenade toward his feet. The explosion sent him soaring back down the hallway, and the roof crumbled, blocking the way. I turned off my comm, I had to be focused.

I straightened and smirked at Jasper. He was nothing more than a trained beast, unable to have a thought of his own. Now that he didn't have the mist or surprise on his side I could take him.

His eyes glinted as he looked me over. I could see his malicious glee, and it was enough to ignite the rage within me. I rolled my neck, shook my arms out, and lowered myself, making sure my stance was firm. Grabbing the gatling gun at my feet I swung it in front of me. I couldn't help but smile wider as recognition flashed across Jasper's features. I gripped the trigger, and he tried to turn out of the way, but the bullets ripped into his back and side before he managed to throw himself down.

"Hello, Jasper." A crazed laugh escaped me. My body thrummed with a type of electricity I'd never felt before. I wasn't scared. Jasper would fear me now. I pulled the trigger again and he tugged the crumlped door up and crouched behind it. His eyes peeked over the edge when the gun jammed.

He stood and grabbed a corner of the door. He spun, using the momentum to hurl it directly at me. It connected, and I went crashing back into the wall behind me. I saw more of his men starting to fill in behind him. I couldn't get distracted. This was my job—stopping Jasper.

Standing, I swiped at the dust from the crumbling cement that covered me. Jasper made a motion to say I was his. His men turned and headed in another direction. We locked eyes, hate clear in his, and I winked to him. I pushed off, racing toward him, using my speed and power to match his bulk. My shoulder hit him right in the ribs, and we went sprawling across the floor.

He reached for me, but I grabbed his wrist and flipped, snapping the bone in the process. He roared in pain. I slammed into him with my right then left knee, my elbows, the blows raining down faster than he could react. Each impact pushed him back, one step at a time.

With an annoyed growl, he knocked me to the side with his meaty hand. As I was off balance he grabbed my leg and threw me out of the front doors. I smashed through one of the still standing door jambs, and the side of the opening started to crumble.

He followed me out, his bulk a dark form in the middle of the spinning dust and flickering lights from inside. I stood up, doing a quick check, feeling completely fine. Just a drop of blood dripping from a cut on my lip. I wiped at it with a sneer.

"Is that all you have?" I asked, laughing.

Midway through the doorway, he grabbed part of the jam next to him. It crumbled in his hand as he roared again. "You aren't getting out of here this time."

"Whatever you say." I pushed against my back leg, springing at him again. He jerked his arm up, clotheslining me, and I went crashing back to the ground. He slammed his fist toward me again, but I grabbed it and used our momentum and his weight against him, launching him into a pile of rubble.

He coughed and worked on extracting himself from the pile of debris. I found a pipe ripped from the wall and picked it up. I tossed it and twisted it around a few times to test the weight. I wasn't on defense anymore.

"Well, Jasper. I just wanted to say thank you. I've been

feeling amazing, and I'm pretty sure I have you to thank for it." I slammed the pipe down toward his head, but he caught the metal before it could connect.

We locked eyes, and I could see the rage and annoyance festering in him.

"You should be dead." His voice was like acid washing over gravel.

I laughed. "Don't you know by now? Every time you try to hurt me, you make me stronger. I am like this because of Esmeralda. Make sure she remembers that." My voice was quiet with just the two of us clashing outside. "I will destroy you." The venom of my hate was almost thick enough to drip from my lips.

I let loose attack after attack, most knocking him back. He only managed to block a few. I didn't stop. I didn't slow. I pushed him back more and more. For the first time, he was on the run from me, and I could see the fear under the anger. His motions became wild, his focus fracturing.

Yet, he got lucky, and one of his punches that connected with my jaw sent me crashing to the ground. Before I could get up, his meaty fists came raining down on me. I had my arms up blocking my head and face to try and stave off some of the impact. As I was curled into myself, I managed to see his feet. I snapped a kick out straight into his ankle, and he went down.

I grabbed another pipe nearby, this one with a jagged edge from being ripped away. My entire vision was red as I held it aloft, standing above him. I could see him calculating how to knock me away.

I felt a wave of calm looking down at him. This was the true way of things. I wouldn't be stopped. I lifted the pipe and sliced it toward his jugular.

"Vi! Where are you?" a scream came from the school.

Marissa Allen

My focus broke for just a moment, but it was enough for Jasper to knock the blow away with his forearm. He managed a kick into my side, sending me flying and the pipe dropping from my grasp.

He was breathing heavily as he stood. I got to my feet as soon as I could ready to take him on again. But he turned and sprinted away from the school.

I screamed after him in frustration. The coward. I went to follow, but I heard my name again and looked back, my face contorted with rage. I was ready to attack whomever it was that distracted me. Then, I saw Chase covered in debris, sweat carving streaks down his face. He was startled and took a step back when he saw me.

He had never looked at me that way before.

I whirled back toward Jasper, but he was gone. I couldn't catch him even if I went after him now. My veins were on fire with the thought of losing him.

25

As Chase followed me back into the building, I could tell he was being cautious. I felt as if heat was rolling off me in waves. I couldn't calm down. I was so angry I couldn't see straight.

I had him. I had Jasper until I had been distracted. I knew it wasn't Chase's fault and I shouldn't blame him, but a part of me, in this moment, did. I had Jasper. I wanted to destroy him so badly, and he slipped through my grasp.

I tried to take a deep breath, and another, attempting to get myself under control.

"Vi." Chase's voice was quiet, like he was approaching a wild animal.

Was that what I was?

He snapped his gun up and hit someone down the hall, who was sighting us with his own. The man screamed as he fell, holding his leg. Chase trotted over and grabbed the gun from the man. He hit him with the butt of the rifle to knock him out.

"Vi." Chase's voice was firmer this time.

"I had him," I snapped. "I had Jasper, and you got in the way."

The look on Chase's face stopped me in my tracks. I had never spoken to him that way before.

I sighed and took a big breath as we walked along.

"Look, I'm sorry," I said. "I'm not totally sure what is going on with me, but that was our best chance to get him. He was right there."

"I'm know, but that's not our priority right now. I need your help to search and make sure we get everyone out," he said firmly.

Just then, I heard someone down the hall. On instinct threw a dagger, and a man toppled to the ground. He'd had Chase in his sights. "I disagree. Taking him down now could have saved so many lives."

"The lives here and now need you. Get it together," Chase snapped back at me as he raised his rifle and shot another person turning the corner in the shoulder, who went down. "Do you hear anyone else?"

I shook my head. "Nothing yet." As I looked over to him, I could see the dark bags under his eyes.

"They have to be afraid to attack like this. Before, we were annoying. Now, we're a force to reckon with. Things are going to keep escalating from here until they boil over everywhere. This is the point of no return," he finished in a whisper.

"Marco said something like that," I muttered.

"When you guys went off together?" Chase asked.

I nodded.

"What is that guy's deal?"

"It's personal for him too, apparently," I said.

Chase glanced at me quizzically. "I'm not sure about him."

Made Immortal

"I am. We have the same goal." The look I gave Chase I hoped he understood the conversation of Marco was over. He needed to trust me on this and I didn't have the patience to explain everything to him right now. My jaw was still clenched tight, the anger was still boiling in my veins.

"Are you okay?" he asked me after a while.

"I'm fine," I snapped. I took a deep breath, trying to calm myself "Is everyone else okay?"

"Benson is with Jupiter and Naya. David and Joseph got out with the evacuation. Gwen and Atty cleared out not that long along ago. I think there are only a few of us left," he said.

I remembered my comm and turned it back on. "Why did they do it this way? They could have thrown so much more at us," I pondered.

"What do you mean?"

"Why wasn't this harder to fight off?" I asked. We looked at each other. "Where did their teams go? Where were they headed?"

Then I changed what I was listening for, and there it was. A consistent beeping, in multiple parts of the school.

"They ran... The building is coming down." I grabbed for my comm unit. "If anyone is left get everyone out! Everyone needs to get out now," I screamed, but as soon as I did, I heard the final beep. On instinct, I turned and pulled Chase to me and covered him as much as I could. The heat hit me first, then the blast of debri.

Chase's cough brought me back to consciousness. He gasped under me, and I tried to push myself up, but there was a slab of concrete on my back. I could feel Chase strug-

171

gling to breathe. With everything I had, I heaved myself up, giving him the few inches he needed to take a deep breath.

"Are you okay?" I gasped as the cement weighed heavily on me. I felt like my arms might give out beneath it, but I couldn't. I wouldn't let him be hurt.

"Yes." His voice was clipped and shallow, but he seemed to be breathing easier.

I used the remaining strength I had to lift myself farther, getting a knee under me and shifted my hands up by my shoulders. Finally, with a scream of effort, I stood. I pushed the slab off of us. Then, I offered a hand to help Chase up and away from the danger. As soon as he was free, I twisted so we both escaped the collapsing rubble.

He grabbed me and pulled me to him. Throwing my arms around him I hugged him tightly. He tightened his arms around me too. We just stood hugging each other for a moment. Fires burned around us, and I couldn't see through the dust and the smoke.

I grabbed his face with my hands, closed my eyes, and laid my forehead to his. He leaned heavily against me, and we continued holding each other.

"We need to find the others," was the first thing out of Chase's mouth. I nodded, and we started to crawl through the hallways, making our way around, over, or under piles of debris and listening for anyone who might be trapped.

I heard someone down the hall, and we both headed that direction. Chase was able to grab them and pull them to safety as I held the debris at bay.

It took us the next few hours, but we were able to rescue a few more rebels. We found some we weren't able to save. Luckily, almost everyone had already evacuated before the bombs went off.

Made Immortal

Once we were done with the search, we made our way out to the track at the back of the school.

The fires were spreading. The walls and upper floors crumbled down into the building. I stood there with my arms on my hips, looking over the destruction. It was like hell had escaped and its flames consumed this place of refuge. I glanced at Chase who appeared horrified. As I watched the smoke rise, the only thing I could feel was my hate for the Esmerelda's father rising. I could see where her own tactics came from.

I was creating a list. A list of everything they both had to be held accountable for when this was over. I would make them pay for it all.

26

We gathered everyone we found, many helping those more wounded than themselves, and made our way away from the building. A hole in the wall caught my attention, and I realized it was to one of the storage rooms. I quickly ran back to grab blankets, parkas, coats, anything I could to cover ourselves when we split up. There were evacuation plans in place, and the group split up to take a few different ways to the next base. They would be out of safe places to hide soon Especially as the amount of people coming to them for care was growing. Chase and I split up, him protecting one group and I went with the other. I wouldn't be surprised if the military came back soon with reinforcements. We needed to be long gone before then.

Guilt coursed through me for feeling slightly lighter after we split ways, still not over my frustration. Although, I was incredibly relieved he was okay. I didn't know what I would do if anything happened to him. I was struggling with my emotions since I had fought Jasper. I had never experienced a frustration like this. One that I couldn't just push away, especially if it was with Chase.

Made Immortal

I pulled the hood up to cover my face more as we trudged their way back to safety. I couldn't even feel the cold. The only things that chilled my veins now were the thoughts I had wondering whether I was becoming what I was fighting. If that's what it took to win this war, could I accept that? I'd have to pay my penance once the war was over, or in the next realm if death claimed me in this fight. Could I stay with my friends if I did? Would they still accept me?

As we walked, I kept my eyes on the others. Even through the pain of their wounds, they had a hard look about them, showing that this only fueled their resistance to the king. I heard them whispering to each other words of hate, worry, and plans for what they would do to the next solider or guard they came across. I smirked in the shadow of my hood. I might not be from this country, but these were my people.

One of them who had been keeping to themselves in the back stumbled and fell. I reached out and grabbed their elbow to help them up. It was a boy who seemed to just be hitting a growth spurt. Like he was still getting used to his new sized limbs. His eyes snapped open as he saw my hair spill from the shadows, and he caught a glimpse of me.

"I... I didn't realize that was you." He gasped.

"I'm nothing special, just helping you all get there okay." I laughed. As he got to his feet, I looked around, to check no one was taking notice of us. "Let's hang back a bit, so we all look less like a group. Just make sure you can keep sight of them in front of us. Do you know how to get there if we get separated?"

He shook his head. "No, I hadn't been there long."

"Well, then, keep with me if anything happens." I gave him a small smile

175

He nodded, and I heard him gulping. I could feel the nervousness spilling from him.

I put my arm around his shoulder and gave him a quick, tight squeeze. "What's your name?"

"Doug." He glanced at me again, his eyes wide in amazement.

"Well, Doug, what do you want to be when you grow up?"

The look on his face told me he hadn't thought of an answer to that before. His answer broke my heart. "I don't think I'll get to grow up."

"You will if I have any say in it," I said firmly. "Now, if everything was better, what would you want to do with your life?"

He seemed to mull that over. "I want to be you."

I laughed. "That is something no one should want. What brings you joy?"

"I'd like to help people. That's what you do, isn't it?"

I chewed on my lip, but figured I'd tell him my truth. "I hurt people. That's my job. If you want to help people, there are so many better things to spend your time on. You could watch the children, help them deal with the trauma they've been through. It could help you at the same time. Helping others often heals yourself. You could get supplies to the elderly or just sit with them and learn from their lives. You could collect resources for those who need them. You could become a doctor like my friend Joseph. Or you could find someone and just love them. Love them with your whole being. That could be enough." I looked down and saw him really processing that information, like he was seeing other paths ahead that could lay in front of him. "If you have enough, share, protect those who need protecting. Just do something good in the dark, with no need for recognition.

176

Made Immortal

You seem like a good person; I don't think it'll be hard for you to find something that brings joy to you and others."

"You do more than hurt people, you know," he said, glancing my way with a serious expression. "You've saved so many of us, you've brought us hope, you've helped everyone here."

I chuckled again. "That's my friends. I got lucky with them."

He shook his head. "If you feel that way, let the help heal you too. I think you need it."

I hugged him tightly. I set my cheek against the top of his head for a second, taking a deep breath, trying to fight off the tears attempting to break free. "You're a pretty smart kid, Doug. When we get there, will you do me a favor?" I asked him, and a bright smile broke across his face.

"Anything!" he said, bouncing slightly at the request.

"Can you check in with the kids? I think they're going to need someone to give them confidence that everything will be okay, and I think you're the man for the job. It's been a long couple of days for them."

He nodded vigorously, and I shook my head with a smile on my own face.

"We're almost there." I pointed to the others. "Go catch up."

He nodded again, and then he turned to give me a salute before running to the group.

I used my enhanced hearing to see if anyone was around besides the rebels. I didn't hear much—some people just living their lives nearby, some watching the Nerian news, gasping at the videos of the burning school and reports of tip lines being open for people to call in if they saw me.

I looked to the tall building next to me, and I pushed

myself inside, breaking a lock on the front door. It was quiet, some sort of office. I made my way into the stairwell and headed up to the roof.

With a quick snap, the chains on the door that led to the roof broke in my hands. I were still a few blocks away from the new base location for the rebels. Walking to the edge of the roof, I stood on the lip, setting my hands on my hips, and surveyed what I could see. The group was making the last turn to get to the building where the rebels would hole up in next

The smoke and dust of the school was visible from here. It wasn't the only view of a fire; they were still smoldering in multiple parts of the nearby city. Sirens echoed from the areas by the blockades. Nothing that would be coming to help us. I also heard the military using PA systems to make announcements.

They were instilling a curfew, threating to arrest anyone who looked suspicious and execute those found helping the rebels.

Screams. There were so many screams. I couldn't catch my breath, and I dropped down to one knee. My breathing was shallow, quick. My vision started to blur, my chest was tight, terror washed over me in a wave. Panic.

I scrambled down and pushed my back to the lip of the roof. I knew I was having a panic attack; it wasn't the first by any means. Tears came unbidden, and I put my head on my crossed arms atop my knees. My body shook with the sobs. I looked to the sky as rain started to fall, which would hopefully help put out the fires. As the raindrops mixed with my tears and slipped down my face, I couldn't take the pain I felt from the people here. Of the people at home. The rebels, the children who didn't deserve this, my friends. Flashes of the people buried in the rubble of the school

Made Immortal

came to me. Their lifeless bodies, their faces twisted in fear. The panic burned away to rage. I screamed into the sky and slammed my fists into the roof, leaving craters in the cement where they hit. I screamed again, and again, and again. Howling my pain into the storm.

I had failed again. My mind focused on the outline of the beast in the doorway of the school. Jasper. His days were numbered. As much as I wished I would have stopped him then and there, Chase had a point. They must have sent him to keep me occupied while they set the charges. That thought me feel even worse.

As the rain soaked me, I finally made my way to my feet. I looked back once more over the city. My heart having to harden again. Instead of heading down through the building, I walked to the lip, took one step off, and dropped. I landed hard on the sidewalk, just barely a bend in my knees as I did. I pulled my hood up and started slowly toward the new base—a condemned apartment building.

As the storm grew in power, the wind began to wail through the streets. I felt its power mix with my rage, a promise that I wouldn't be stopped.

27

I slipped into the building quietly, which wasn't hard because the place was filled with a cacophony of voices and noises. I tried to refocus my hearing, to ignore the metal bangs, the cries of the children, people shouting over one another attempting to get everything situated. I heard Jupiter getting a count of everyone who made it, and I headed toward her voice.

I made my way up a few floors to what seemed to have been a recreational room for the building.

"We need to get more computers; we need to get security back up and running. For now, we'll have guards on every entrance and stationed in the surrounding streets. Silvie, where is your team on getting us the new tech?" Jupiter asked.

"We've already reached our contact. They said in the next few days, but they should be able to get us some tonight," Silvie replied.

"Good. Lilly, please go down and get a count of the children. I need to know if anyone is missing," Jupiter said. The

Made Immortal

girl nodded, but before she rushed out of the room, I managed to catch her arm as I passed her.

"Find a boy named Doug. He just got here a bit ago, and he'll be able to help."

Her face brightened as she saw me, and she nodded before rushing out.

I stumbled as Gwen launched herself at me and held me close in a tight hug. I laughed and tightened my grip on her, not wanting to let her go either.

"Oh, thank the gods you made it," she said before letting me go.

The entire group was here. It seemed I was the last one to make it. I even saw Marco covered in dust leaning in and talking with Naya, who had blood running down from her hairline, making its way through her own dust covered skin. Everyone looked a bit worse for wear, but Marco's eyes shone with determination.

Chase was leaning against a wall. His eyes brightened as he saw me, but he didn't move to come to me. Naya's head snapped up and looked me over.

"Good, you made it," she said as she and Marco both turned to me at the same time.

"What's the next move?" I asked.

"We're attacking the supply chain and depot at dawn," Marco said firmly, and everyone nodded. "Things are going to be changing quickly from here. The city is at its tipping point, this is going to be a cry to arms."

"I wish we had more time for you all to recover, but this can't wait. We need to make a show of force. We can't let this stand," Jupiter said.

"We'll be ready," Atty said, his face fierce.

I could tell we were all a bit haunted, thinking of the

181

devastation from the last few days. We had been doing nothing but reacting. The military had just continued attacking since we had gotten here. We had to make a stand and hit them back.

"Vi," David said, jerking his chin over his shoulder for me to follow him. I nodded and trailed after him and Joseph.

Jupiter returned to discussing the plans with the others. I heard Chase chiming in, working to figure out the best strategy.

We walked into a nearby apartment. The room was dark, the only light coming from a streetlight outside and flashes of lightning. David and Joseph walked toward the window. I realized I had been able to see but they couldn't when David caught his knee on the side of the dust-covered couch in the middle of the room and Joseph reached out to catch him. His hands lingering just a bit longer than necessary.

I couldn't help but smile at the two of them. I was so happy David found someone who got him so well. They were a great pair. I wondered if they would become more than just colleagues.

"How are you feeling?" Joseph asked.

I started to explain the things I'd experienced. The fight against Jasper, the strength against the rubble, the jump from the building, the fact that I could see fine in here now.

"But how are you *feeling*?" David asked me, his intonation telling me he didn't mean my physical wellbeing.

"I'm fine." I crossed my arms in a huff.

"No, you aren't. Talk to me," David said quietly.

"At times, I've been feeling out of control," I mumbled.

"How do you feel out of control?" Joseph asked.

"Sometimes, this rage just comes over me. I can't pull

Made Immortal

myself away." I sighed. "When we're in the thick of it, it's like everything goes red, and then I can't turn it off. I was mad at Chase when he got between me and getting Jasper for good. Insanely angry." I was sure my face was twisted with the guilt I was feeling.

David put a reassuring hand on my shoulder and nodded. I wondered if Chase had talked to him before I had gotten back. I wouldn't blame him if he did.

"It seems that the changes happening to you also have sway over the chemical compounds in your body. It's like a heightened fight-or-flight response," Joseph said. "Luckily, I have a backup of our work on my servers in Soland. So, it wasn't lost in the raid when we destroyed the equipment. Once I can get back into it, we could start running tests for serums that might help you control it."

"It might not just be while fighting. We don't know what this might do to your other emotions, so I want you to let us know if anything happens," David said seriously.

I nodded and sighed. "Okay, I promise."

I knew he was worried and trying to do what was in my best interest.

I looked over, sensing someone join us, and saw Chase enter the room. My chest tightened. His eyes raked over me as he came closer. The thunder and lightning cracked across the sky, and I bit my lip at the sight of his sharp features in the quick flash.

"I should get going and help out with the wounded," Joseph said, giving me a small smile.

"I'll come too." David clasped arms with Chase as they passed each other before heading out after Joseph. He winked at me before he closed the door.

"You took a while," Chase said as he leaned in, his arms

183

caging me against the window. He dipped his lips toward me, his breath tickling my neck. "I was worried."

"I just needed a minute to myself." I trailed my fingers across his cheek, to his neck, along his shoulder, and down his back. He shivered beneath my touch. "I'm sorry for how I was acting."

"I know." His lips grazed the delicate skin of my neck. One of his hands snaked up to tangle in my hair, the other grasping me around the waist and pulling me tight against him. I wrapped my arms around his neck and brought us closer.

He groaned as he crushed his body against mine. We devoured each other. The last few days had left us both on edge, it seemed. I just wanted to lose myself in him and worry about the world later.

Chase grabbed my hips, turning me around and laying me on the floor in the light coming from the window. He took my wrists in his hand and held them above my head. His other hand roamed along my waist. He arched to get a view of me below him.

Biting my lip, I stared up at him. His eyes blazed as he stared back. He leaned toward me, his kisses soft but filled with such passion it made me shiver. Fire erupted on my skin as his fingers ran down my ribs to my waist. His thumb slipped under my shirt and started to inch it up.

I moaned against his lips as we kissed.

He pulled back, and I felt his chuckle rumble through his chest. "If anything happens, I just want to make sure you never have any doubts about how I worship you. I love you, and I'm going to remind you just how much."

My head spun as I breathed him in and became lost to his touch.

"You are my everything," I rasped. My eyes fluttered

Made Immortal

open again to see him looking down at me; the love in his eyes was fierce. He smirked before he brushed more kisses along my skin. We took this small moment for ourselves before we needed to jump into the fight once more. Plus, for once we finally had a real door.

28

Naya had called in reinforcements from the rebels farther in the city. We were all closing in on our positions around the supply depot just before dawn.

Atty and Gwen were one of the farthest teams as they would lead the others in working to make the routes to the building unreachable for blocks in every direction.

The rest of the troops were going to surround the depot, planning to get as many resources as we could before we razed the building to the ground and blocked the military from this section of the city.

Chase and I were on the assault team while Benson, Jupiter, and Naya were on the extraction team to get the supplies out.

As we crept into position, I tapped my wrist and my suit started to slide across my body. Chase tapped his own suit, and it started to cover him. I felt better knowing the team finally had their own for protection.

I left the mask down, letting my hair spill free. They would know who was responsible for this.

186

Made Immortal

Over comms, the units called in, saying they were in position.

Jupiter's voice came across. "All teams, prepare to launch. May the gods bless you all. Breach in three, two, one."

The rebels roared as multiple explosions erupted around the building. I was the first to the doors, with Chase and the others behind me. I ripped the door free, the hallway before us hidden within the smoke.

I pulled my rifle up and made my way into the building. I could hardly focus because the noise was more than I could handle. I flinched as I moved forward, trying to get an idea of what was in front of us. Half of the team split down another hallway.

Chase tapped my arm, and I nodded as he went in front. I kept my rifle aimed over his shoulder as we walked farther into the building. Movement in the smoke ahead of us caught my attention. I tapped Chase, and he lowered his stance. I shot down the hallway, and a scream rang out as a man went down, grabbing his leg.

There were flashes of muzzles and ringing of bullets as the men behind the soldier fired at us, and our rebels shot back. I raced forward, sliding under most of the fire, spraying at the enemies knees. Men screamed, and I launched myself up with a knife in my hand, going right into the man in front of me. I roared and shoved him to the wall, ripping the rifle from him and throwing it away. The others noticed me and swung their guns toward me, and I pulled the man in front of me as a shield. I pushed my way into them, knocking a few down with a kick or a hit with the butt of my own rifle.

The fight had dispersed some of the smoke in the area, and there was fear on the faces ahead as they saw me. One man fired a shot, and I ducked and slammed a fist into his stomach. He dropped to the ground, unable to breathe. I smiled, and the rest of them whirled and raced away from me. I gave chase, leaving the other rebels behind. I could hear them heading down another hallway, Chase with them.

Who I was looking for, I wanted to meet him alone.

I slammed my shoulder into the closest man, knocking him off his feet. His rifle strap was over his shoulder, and I grabbed and twisted it, catching his neck in it and pulling. He struggled as he fought to breathe. When he stopped, I dropped it. He wasn't dead, but he wouldn't get up for a while.

The others had turned a corner, and I took off after them again. As I rounded the same corner, they shot at me, but I threw up a shield up and jumped above the volley aimed down the hallway. As I landed, I was able to throw a punch, rendering one unconscious. Turning, I received a kick straight to the stomach, but I could barely feel it. I glared at the man. His eyes widened, and he went to run. I grabbed his vest and yanked him to me, growling as I slammed him into a wall and dropped him. He was moaning as I left him, heading deeper into the building.

I tried to focus, to find the sound of Jasper's steps—his loud, slow trudging. There was so much going on that I was having a hard time hearing what I needed. But then for just a second, that had to be him. My head snapped toward the way it had come from, and I didn't hesitate to set off in that direction.

The sound of the comms added to my confusion, so I switched mine off, making it easier to tune out noise from farther away in the building. I heard him, closer this time. I took a right and saw flashes of gunfire. Behind me, there was

Made Immortal

an explosion that scattered more debris into the hallway. I took a left and pushed into a large room stacked with pallets and machinery.

In the middle was Jasper. He smirked as he saw me come in. He pushed one hand into his other fist and cracked his knuckles.

I walked toward him, looking around the area, the lights flickering above. He opened his mouth to say something, but I just launched myself forward with a scream. I slammed into his chest, knocking him back. I pressed my advantage and swung a punch into his jaw.

With a grunt, he grabbed the nearest thing and flung it at me. The metal of the container dug into my chest, tossing me back.

"I'm going to enjoy destroying you." He growled. He struck at me again, but I dashed out of the way.

I pulled a knife from my suit and slashed at him, catching him with a knee as he tried to get out of my range. He pulled his arms up in defense, unable to keep up with the speed of my attacks.

All he needed was one good shot though, and he got one. His fist connecting under my chin, throwing me backward through the air. I tried to take a deep breath as I landed, trying to get over the shock of the blow.

His beefy arm arched through the air toward me. I rolled and twisted out of the way as his fist crashed into the floor. Like a feral cat, I pounced. My fingernails raked across the skin of his face as I tried to bash my knee into his side.

Jasper roared in pain, grabbing me by the neck and pulling me off. He held me above the ground, my toes unable to reach the floor. I tore at his hands, but I couldn't get a grip.

189

"You have been nothing but trouble. It's time to get rid of you for good." He growled.

My lungs were on fire as I tried to free myself. There was no way to break his grip this way. Changing tactics, I dug my thumbs into his eye sockets. He howled in pain and dropped me, his hands wiping at his eyes.

I landed, my gun was within range and I snagged it, pulling the trigger, spraying bullets at Jasper. Unfazed, he stomped forward. He ripped the gun away, and I sprawled to the floor as the strap was twisted around my wrist and sent me tumbling. He took the butt of the rifle and smashed it into my temple .

I tried to fight my way through the confusion. I couldn't see straight as I attempted to gather myself. Jasper reached out and grabbed my leg. I tried to grasp something to pull myself away, but he jerked me up and then slammed me into the ground. After a sickening bounce and a beat to breathe, I twisted and kicked out my other leg, catching him in the chest.

I conjured two daggers and jumped on him. I slashed out, cutting his face, ripping his clothes, and stabbing deep into his flesh. He pushed me away from him as he cried out in pain.

We both stood there for a moment, both of us catching our breath and wiping at the blood on our faces.

"Why? Why do you work for her?" I gasped between deep breaths.

"She gave me everything. She is the queen; there is no higher honor," he said gruffly. "You are nothing but a traitor and must be punished."

"She experimented on you!" I knew I would never get through to him. I wondered what he was like prior to what she had done to him.

Made Immortal

"She saved me. I was nothing, and now I am the right hand to the queen, here to do whatever she wishes. And she wishes for you to be removed." He jumped toward me, and I stumbled backwards.

I ground my teeth as I jumped and landed upon a tall pallet of cinder blocks. Looking at my footing, I grinned and ripped one through the plastic wrapping. I launched it down toward Jasper. He moved just in time, so the block broke into pieces as it hit the floor.

He zigged and zagged as I continued throwing blocks at him. "Just stay still you stupid oaf," I screamed.

Eventually, he growled and ran straight for the pallet I was on, knocking it over. I flipped, landing on my feet as it scattered around us.

He charged and rammed into me, and we both went sprawling. I laid there for a moment, trying to catch my breath. I saw him moving to get up and groaned as I move to do the same.

We crashed into each other, the fight turning into nothing more than an all-out brawl. We traded blows, bones cracking, blood rushing from cuts, things already swelling shut. For everything I gave, I got it back.

I couldn't help but growl in annoyance. My head snapped around as the door on the other end of the room burst open. The rebels were on the run as soldiers fired after them.

Jasper laughed, and we shared a look. He smirked like he knew I had no choice. I turned and raced to block the rebels from the oncoming soliders, giving them time to get away. When I could spare a glance, I saw Jasper was gone.

I pulled knives into my hands again and raced through the soldiers, cutting their weapon straps, belts, and into some of the vests before they even knew I was there. I tossed some of their rifels to the ground and landed a few punches along the way. When I was done, I saw the rebels were gone too.

I looked around, trying to figure out where Jasper went. I moved to the door at the other end and stalked out to track him down.

I heard many people racing to the exits. I turned my comms back on and heard Jupiter's voice calling for everyone to evacuate.

I cursed my luck and headed toward the closest exit. It was time; they must have gotten what they needed, and our finale was about to blow. Since we arrived, Gwen and Atty had people placing explosives throughout the building and the nearby streets. Once we were clear, everything was going to blow.

I could only hope Jasper would be caught in one of the blasts. As I ran, I tried to make sure none of the rebels were still here.

"You, this way!" I yelled as I saw two people. They turned and headed my way. I held the door open and rushed them along.

We made our way to the closest exit route, and before we had made it very far, the bombs started going off. The depot building had bombs set on the weight bearing columns, and the building collapsed just like the school had. The charges on the streets went off as well. The explosions ripped up the pavement and nearby buildings for blocks.

I pointed ahead to the others, and we raced along. Finally making our way past the explosions. It would be a while before anyone was going to get anywhere near this part of the city due to the damage. Giving the rebels just a bit more breathing room here.

29

I made my way behind the apartment complex the rebels were using for the base now. The trucks had pulled up with the supplies we had managed to get from the depot. We made an assembly line to pass it all inside. I stood in the truck, dropping things down to the others. We had food, medicine, radios, other tech, weapons, and ammunition. It was a huge win for the rebels today.

It was almost noon by the time we got everything inside and the trucks moved out. All I wanted to do was sleep for the next week. I rubbed the back of my neck as I made my way inside, looking for Jupiter. I touched the side of my face, I could have sworn it was swollen from my fight with Jasper, but it was already barely noticeable.

As I wandered through the building, I heard music and the sounds of dancing. I followed the noise and came to another large room. Many of the rebels were drinking, tapping their glasses in cheers, dancing, and laughing. I smiled and found a spot on the wall to just sit and watch.

Chase slid up next to me. I leaned my head against his shoulder and took a deep breath.

"Glad you're okay," I said.

He kissed the top of my head. "Everyone else got back okay too."

He pointed to some couches, where the rest of the team were laughing together. I relaxed, seeing their faces. I took another deep breath, smiled, and turned to Chase, but his eyes narrowed with concern.

"You're bleeding," he said.

I touched a hand to my head, and it pulled away sticky with half-dried blood. "Oh, I hadn't even noticed," I mumbled.

He pulled me along, seeming to know where he was going. I hadn't even really had time to figure out where anything was here yet. We went up a few floors and he grabbed a first aid kit in one of the rooms and sat me down. He got the gauze and wiped at my forehead, but his eyebrows turned down. He wiped a few more times before pulling away.

"It's gone already," he said.

I shrugged and chuckled. "Not super surprised at this point."

He started to put everything back.

"You should get cleaned up." He pointed at a bathroom connected to the room.

"Is this our room?" I asked, and he nodded. I smiled, my shoulders dipping. "Oh, good. I'm exhausted."

I headed to the bathroom and started the water in the shower. It sputtered for a bit, and I wasn't totally sure the water was clean when it came out, but I just wanted to get some of this grime and blood off me. I didn't stay any longer than absolutely necessary and hopped back out. Chase had left some fresh clothes for me to change into.

I returned to the main room, but I wasn't sure where he

194

Made Immortal

had run off to. There wasn't any real furniture in here, but there were blankets on the ground. I grabbed a backpack and used it as a pillow, curling up on the floor. I was out within moments.

I woke up to light starting to stream into the room. I wasn't sure how long I had been asleep. I rolled onto my feet, pulled my shirt straight, and ran my hands through my hair. I walked out of the room to find the hallway empty. I listened, trying to see where people might be, and heard something a few floors down, so I headed that way.

I ended up in the main room I had seen Jupiter in before the attack on the depot. Jupiter, Naya, and Marco had their heads together, whispering. They all looked up as I came in.

"Ah, you're up. How are you feeling?" Naya asked.

"Fine, actually. What time is it? How long was I out?" I asked.

"About fourteen hours," Jupiter said, and I nodded. At least that question was answered; it looked like it was the next morning.

"How did it go? I didn't have comms in for most of it," I said.

Marco nodded with a smile on his face. "Well, the raid got us more supplies than we were expecting. We've heard chatter that we put the military back months by cutting off this depot. We have better news though," he said, his eyes shining.

"What's that?" I asked as he seemed to be waiting for me to do so.

"With this hitting the news, the rebels have had an

influx of volunteers. In the next few days, the cells all over the city are going to be ready to coordinate. This is it. We're ready," he said excitedly. "We knew you would help, but I didn't expect the push you being here gave us. I wanted to thank you." He put out his hand, and I shook it. Again, I wanted to say it wasn't me, but I just left it.

"That's great. What is the plan?" I saw Jupiter behind him chewing on the end of the pen staring down at a map. I walked over so I could look at it with her.

"The cells are set up roughly every few miles on the exterior edges of the city," Naya said, pointing to certain places on the map. I saw her hover over her own cell, where we had originally ended up after the summit. "We're going to do a synchronized attack pushing toward the inner city." She stopped and glanced at me with a question seeming to hang on her lips.

"What?" I asked.

"Well, while this is going on, we have a request for your team to lead some others in an attack against the palace. They will send more men out to deal with us, leaving an easier path to the king," Jupiter said.

"You want to take out the king at the same time." I laughed at the audacious plan. I was impressed. "That could end everything. End how it is now, anyway. Are you planning to take power? It'll be chaos in that vacuum," I said, thinking out loud.

"Yes, we'll..." Jupiter pointed to the three of them. "Be with you. We plan to have another team taking over the media control center at the same time, so we'll announce we're taking the country back for the people, to be led by the people. Marco will get that set up and then meet us at the palace during the raid. Once we have control we'll let the areas of the city vote for their representatives, and we'll

Made Immortal

work together to try and fix this country. It'll still be a fight, but we'll finally have the upper hand."

"Sounds easy enough." We all laughed. "We're not going anywhere as long as you need us. I assume you probably talked to the others already?" I asked.

They nodded. "Everyone is on board."

"When is the attack?" I asked.

"We'll finalize the plans over the next few days with all the cells. Within the week, I would assume," Marco said, then he and Jupiter went back to analyzing the map.

"Okay, just let us know when you need us," I said. They nodded but never looked up. I couldn't help but chuckle as I turned from the room in search of the others. I made my way to where I could smell food.

As I entered the lobby, the smell hit me in full force and my stomach started to rumble with hunger. I was already salivating. There were a bunch of people around, most running a buffet style breakfast, many cooking more behind the tables. They had set it up down here so they could feed anyone nearby in the city who needed it too.

I saw the team gathered on the floor, eating their own breakfasts. I grabbed a plate and went to sit with them, taking a place next to Chase.

"Morning," everyone said.

Gwen and Atty both had some cuts and bruises. Benson had a large cut across his cheek that someone had stitched up. Chase had a bruise around his eye I hadn't noticed yesterday.

"Morning," I replied. I blew on my cup a bit before moaning as I tasted my coffee, and the others smirked at me. Another day we were safe and together, no matter how banged up. I had to be thankful for every one of these we had.

197

I leaned into Chase's shoulder while I enjoyed just watching and listening to everyone chatter about the mission the day before. Gwen and Atty had been ambushed on one of the side streets as they were placing charges. Gwen had taken care of them, but most of their bruises were from not getting far enough away before setting off the explosions. Benson had run into a pack of soldiers while they were loading the trucks, but they hadn't posed much of an issue to him. Chase has run into a bunch of resistance, but he and some of the rebels managed to clear out his section of the building with relative ease.

I saw the others look behind me, and then I heard a gaggle footsteps coming our way. I turned to peer over my shoulder and saw a group of teens, including Doug, Lilly, and Jessie. Jessie's little sister, Cecily, was with them too. There were a few others as well, who I hadn't met.

"Can we sit with you?" Doug asked.

I smiled and patted the ground next to me.

"Of course," I said, and his smile was so wide I wasn't sure if he'd be able to make his face go back to normal afterward. "Have you found something you like to do yet?" I asked as he settled down next to me.

"We've been with the children, telling them stories and trying to keep them calm when they hear gunfire or explosions. Just like you asked," he said, nodding gravely, knowing it was an important task.

"Good. Do you like helping them?" I asked, and that smile broke out across his face again.

"I do, and Jessie and Lilly are really helpful. Have you met them?"

I waved to the girls and smiled as they waved back. "How are you?"

198

Made Immortal

"We're fine. We wish we could help with the fighting though," Jessie said, seeming slightly downtrodden.

"There are tons of jobs to do here. Fighting isn't the only thing you can do to help," I told them.

Doug perked up. "Yeah, keeping up morale is important. Someone has to stay and protect the kids and make sure they aren't scared," he said gravely, nodding as he did so.

"Exactly." I winked at him.

"You and those kids are the future; we're trying to build something for you. Give you the access to take control and rule with peace and compassion. That's going to be your jobs before too long. It's a serious task, and you can help the younger kids learn what it means to be a good leader," Chase chimed in.

The teens all nodded, staying quiet, mulling over that bit of information.

Gwen looked over at me then over the group of kids surrounding us and giggled. "You sure have quite the following here, Vi."

I shrugged and leaned back against Chase's chest, and he wrapped his arms around me. "No accounting for taste here in Neria, it seems."

We all laughed and watched on as the teens told us about what they had been living through here in the city. I added every one of their wounds to the toll of what I would take from Jasper and Esmeralda, not to mention the king.

30

I had never heard the song on the radio before but it was catchy. Although, It stopped abruptly, and just as I was getting into it.

"This is a mandatory broadcast from King Edgar Ravensbone," the voice said, and then there was a moment of silence. "Good people of Neria, I am coming to you today with terrible news. As you have seen on the news, we are under siege. Terrorists have attacked the security we bring you, and have proven how evil sits within their hearts. There was an strike on a warehouse that had months' worth of medicine, food, and supplies taken. Stolen from you, my good people. My heart is saddened by the ruthlessness of these terrorists. We will not stand for it any longer.

"Anyone found helping or housing these terrorists will be executed swiftly. Make no mistake, these are people who want to destroy our country and way of life. We will not let them take an inch. I implore you, please reach out to our special division with any tips on where we can find the terrorists or the stolen supplies and medicine that was destined to help the weak and the poor.

Made Immortal

"Hear this now. We will not be defeated. This rabble rousing will be put down immediately with the force of our great nation. Please call in if you see any hint of the terrorist Genevieve Astor, who has come here from Kabria. It seems that attacking my dearest daughter, Queen Esmerelda Astor, her stepmother, was not enough. She has now brought her addled mind here to Neria to upset the peace we have so long endured. This will not be tolerated, and we expect to have her in custody soon. Keep the faith, my good people. Neria is stronger than any other country, and this shall not define us."

The message cut off, and the music resumed. One of the rebels near me spit on the floor, and many grumbled about the propaganda the king was pushing. Anyone living near the outskirts of the city knew the lies in what he said, but many elites or even those in the middle class wouldn't know the difference. We'd have to be even more careful as we would have even more eyes on us than before.

Yet, he had done us a favor. The marginalized, those who knew those supplies would never have reached the people in need, those whose families had been kidnapped, killed, or still missing... We knew the truth. And I wouldn't be surprised if the rebel cells would be flooded with even more recruits, with those ready to fight back against the brutality of the system that left them hungry, hurt, and cold.

I couldn't help but smile, thinking of the attack that would soon come. I worried for those who would fight, but I knew, just like myself, that dying for this cause would be a worthy death. The king would see the might of his people pushing back against his iron grip and hear their cries of defiance.

I looked up as Naya walked into the room. She searched for a moment before her eyes landed on me. She jerked her head, and I got up to follow her. I had been lazing in the communal area with the other rebels, just basking in seeing them enjoy themselves with the little we had. They seemed so happy and free here.

As I followed Naya, she headed toward the war room that had been set up. The room where Jupiter, Naya, and Marco had been looking over the details of the upcoming plans.

Benson had a roll of waterproof tape on his arm and was cursing as water dripped on him while he tried to repair a pipe in the ceiling. Atty sat on the floor with a smile on his face, making no move to help. Gwen walked over and kicked Atty in the shoulder, and he groaned. Then, the three of them worked together to fix it.

"Hey, you found her," Jupiter said, turning to us.

"What's up?" I asked. Marco and Chase weren't around. I hoped they were getting some sleep. We had been all running on empty for the last few weeks with everything that had happened since the summit.

"We want to take you to the other cells. Boost morale before the attack," Naya said.

I tried not to roll my eyes, and I internally groaned at being paraded about. I didn't see why everyone thought I was doing something special. They were doing most of the work without me. Yet, I would do whatever was needed to put them in the best spot for success. "When would we be leaving?"

"Tonight. It'll take some time to navigate to them. We'll move you around and end in the most internal cell to have the easiest route to the palace," Jupiter said, pointing first to Naya's cell on the map, then her last tap landed on the large palace on the northern edge of the city. It towered over the executive district, the rich living lavishly around it.

Made Immortal

"Of course. Whatever you need." I caught a glimpse of David and Joseph walking past, and David caught my eye, giving me a look that said he wanted to talk. "I'll be right back, but I'll be ready for tonight."

Naya nodded, seemingly lost in thought again.

I trotted over to David and Joseph and followed them down the hall to another apartment. When I walked in, I saw they had computers set up again. I grabbed a stool and scooted toward one of the screens Joseph neared.

"We got the data, from the monitors David had added to your suit, of the supply raid," Joseph started.

"You barely had an elevated heart rate during the entire raid, even though you did have an elevated chemical release of adrenaline. Your oxygen saturation was normal, even after the extended fight. You were pretty much just level, no real changes that we should see after that type of altercation," David said. "We want to keep collecting data over a broad range of your activities. To see what we can learn. We can obtain the data even over a great distance."

I quirked an eyebrow. "How far away do you expect me to be?"

"Well, that's the thing. This base is one of the closest to the Soland border." David rubbed his neck like he did when he was telling us something he didn't think we'd want to hear.

I waited, knowing he'd get around to it eventually.

"We're going to stay here and work on setting up evacuations, but then we'll be going with them on the last caravan," David said quietly.

I bit my lip. So he wouldn't be leaving with us to head to the next cell. I had known this was coming. I knew he was going to go to Soland. It didn't stop my heart from breaking. Our little trio had been together as kids, and again once they

203

rescued me. So outside of my imprisonment David had always been by my side. I bit the inside of my lip, not wanting to show my greif. I nodded and rushed over to grab him up into a crushing hug. He gripped me back tightly.

"I'm going to miss you," I whispered.

"I know. I'll miss you too, but there is so much I can do from there. I can have the time to work on the nanobot tech. I can help settle those displaced. I can finally have the time I need to do the things I have to for us to win this war."

"I know." I sighed. "I know you can, and Chase and I will be going back to Kabria right after anyways." My voice cracked.

"I'll come home soon," he said, pulling back and catching my gaze, but I saw in his eyes he wasn't totally sure if he would. I wouldn't be surprised if he got caught up with his new life with Joseph for a while.

I knew the pain he saw here broke his heart and he wanted to do something to help. He was never a fighter. He and Joseph could help in another way, not just Nerians but would help Kabrians as well.

"I'll still be working on tech for you. I'll make sure you will always be as safe as I can make you. The entire team. I'll video call you all the time. So much you'll get sick of my face," he said.

I reached out to cup his cheek and gave him a sad smile. "Never."

I hadn't known Joseph terribly long, but he had changed my life, and the lives of all of us, especially David. I reached over and pulled him up into a tight hug. He chuckled awkwardly before returning the embrace.

"You keep him safe, you hear me?" But I knew he would. If he knew what was good for him, anyways. No one hurt my boy. "Does Chase know?" I asked.

Made Immortal

"Yeah, I just told him a bit ago," he said.

I pulled him close again, memorizing the feel of his arms around me, the look of him now as a man choosing his own destiny. I couldn't stop the tears slipping down my cheeks. I wiped at them and then straightened his jacket, swiping at his shoulders even though there was nothing to clean from them. I nodded before turning on my heel to head back out, but I looked over my shoulder quickly before I left.

I saw tears shining in his eyes as well. Joseph grabbed his hand and squeezed, and David smiled at him for the gesture. "I'm going to find you before you leave," he called after me.

I tried to remember how to get to the room Chase and I shared. I wasn't paying attention to my surroundings and ran straight into someone. I went to apologize but looked up and saw Chase staring at me.

He grabbed my hand and pulled me along to our room, as if he knew exactly what I needed. He shut the door behind us before I fell apart. I collapsed to my knees, on the verge of hyperventilating. Chase came to me, wrapping me in his arms, and I let myself cry.

I felt like all I did these days was break down. I hadn't cried this much since my first few years held captive. Chase rocked me and rubbed my back, murmuring that it would be okay. My entire world was swinging off its axis though.

"She's taking everything from us," I sobbed. I had never met her father, but I had to guess the apple couldn't have fallen very far from the tree. If she hadn't been using her fathers power and country for her own gains, kidnapping all these people from Neria for her testing, using Jasper as her tool here and at home in Kabria. What would life have been like if she wasn't on her warparth? I would have had my life,

205

David would be home, we woudln't even had needed to be here. I was just so tired of losing the things I loved. She was wicked and had poisoned everything.

"We won't let her get away with it," he said firmly and grasped my chin, turning me toward him, a fierce look in his eyes. He pressed a kiss to my lips before pulling back and running his thumb across my cheek, wiping away the tears. "That entire family is going to pay for the chaos they've wrought."

I nodded and leaned into him as he folded himself around me. Slowly, I calmed, feeling safe in his arms. "I'm happy for him though," I said quietly. He had been batting around ideas of ways he could provide more help, and he had a soft spot for the children affected by everything. They would be setting up a school on top of doing their research together, taking in orphaned children to give them a safe space to grow in Soland.

"Me too Vi, me too. We'll see him again," he whispered into my hair.

We just sat there wrapped together, watching as the sun passed across the window of the room. Just basking in this moment of calm. Tonight, we'd be off again. The next week, I was sure, would be a whirlwind of noise and movement until the day of the palace attack.

31

The smell of dinner wafted through the building. We must have fallen asleep, but it couldn't have been for too long. I kissed Chase awake, and his smile that was just for me spread across his face.

"Hey, beautiful," he murmured, still waking up.

"Dinner is almost ready, I think," I said, and he nodded. I pushed myself up and held out a hand to help him up too.

As he stood, he wrapped an arm around my waist, the other tangling in my hair as he pulled me into a heated kiss. His touch was electric against my skin. The feeling lasted long after his hands moved away.

"I'm more interested in the meal right here." His voice was thick with longing, and his kisses trailed down my neck to my collarbone.

"We've only got tonight with David. You can get your fix at the next stop," I promised him. The look in his eyes told me he would keep me to that promise. I pushed myself up to my tippy toes to kiss him once more before we headed out the door.

As we closed it behind us, I glanced to Chase with a mischievous glint in my eyes.

"Race you," I said, then took off down the hall. Chase was right on my heels and managed to trip me up and make it to the doorway to the stairs first. He crashed through it and started to descend. I smirked as I came to the stairwell, giving him some time to get a good lead. "Ready or not, here I come."

I cackled and threw myself over the railing and dropped straight through the gap in the stairwell to the main floor. As I landed, I looked up to see Chase only halfway down.

"That's cheating." He growled.

"You'll have to catch me to punish me." I laughed and took off toward the main lobby. I heard him hit the landing and jogged after me. He knew he couldn't catch up.

He slammed the door open as he made his way into the lobby, and his glare was offset by his smirk as he made his way to me.

"For now, how about a kiss for the winner?" I laughed, and he came up and kissed me deeply to a chorus of kids groaning in our direction.

We broke apart, and the children were giggling behind their hands, some pointing at us. I winked, and we looked for the others. The group was already sitting in the same corner as before, the teens already in their spots surrounding them. We grabbed our plates and headed to join them.

The conversation was about the evacuation to Soland, so David must have already told the others. His eyes snapped to us, and everyone made room for us by him. We sat on either side of him and squished him between us, wanting to be as close as we could now before we wouldn't have the chance any longer. He reached his arms out

Made Immortal

around our shoulders as we did. I caught him with a hug around the middle. He kissed both of our temples, and then we let each other go and started to dig into our dinner. Although, David wasn't really eating, just moving his food around his plate.

"Not hungry?" I asked him, and he shook his head.

"I know it's what is best, but I'm going to miss you guys," he said quietly.

"We're going to miss you too, but we'll see each other again soon," Chase said, and David smiled at that.

"If you're not going to eat that, can I have it?" I asked, already pulling his plate toward me.

He laughed, a big deep laugh that I hadn't heard in a while. "Yeah, all yours," he said, and I pounced on it, shoveling it into my mouth.

Meals here were leaner here than back in Kabria, and I was trying to only eat my share, but at times, man, I was starving. Everyone had been offering part of their rations here and there when they saw I needed it. I still needed more sustenance than normal because of my metabolism. I burned through everything so quickly, but I felt guilty taking more than anyone else when there wasn't nearly enough. I moaned as I gobbled down everything in minutes. The whole group laughed as I did.

I saw the teens keeping an eye on us as we ate. I figured they had heard we'd be moving out soon.

Finally, Doug straightened his spine and looked at me. In a firm tone, he said, "We'd like to come with you and fight."

The others behind him nodded.

"You all are needed here for very important tasks," Benson asked pointing to our friends.

"We're just babysitting." Lilly whined.

209

"You're protectors," Atty added. "Every cell is going to be pushing into the city. It'll leave the bases mostly empty, and we need someone to make sure no one doubles back and hurts the kids or steals any of our supplies. You are the line of defense for the future of Neria; it's a very important job."

"I'd say you have the most important job of all," Gwen said, smiling.

The group of teens leaned in and whispered to each other, some getting a serious expression. Doug nodded, looking at Lilly and Jessie who returned it. I smiled, seeing the little cohort being created right before our eyes. Pride swelled within me for these young people. These would be relationships that lasted over years. I tried not to think of the possibility of the base being attacked while the last push was happening. I just needed to have hope, like everyone else here. Hope was what pressed all of us forward.

"You just need to remember what we've been showing you," Benson said firmly. The teens nodded, and I looked at Benson surprised. I hadn't realized he had been working with the kids, but I was happy they had. He caught each of their gazes, making sure they knew this was important. "You know how to use the weapons if you need to, but you only point them at something you are willing to shoot. Do you remember how we showed you to blockade the area?"

The teens all confirmed they did.

"Good, that will be the first thing you need to do if anyone comes here while you're in charge."

"Yes, sir," one of the boys shouted. The others took up the call, hooting and hollering, ready to take on the world.

We all smiled, but we also shared a worried look between us for these kids. As we finished eating, the team regaled the young ones with tales of missions and hair

210

Made Immortal

brained pranks we had played at the headquarters in Kabria. The stories brightening the somber mood.

"Were you really kidnapped?" one of the girls asked me.

My heart clenched. I still didn't like to think back on my time in Esmerelda's clutches. "Yeah, for six years. Before my friends found me and brought me home."

"Were you strong back then, like you are now?" a boy asked.

"No, and I was just a kid, about your age," I replied.

"Then, what happened? Can we be strong like you?" another asked.

"You know the people who went missing?" I asked them, the look they gave me said they did. I wondered how many of them had family that they still didn't know where they were. "Those who took them are the ones who had me."

"Here in Neria?" One gasped.

"Sadly, it's not just happening here. It's happening in my home too, back in Kabria," I said, flinching, thinking of the ones we would never get back.

"The ones we saved, your friends and family, they're going to need you to show them how much you love them. They'll need all the love they can get to heal some of the wounds you can't see," David said, looking at me with pain in his eyes.

My heart broke at the looks on their faces, showing they knew that, and that some of them probably needed a bit of that love themselves. "All of you are already as strong as me in the ways that count. I wouldn't wish this on anyone. We're making sure no one else ever has to go through that."

They sat quietly, seeming to take that in.

"I don't know if you've heard yet but when Joseph and I leave, if any of you want to come with us, we're going to be going to Soland, creating a safe place for the people who can't be in Neria any longer," David said, and Joseph nodded. "One of the things we'll be setting up is a school. All of you are welcome; you'll have a safe place to live and learn. You can develop your skills to come back and help rebuild Neria once it's safe."

A few of their faces lit up. I was glad I got to see when they found out.

"We'll be leaving after the last push," Joseph said, glancing our way.

At least I'd be able to keep track of them after the chaos. I looked up and saw Marco headed toward us.

"I think all of you have some things to do," Marco said, looking at the teens. They all waved to us as they got up and headed off to drop off their dishes. "We're going to be loading up soon," he said pointedly, and we understood the time had come.

As we stood, David caught me in a bear hug. I closed my eyes, savoring the moment, waiting for him to let go because I wasn't going to be the one. I'd hold on as long as he wanted. He finally pulled away and hugged Chase before gripping the back of our necks and looking at both of us with so much emotion.

"I'll see you soon," David said. I had to swallow past lump in my throat, but we weren't going to say goodbye. That was something I wouldn't be able to do. Chase and I gripped his shoulders, and we put our foreheads together, just holding on for one last moment.

We broke apart, and David said his goodbyes to the others as Chase and I went to Joseph.

"You keep him safe, okay?" I begged. "And yourself too."

Made Immortal

His look let me know he would do everything in his power to do so.

"Both of you stay safe." Chase held an arm out, and Joseph clasped it.

"We'll be working around the clock to help in any way we can," Joseph told us.

"Our ride is here," Marco called out.

Gwen squeezed my hand as the five of us headed to the doors that led to the alley behind the building. David grabbed Joseph's hand, and they waved goodbye. I returned it enthusiastically until I couldn't see them any longer, unsure when we'd see them again... if we ever would.

32

Outside waited a jet-black armored van. I smirked; it was a beauty to behold. Marco unlatched the back, and we climbed inside. When the door swung shut, it was still surprisingly roomy with the six of us.

"Naya is on her way to her base. You'll regroup with her as the last stop before the attack. She'll have supplies ready for you," Marco told us as the van started to move.

"You aren't going to be with us?" Gwen asked.

"I'll be with you most of the way. I'll be staying at the second-to-last base, which will be the team in the inner city taking over the Media Control Center," he said.

Chase had a pensive look. I was sure he was going through all the plans yet again. He'd had been working with the leaders on this strategy since they asked for our help back in Naya's base. Marco said he had the contacts to help put things in place for taking over the airways, which didn't surprise me.

Atty's knee bounced in a steady beat as his fingers were twisted in Gwen's. She laid her other hand on top of his arm, seeming to try to spread her calm through him. Benson

214

Made Immortal

had his head leaned back against the wall of the van with his eyes closed.

I couldn't pull my gaze away from the window. I watched as the city passed us by. People huddled, sleeping on the streets, buildings on fire, the sounds of gunfire echoing throughout. The next base was only a few miles away, but it took us over an hour to make our way there. We pulled up to an old factory that looked like it had been abandoned for a while. Some of it had been shelled and was falling in on itself.

Our drivers told us to wait to exit the van. They got out and confirmed we were clear before they opened the back door. We poured out and rushed to the door of the factory. Someone almost as big as Benson stood beyond it to block us from going any farther. The door closed behind us as soon as we had all piled inside.

"Alejandro," Marco said in greeting.

The large man smiled and gave him a quick salute. His eyes washed over the group but stopped when he saw me.

"Princess, it's an honor," he said.

"Please call me Vi." At his shocked look, I begged, "Please."

He seemed uncomfortable but nodded.

"Of course, Princ—er, Vi," he stuttered. "If you'll follow me, everyone is excited for your arrival." He spun on his heel and headed into a large open room. It looked to be the main area of the factory, but the machinery had been removed to make space for the rebels' camp.

As we made our way in, heads started to turn and whispers floated through the room as people started to point in our direction. It felt eerily similar to walking into that infirmary and having people reach out to skim their fingers across my skin as I passed by.

215

The others followed Alejandro as he walked through the room. I fell back and spent time with the people I passed. I didn't manage to say anything, but their hands were squeezing mine tightly. Pain filled their eyes, but there was hope in them too. Some had their arms crossed but gave me a quick salute in approval. A child ran up to me, stopping right before knocking into my legs. The little girl pulled at my pantleg, and I dropped down to be on the same eye level as her.

"Are you the princess?" she asked.

I laughed and nodded. "I used to be."

"Do you have a charming prince?" she asked.

I glanced over her shoulder and caught Chase's gaze. We shared a smile, and then I looked back at her. "I do. He's my knight in shining armor."

"I hope to have a prince of my own one day," she said.

I took her hand. "I'm sure you will, but until then, do you know what?"

Her eyes went wide. "What?"

"You can be your own knight. You never have to wait for anyone to come save you," I said with a smile, and she clapped her hands to her mouth.

She gasped. "I could be a knight?"

"You can be whatever you want." I laughed as she squealed. She turned and ran off to a group of other children and started to tell them all about it. I stood up and headed through the room again. The eyes of the adults around us trailed me as I slowly made my way to my friends.

I finally reached a blanket wall that roped off an area that seemed to be where they did their planning. Alejandro had slipped in, and so had the others. I ducked into the room, and Chase patted a seat next to him on a milkcrate.

216

Made Immortal

"Thank you for that. It means a lot to them," Alejandro said, dipping his head to me.

"I'm starting to see that seems to be the case," I said, shaking my head in bewilderment at it all. "I'm just not sure what else I can do exactly." I shrugged.

"Just a little speech before you go back out tomorrow, letting them know they aren't alone," Alejandro said.

I looked at Marco. "No one said anything about speeches."

He shrugged. "You'll do fine. We don't have a lot of time, and this is going to help."

"Is this what I'm doing at every stop?" I felt sick to my stomach just thinking about it.

Chase shrugged and smirked at me. I was going to have to get him back for this later.

"Why can't one of you do it?" I asked Alejandro and Marco.

"Honestly, your face has been plastered everywhere for weeks. They've seen the blows you've landed against the military. It's going to mean more coming from you," Marco said firmly.

This was my dad's fault. He had told me to show my face to cause chaos when he sent us for the mission. Well it had worked too well. We were just supposed to be here for the summit and now I was the face of a revolution. I think I was finally seeing what his intention might have really been. This was probably his plan the entire time. I kicked out at nothing with a growl. We would be having quite the discussion when I got home. "Fine, fine. Okay, so, when do I make this speech?"

"Tomorrow, after breakfast, right before we head out. For now, just go spend some time with them." Marco held out his hand toward the main part of the room.

217

Chase grabbed my hand and the five of us headed out there. Benson pointed toward an area that had fires lit in trash cans, people standing and sitting around them. We made our way over, and the crowd hushed as we neared them.

"Can we join you?" I asked. Some of the people who hadn't noticed us jumped up and brushed off their clothes, looking surprised. I *really* wished everyone would stop acting like this around me. All I ever wanted since I had been rescued was to be normal.

"Oh, yes. We can leave if you want to have this to yourself," one said quickly, sounding worried.

"We were actually hoping for some company if you'd stay with us," Chase said, leaning over my shoulder and wrapping his arms around me.

I couldn't help but laugh and kiss his cheek. The slightly flustered group of rebels managed to make room for us.

"It's been a long day. Does anyone have a drink?" I whined, and four people instantly pushed bottles toward me. I was so startled I gasped and tried to laugh at the same time, which just caused me to sputter instead. I wiped at my mouth and grabbed a bottle quickly before the team fell into giggles. After a beat, the rebels joined in, and it wasn't long before they clearly felt more comfortable around us. No one needed to know I couldn't get drunk because of my metabolism. They just needed an ice breaker, and I wanted to seem like one of them.

I sat wrapped in Chase's arms as we passed the bottles around, and I basked in the warmth of the fire. We hadn't been anywhere with heat in a while, and it was starting to get cold at night. I stayed quiet, just watching as my friends laughed at one of the stories the rebels were telling.

Made Immortal

Which launched Benson into his epic tale of when he used to fish with his bare hands growing up. I always loved this story, trying to imagine what a young Benson looked like, jumping in the creek and having fish slip, slide, and probably smack him in the face at least once or twice.

The the heat of the fire, and the love I felt all around me, lulled me into a sense of calm I didn't think I would manage today of all days. This helped me remember that David wasn't disappearing completely from my life, my friends would still be here. Our lives might change, but they'd still be entwined. He was figuring out what he wanted from life, and I was happy for him because of it.

I tried to cover my yawn, but Chase noticed of course. He stood and held his hands out to help me up.

"I believe it's time for bed. I'm exhausted," he said with an overexaggerated yawn. There was no doubt they all knew it was because I was tired. Everyone waved, and I thanked the rebels for letting us join them before Chase tugged me off to a cot along the far wall. I crawled in quickly, and he threw a blanket over me. I gave him a quick smile before I drifted off, complete exhaustion overtaking me.

33

The early morning was quiet at the camp. I stretched my arms high and then twisted my back to crack it. I pulled Chase up after me and held his hand as we made our way through the building. Away from where everyone was sleeping, a door was propped open, and we slipped outside. Chase wrapped his arms around my waist and spun me before catching me against him and kissing me lightly.

"Good morning," he whispered.

I smiled at him as I ran a finger over his cheek, pushing myself up to sneak a quick kiss.

"I see you are quite the early bird, aren't you?" Marco laughed as we looked over to where he leaned against the wall, a steaming cup held in his hands as he watched the sun rise over the skyline.

I thought of the breakfast at dawn at the summit where we had first met. Was that only a few weeks ago? It felt so long ago now. Other than my friends, I didn't know anyone here longer than that. Yet, I had forged some strong bonds with the rebels I'd met. I hoped they succeeded in their quest to get power back to the people.

220

Made Immortal

"I'm not fond of not being able to see the sky," I said, thinking of my years in the prison, the tests, the torture, and never, ever getting to go outside.

Marco nodded, making a soft noise in agreement. "I've heard Kabria looks much different than it does here. I never managed to visit. Always locked away in my labs working—for far too much time, now that I look back at my life. Can you tell me about it? Is it really as beautiful as they say?"

"Yeah," I replied. "Everything is green. or has bursts of color. It's bronze in the fall and white in winter. The only things that break the horizon other than the capital are mountains or forests. We live with the earth; we don't just use it."

"It sounds wonderful. I'd like to see it once before I die." He kept his eyes locked onto the sunrise.

"If you think that's something, wait till you can see the stars." I hoped one day I could bring him there. Show him the beauty of it all.

"We're all so different. Kabria and its agriculture, Neria and its technology, and Soland, well, the artists and scientists made that place damn gorgeous. Not always useful, but a thing to behold." He chuckled, and I had to agree.

Chase and I both nodded. We'd spent some time in Soland over the years when we went to visit Nathan and his father. The entire city seemed covered in gold, silver, and the most brilliant jewels. The buildings were works of art, and the pathways were normally more garden than street. It was an amazing place to visit, but I wasn't sure if I could ever think of living there. Kabria is a little more direct and to the point, and I enjoyed that bit of life.

"Trade is good, but think what it might be if we all worked in harmony one day. No borders, just one people.

We had to have been united at some point, don't you think?" Chase mused.

Marco snorted. "Wouldn't that be something? But that dream is just a little too big for us humans to manage. There will always be a fight somewhere over something. It's just how we work." Marco dropped the hand holding his empty cup and pushed off the wall to go back inside. "Don't be too long; you've got work to do, kid."

I sighed and leaned back against him.

"I can't believe you didn't tell me about the speeches," I grumbled, turning around in his arms to look at him.

"I just wanted to see your face when you found out." He laughed and jumped out of the way as I threw a light punch at his side.

"You're lucky you're cute," I said before I pulled him back in by his shirt for a kiss.

"Are you doing okay?" he asked quietly. "Just, with the scars and we've been on the move basically since, I wanted to make sure you are okay." His eyes were soft, his gaze worried.

I leaned my forehead against his chest. "Some days, I am. Some days, I'm not. I don't get much time to think about it. I'll be better if this works. If we can do some good here."

"We've done good."

I could feel the words rumble through him.

"Not enough. Not yet," I replied.

He tightened his grip around me.

"It's never going to be enough for you, you know that? Your heart is too big. We are going to have to go back soon. We have to do this for Kabria too. We have to take the fight back to her. We'll be leaving people here who are hurt, and you won't be able to fix it all." He rubbed my back as he spoke.

Made Immortal

I chewed on the side of my lip. "I know. I'll cross that bridge when we get there. Let's just help these guys take down her dad and cut off her help. Then, I'll be ready to go home." I nodded, it was time to get to work. I gave Chase one more peck on the cheek before heading back inside to help serve breakfast before I grabbed some of my own.

The looks on everyone's faces as they came through the line so I could shovel some eggs onto their plate made my day. I still didn't totally get it, but I couldn't miss the grateful attitudes of the rebels. It was infectious. Once the line died down, I went to make my own breakfast plate and gave myself an extra serving of eggs since luckily there was still plenty. I couldn't wait to eat.

I found the closest seat and dropped into it to start scarfing everything down. The others sat next to me, all quiet as we ate, prepping for another long day of traveling and meeting people. We were supposed to be in the next cell by the afternoon.

"What am I supposed to say?" I asked, finally looking at Chase.

He took a moment before answering. "Something from the heart. You understand what they're going through, you'll know what to say."

"Very helpful, thank you. I feel super confident about this now." I couldn't help but roll my eyes.

The group broke into giggles before we saw Marco heading our way. "We're going to need to leave soon," he said. "When you're ready, I'll take you to where you can talk to them."

"Where is that?" I asked.

He laughed and pointed to a pile of crates. "We have a megaphone, and you can stand up there."

223

I balked and turned to him. "Cool, just climb on a soap box and yell at everyone. Got it."

He smirked and shook his head. Chase grabbed my plate and took both of ours back as I got up and brushed the debris off my pants. Marco started off, and I followed, knowing the others would catch up.

As we came up Alejandro held his hand out, and I shook it. He nodded gruffly before turning around and calling for attention. "Everyone, quiet down! You all know Genevieve Astor is here with us. Many of you got to spend time with her these last few hours, and we'd like to thank her and her friends for coming to see us before things start moving."

A cheer went up from the rebels, all ready for the upcoming attack.

Marco held out a megaphone and pointed toward the crates. I glowered at him but jumped up. Everyone was watching in rapt attention. I held the button, but the megaphone squealed. I stopped and put my hands to my ears as they rang. Frowning at it, I tried again.

I started to speak but my voice cracked, so I cleared my throat. "I would like to thank all of you for being so welcoming to me and my friends. I know I'm not your countryman, but I do know your fight. At home our people are being kidnapped as well. I was one of those people. I understand the stake in trying to find them. Someone thought they wouldn't be missed. They were wrong. Our people! That's what you are doing here. Are you not?" I yelled, and the crowd roared in confirmation. "I understand the anger at not having your liberties protected. I understand not being able to get food, medicine, and safe places to sleep. We are all here to fight to bring these basic rights back to

Made Immortal

everyone in Neria." Fists flew into the air with another cheer erupting.

"They cannot bind you forever. Their hold is breaking, shattering, and they are so full of themselves they don't even notice. That is our advantage. They have underestimated us. We have struck at them with small cuts, so small they weren't even noticed by our enemy, but they have fortified us. Their treachery brought all of you to the tipping point, and they'll fall under the weight of your power. You are fighting for what's good and what's right, and you will prevail. Just know, I am here with you, fighting your fight, and I will not stop until you are free." My voice had built until I was shouting, and the room exploded with screams and chants from the crowd below me.

I took a deep breath and dropped the megaphone into Marco's hands before jumping down after it. He smiled at me and put a hand on my shoulder. "Not too shabby, kid. Not too shabby. Now, just a dozen more like that."

34

The days were a blur of shaking hands, giving speeches, and being in the van hauled across the city. Yet, the longer it went on, the more my stomach twisted in knots. I had felt a connection with these rebels in Neria before I even encountered any of them. Now, after spending time and really getting to know them, they reminded me of the people in the resistance back in Kabria. I got to know their stories, meet their families, grieve their losses. Through all of this, I knew so many of them would be dead in the next few days. There was just no way around it, and it cut me up inside. I wished I could take on this entire army for them. I knew their resolve was just as strong as mine. They knew the risks, and this was worth it to them.

The van rolled to a stop, bringing me out of my thoughts. When the door popped open and we jumped out, I had to cover my face with my shirt because of the thick smoke and debris. We were headed where we would leave Marco. The cell that would attack the media control center. The only issue was that we couldn't get the entire way there

Made Immortal

in a vehicle. There was so much damage to this area of the city we'd have to go the rest of the way on foot.

The group with us was making sure it was clear before they let us out. As the door swung open I held a hand out to Marco to help him down. He had a bulletproof vest on like the other rebels, while my team was in our suits. My mask was still down; it was every time now. I had to make sure my face was plastered all over the news if it came to that.

I adjusted the grip on my rifle and looked to Marco. "Remember, do exactly as we say. Stay quiet, low, and on my hip."

He nodded and crouched as we started to move out. There was a squad of rebels leading the way, with my team surrounding Marco as we moved.

I focused my hearing, but all I heard was the crunch of gravel under our boots, the skittering of some small animals, and the crackling of fires that had yet to go out. Every once in a while, I heard the grinding of rubble falling. All things to be expected out here. I moved slowly, trying to keep track of sounds surrounding our path to make sure there weren't any incoming forces.

Chase spared me a glance, and when I nodded, he pushed forward. The rebels ahead of us announced the area was clear quietly, then we fell into an easy rhythm.

"Hang a right at the next street," one of the closest rebels told Chase.

We were almost to the turn when I heard a loud noise from what might have been on the other side of the park across from us. I waved my hand, motioning for everyone to stop. I pointed to my ear and then toward the park.

We silently split, moving to hide behind cars, pieces of cement jutting out, and even a downed sign. The leader of the rebels with us poked his head up and swore as he slid back down.

"It's a freaking tank." He growled.

I silently shook from a crazed laugh I couldn't let escape. I ran my hands through my hair. I could hear the loud grinding of the treads tearing up the ground beneath them.

"Perfect," Benson groaned.

"Perfect!" Atty exclaimed with a wicked smile.

Gwen glared at him. "You're going to do something dumb aren't you?" He smirked, and she pulled him in quickly for a kiss, which stopped him in his tracks. "I'll have your back. Do what you need to do."

Atty's cheeks blushed bright pink before running off, working his way closer to the street nearest the tank. Gwen went after him, keeping low and scrambling up to the top of a pile of rubble.

"You all need to get rooms," Benson muttered under his breath, but we all exchanged smiles.

Chase jerked his chin over his shoulder, and we crouched to follow him, slipping behind different cars to make our way to the corner. Benson followed last behind Marco as we crept along. Marco seemed pretty composed if not slightly pale at our current situation.

"Don't worry, we've got you," Benson said.

Marco swallowed and nodded, keeping close to me. Chase checked around us and motioned for us to follow before he hurried across the street and behind another car on the other side. Benson kept watch for us as I grabbed Marco's hand and pulled him along after me.

Benson crept up behind us as we waited for Chase to pick where to go next. He started to move ahead, but I grabbed his shoulder and pulled him back down. I put my

228

Made Immortal

fingers to my lips so everyone could see. I closed my eyes and listened to the quick steps crunching on the gravel, moving our direction, and it wasn't the rebels.

"Take cover from our six." I spun around, popping up and spraying bullets behind us.

There shouts of alarm telling me they hadn't expected someone to attack them first. I saw someone go down, holding their shoulder. Benson pulled Marco around a car to block him from the shooters that had come up behind us. Chase and I laid down cover for the others as we moved backward but still headed toward the media building. Benson led Marco by the front of his vest, and Marco was trying to cover his head with his arms as they ran.

More bullets came from above, and I cursed as I saw snipers. Yet, just as I noticed one, he fell from his perch, and I looked to see Gwen picking a new target and dropping another. I burst up again, laying down a line of fire.

There was a giant explosion that I felt in my bones as I was tossed away from where I had been standing. I landed hard on my elbow and ribs and gasped for air. I gave myself just a second to reorient myself before pushing to my feet and trying to get my bearings. Pieces of the tank were falling back to the ground from the explosion, and I heard Atty whooping in victory.

I wiped at my face and stumbled for a moment before I remembered my rifle and grabbed it, looking around me. I dropped quickly as bullets came flying our way from a band of soldiers that had caught up to us.

"Get down!" I heard Benson cry as there was another burst of gunfire. Then I heard some impacts and a grunt from Marco. I raced to them. Luckily, all the bullets had hit his vest. He'd be sore, but he was fine.

"This way. We're close, just keep going." Marco

sounded out of breath, but he kept on, and we kept pace with him. "There is a plan in place. Just get to the building."

The large tower loomed above us less than a block away.

I saw Gwen make her way down from a hill of rubble, and Atty shot at a few people, giving her cover, then they made their way to us. Chase held open the door as we all ran through, the last of the rebels catching up with us and pouring inside.

"Now!" Marco shouted, and within moments, explosions rocked the streets outside the building. I was tossed forward off my feet as the floor shifted under me.

"Well, that's one way to keep them out," Benson said, wiping at his face with the back of his hand as rubble still fell here and there from the caved in entrance and the floor and street that buckled upward.

"All right, we're running late. Follow me," Marco said, slapping his hands together and heading into the lobby.

35

Guards lined balconies above us on either side, they must have been the ones responsible for the blast at Marco's order. Their eyes glowing neon blue as we walked past. They kept at their watch, even though it was unlikely anyone would be able to get in that way now.

"What is this place?" Atty asked.

The building was beautiful. The open air of the lobby extended many floors, with the walkways circling the edges of the building and leaving the center empty. The entire building was made of shining metal and glass, and high above was a giant, blown glass sculpture hanging down from the ceiling passing multiple levels. It looked like molten glass made of hundreds of colors was dripping its way toward the ground.

"This was the headquarters of my company until a few months ago. The board moved it closer to the palace for the extra security." Marco's smile seemed sad as he looked up at the sculpture above us. "My son helped create that," he said, pointing toward it.

"Where is your son?" Benson asked.

"He died a few years ago. Well, he went missing and they never found a body," Marco said, his body stiffening, his eyes taking on that hard haunted look again. He glanced at me and caught my gaze just for a moment before walking on. "Come, come. I have some things for you before you move on." He looked to the rest of the rebels with us. "The guards can bring you some food and water. Rest up; you'll be on your way again soon."

He led us to the elevator bay. One had its doors open, and two more of Marco's guards were there, holding their weapons relaxed across their chests. Their eyes were the same neon blue. We followed Marco inside. He nodded to them, and they returned it before the doors slid shut and we started heading up. It took us all the way to the second floor from the top. As we exited, I saw frosted glass walls lining most of the walkway. Marco went and put his hand against a scanner, and the frosted doors slid open. Beyond them was a lab that would have had David salivating.

The rooms were warm, the sounds of machines whirring and beeping, and lights flashed randomly on them, indicating something I was sure I'd never be able to understand. People sat at desks in white coats and didn't even take the time to look up from their work. As I watched, I realized they all had uncannily similar movements. I caught better sight of one of them and saw their eyes glinted blue, and I realized they were the same as Naya's bionic eye.

"I kept the keys and connected the building to my own power supply after the move. It's come in quite handy," Marco said as he continued marching through the rooms. He came to a stop and scanned his hand at another set of doors. This more secure lab within the larger outer one. The doors hissed open at his touch, and we followed him. The guards didn't join us, instead they took up watch. Inside, the

Made Immortal

wall was covered in screens, showing much of the same city CCTV coverage we had access to before, but there was so much more than we had ever seen. My eyes caught on footage that seemed to be coming in from the palace itself. Sitting in front of the consoles in this room were people with the same blue eyes, and the same movements as they typed away.

I hooked a thumb over my shoulder toward the rooms we had just come from. "Sorry to be rude, but is there something weird with your employees?"

Marco laughed. "Caught that, did you?" He walked over to one of the people sitting at a desk. "CC1, stand up and turn around please."

Marco hadn't phrased it like a question, and in one smooth movement, the person stood and turned to us. Other than to stand, they didn't make another movement. At all. It didn't even seem like they were breathing.

A few of the group made confused noises themselves.

"Everyone who is still here is non-biologics. Androids. They work on projects and monitor data twenty-four-seven. In shifts, mind you. They still take rest breaks to recharge and get repair work done," Marco said. "Thank you, CC1. You may sit."

"Thank you, sir. Is there anything specific you need today?" they asked.

Its voice was incredibly pleasing to the ear, but I guessed that was intentional.

"Not at this moment, CC1. Thank you," Marco said, and CC1 smoothly sat back into their seat and started typing again.

"Is it alive?" Atty asked, his head cocked to the side as he watched them.

"I like to think so. They make quite good companions.

233

They are very interesting conversationalists," Marco said, grabbing an empty seat and twirling it around before plopping down onto it. "CC1, please pull up the floor plans of the palace and load them into the units I prepared."

CC1 nodded, and within moments, what looked like arm guards sitting on a nearby table pinged. Marco waved a hand, and we walked over to each grab one.

"We've programmed the floor plans with the secret passages and any rooms of interest. Atty, we've marked the most likely places explosives might be necessary, as well as the guard rotations, a dossier on all palace staff and guests, manuals on all vehicles there that could be used for evac, and a few other things." Marco tapped on one, showing the different sections to choose from. "With the attack being in the next thirty-six hours, I suggest you study as much of this as possible. The goal while entering will be stealth. When you meet up with Naya, she'll have the uniforms for you. The dossiers should help you talk your way out of most scenarios if you have to."

We nodded, and I saw Chase was engrossed in his, quickly reading the data.

"Well, while we have you here, anyone want any augmentations?" Marco said with a laugh, but I was sure he was also serious. Atty bounced on the balls of his feet, looking excited.

"Really?" he asked, eyes wide.

Chase slapped him on the shoulder. "How about after? What would you want anyway?"

"I don't know but something!" He smiled as we all chuckled. "Okay, after it is. I'm gonna hold you to that Marco," he said, pointing to him, and Marco nodded.

"Here, also take these. David had requested we make these up for everyone." He took a box out and handed us

234

Made Immortal

small, odd-shaped triangles "These are high-grade gas masks. Place like so," he said, holding it to his face, and it moved like the nanobots of our suits to form to his face over his nose down to his cheeks and chin. He tapped it, and it retracted into its original form. "We've already sent shipments out to the rebels too."

A weight lifted from my shoulders. The mist was still an unknown, and we had no idea how they planned to use it. The number of options was terrifying. Having these two pieces of protection for my friends helped ease some of my fears.

"Thank you," I said and pulled him into a hug. He relaxed after a moment of shock and returned the embrace.

"I want to thank all of you," he said, holding my hands and looking around at the others. "We'll never forget what you've done for us here." He clapped his hands. "I don't want to keep you. You should make your way to Naya and get as much rest as you can before we move out."

"Do you have everything you need for the media control center? Is there anything you need from us?" Chase asked.

"We've been in control of the center for the last few weeks. Overall, I'll probably have the easiest job. We've been converting employees for years, weeding out the ones we can't get to join our side. Right under Gregory's nose." He threw his head back and laughed, obviously he *really* enjoying taking this from him. "We'll be ready."

Marco walked back out through the labs and led us to the elevator. We all headed down to the basement and through an exit to an underground garage, where the other rebels were already waiting for us. The garage opened at the rear of the building, away from the cave in where we had first entered.

Marissa Allen

We stopped at the exit and turned back to Marco, who said, "Good luck."

"You too," Chase said.

Marco clasped arms with all of us in farewell before we split ways. "I'll see you all at the palace once I'm done." He headed back inside as we made our way into the city.

The night was chilly as we moved in silence. The sounds of buildings burning and gunfire started to quiet. The further we got from the edge of the city, the calmer it became. The shift from the poor to the rich was heartbreakingly obvious. As we made our way toward the center of the city, we pulled our hoods up and separated, taking a few different routes back to Naya's base.

I looked up and in the distance I saw the palace towers glinting with the last light of the sunset. I balled my hands into fists so hard my nails broke the skin of my palms. The weight of our plan settled upon my shoulders, pulling my chest tight. I tried to not think of the things that could go wrong, instead wanting to focus on all the things that could go right.

As the light faded, I took my last turn and quickly slipped inside the final rebel base, going to hunt for the others, to spend our last night together before we took these people down.

36

"Oh good, you all made it!" Naya said as we made our way into the surveillance room. She saw Benson and gave a sigh of relief, and he smiled at her, walking over to grab her hand and squeezing it reassuringly. "Are you hungry? We can get you fed and let you some rest before going over everything one last time tomorrow."

Benson and I both nodded vigorously, and she chuckled before leading us toward the smell of food. It looked like everyone at the base had already eaten, but there was still plenty, so we grabbed plates and started to chow down. The base was emptier than when we were here last. Just the people needed for the mission tomorrow. Naya sat with us, and we filled her in on the last few days. She didn't seem surprised about Marco's robots, but she probably knew about them already. They spent quite a bit of time together, it seemed.

At some point, one of the rebels had dropped off a couple bottles of drinks, and we stayed well into the morning talking, laughing, and just enjoying the company. The last week running from base to base had taken it's toll.

it was nice to have this time together. I was aware that nights like this weren't promised, and I tried to soak up as much of it as I could while I could.

Gwen's cheeks were pink, and Atty laughed, holding her close, as Benson belted out some old sea shanty. We held our glasses aloft and tried to sing along, but no one else actually knew the words. Finishing his tune, Benson leaned down, and Naya gave him a kiss on the cheek, making it his turn to blush. I had taken up my normal spot folded within Chase's embrace. He rocked us from side to side and kissed my temple, then my cheek, then just barely grazed my lips as I turned to him.

As the sky started to lighten, many of us fought yawns. Chase stood and held his hand out to me. I took it, and he pulled me up.

"We should turn in; we've got a big night tomorrow," Chase said, and everyone nodded. We all called goodnight to the others and then broke off into our own little pairs. Atty and Gwen, Benson followed Naya out, and Chase and I made our way to our bunk behind the blanket wall we had claimed before.

As soon as Chase pulled the blanket closed, he spun to me and grabbed me, kissing me as he laid me down on our bunk. I could hear the rebels around us waking up for the day. I smiled against his lips as I wrapped my arms around his neck. He moaned against me and whipped my shirt above my head, leaving my skin covered in goosebumps from the cold of the air along with the fire of his fingers tracing my skin. I clawed at his shirt, pulling it over his head, and spread my fingers wide against his chest. My hands roamed his body just like he was doing with mine, drinking in every inch of him. Memorizing every line and scar.

Made Immortal

I heard Gwen's giggle, and I forced myself to focus just on Chase because I didn't want to hear whatever was going on over there. It wasn't hard. When we were tangled up like this, the entire world fell away and there was nothing but the two of us. He was like a drug to me, and I couldn't get enough.

"If you don't come home tomorrow, I'll kill you myself," Chase said with a growl that vibrated through me as he kissed a trail down my stomach.

"I would never leave you," I whispered before I was sucked in, drowning in pleasure.

I moaned as I stretched as far as I could, still waking up. Chase stirred next to me. I rolled over, draping my arm across his waist and kissed him awake.

"Morning," I mumbled.

"Pretty sure it's at least afternoon now." He groaned and turned to look at me. "Coffee?"

"Mm, yes, please." I grinned.

We both threw on some clothes and our boots and then made our way back out with the rest of the rebels. They smiled and waved when they saw us. One of them filled up cups with piping hot coffee and handed them to us. I gave a smile in thanks, and we turned to try and see if any of the others in our group were up yet.

Benson and Naya sat on a couch in one of the recreation rooms. I slipped onto one of the loveseats, and Chase dropped down beside me. The cushions bounced under our weight. Benson looked up. He had been going over some of the data on his arm guard while Naya read over his shoulder, and they had been whispering together.

239

"Hey, I'm reading up on this manual for this crazy new hover copter. It looks like it would be a good exit vehicle. They have a few by the landing pad in the courtyard." He blew out a breath. "Helipad in the middle a house, jeez."

That sent Naya into giggles.

"It's a really big house if that makes a difference." I laughed. I had grown up in a house that size. So had Chase and David, but for everyone else, I was sure it must have seemed strange.

"Thanks for the context, Princess," he joked.

I pulled up the layout of the palace. "I think mine was bigger," I said, and we all laughed some more.

"I'm gonna go over the dossiers one last time," Chase said. "We can't let this one do any of the talking." He poked me in the side. "You should probably be closer to the back of the pack, actually."

I rolled my eyes, but he wasn't wrong. I pulled up my own and started to look through the patrol schedules. There was already a route entered to get us to the king's living quarters. We would be going in early when he should still be in his rooms. On the rotation, I didn't see any mention of Jasper. I chewed on my lip. He would be my priority if he was there. No one else would stand a chance against him, not even a whole squad. I opened the security feeds within the palace and started shifting through them, hoping to catch a glimpse of him. He was huge, but the palace had an endless number of cameras to go through.

I started to ignore places where gatherings were held. There were no meetings planned that would use them any time soon. I moved to the more internal cameras. As I flicked through, I saw him on one of the hallway cameras. He looked angry. I hadn't been one hundred percent sure

Made Immortal

he would be there today; I had wondered if he might still be out with the soldiers in the city.

I followed his path as he walked into the king's office. There was no sound, but I saw the anger on the King Edgar's face as he started to scream at Jasper. Jasper crossed his arms over his chest and tried to reply, but the king jumped up and just began waving his fist in the air.

I laughed sharply watching the interaction. Chase looked over and smirked as he saw it.

"What do ya think is up his bum?" he asked.

"Us probably." I giggled. "They haven't seen me anywhere in a week, and then the whole street explosion yesterday likely didn't help. That was closer in the city than anything the rebels have done lately."

Chase nodded in agreement before he went back to his reading. I just watched. Eventually, Jasper left in a huff, and I swapped through the video feeds, trailing his path. While the others did their own research, I watched him for the rest of the day. The rest of the group filtered in, and we ended up sitting in a circle, chatting a bit, sharing information we found in our research, going over the plans again and again. The rebels who would be with us joined, and we went through the plan even more. All the while, I kept watch. I took note of every room and hallway Jasper went through. Where he stopped and spent time, memorizing the areas I'd most likely find him when we got inside.

I kept one eye on the time, trying my best to ignore my internal countdown until we had to go. There would be no turning back. We just needed to make it out the other side.

All too soon, it was time.

"All right, everyone knows their job. We're ready for this. Now, let's go. Time to roll out!" Naya called, and the rebels let out a cheer.

241

37

My back was pressed up against the slick, cold stone of this entryway to the palace. There was an entire group of us hiding behind a secret door into the building. We had been holding in place while the alarms blared inside. People yelled, and the stamp of hundreds of feet marched past.

It was all going to plan so far though. We were waiting for the palace to send some of their guards into the city. The rebels had started the other cell attacks over an hour ago. I was terrified about the soldiers running toward our friends, but we needed them out of here. There would still be a rotation of guards in the building, but they would be on a skeleton shift.

Eventually, the footsteps stopped, the alarms quieted, and no one was shouting anymore. I pulled up the security feed on my arm guard and swiped through most of the cameras of the royal quarters and the main security hub. The king was pacing back and forth in his bedroom with the door propped open and his two guards on either side of frame. I nodded and made a motion to Chase that we were

Made Immortal

good to breach. Those behind us squared their shoulders and got ready to move.

Chase looked at his watch, moving in had to be timed perfectly against the guards' patrol routes. When it synced he moved to push the door open quickly. Chase, Atty, and Benson sighted and cleared the hallway before we followed Chase's lead down to the first turn. We kept as quiet as we could, but this many boots on polished flooring made my heart jump at every squeak.

The path brought us along a few different hallways without running into anyone. At one point, we all had to pile into two rooms on either side of the hallway as a pair on patrol came by. As we held there, I pulled up the security feed and started to search for my own target. We couldn't take the risk of any of the groups running into Jasper, I had to keep him busy. Even on his own he was enough of a threat to derail everything we were trying to do here.

Chase prepped everyone to move out again and caught my eye. My heart jumped, understanding this was the moment when I didn't know what was going to happen next, but my friends would have to take care of themselves. Naya gave me a nod, and I returned it. Gwen grabbed my hand, Atty squeezed my shoulder, and Benson gave me a quick hug. Then, I turned to Chase. The time we had spent together had been a goodbye if it had to be, but I would see them all after this was done.

"See you later. Be safe," I said to them all. Chase gave me a quick kiss on the cheek before turning and the others followed him down the hall. I watched them go before turning my attention back to my own task.

With a quick search, I found Jasper; he wasn't too far from my current position. I checked the patrol route compared to where I was and timed my exit to slip through unnoticed. The sounds against the marble of the building made it a little harder to pinpoint where the nearby soldiers were, but I heard those familiar thumping steps and knew exactly where Jasper was.

Naya had given me a tactical shotgun, and I pulled it up as I slowly made my way to the corner he was beyond. I was so excited to try this puppy out. I stepped around the corner, automatically finding the sweet spot and fired. The boom ricocheted through the echoing hall. I stepped forward, pumped, and shot once more. Jasper jerked back with each hit, his arms flailing as he started to fall. I didn't stop. I shot again and again, but then he screamed and his beefy arm hit me so hard I went flying off my feet and slammed into the wall, rattling my bones.

My head swam for just the briefest moment as I pushed myself up, bits of the wall falling off me as I stood. I snapped my eyes to him and snarled. As he got to his feet, he clutched at his arm where blood poured out of the wound. Multiple shots in his chest did the same. He screamed again and raced at me. I grabbed the shotgun like a bat and swung to try and clip him in the jaw but was too slow, just knocking his shoulder, which plowed into me seconds later. I had enough time to slip sideways, and we spun. His bulk went through the wall, crashing into the room beyond with me falling after him.

I got to one knee as he pushed himself to his feet. He tried to land a kick to my side to send me sprawling, but I managed to grab his ankle and redirect him, pulling his other leg out from under him. I could see the rage in his eyes as he got away from me and knew that would make him sloppy, which gave me the upper hand. I stood and pressed my advantage, ramming a knee toward him, catching him in the side, knocking him over. I slammed my fist down, but he

Made Immortal

spun away, and it smashed into the floor, the marble splitting beneath it.

We snarled at each other like animals. Both of us charged into one another, locking onto each other like boxers trying to get in any hit we could. My skin broke from his blows and from my own, and blood coated us. He tried to grab me when he could, but I kept slipping from his grasp, my speed too quick for his bulk.

But this time, he got me by the ankle and threw me through the door and out into another hallway. Though, as I looked around, I realized it was more like a balcony. Before I could account for that, Jasper was there, running at me. He slammed into me, and I cursed as we both went flying over the railing and sailing toward the ground below.

I landed flat on my back, and the breath rushed out of me. All I could do was gasp and shudder for a moment while Jasper coughed from where he lay a few feet away. I heard the snap of weapons raising around us, and I finally opened my eyes and looked up.

Palace soldiers surrounded us.

"There has been a breach. All units be aware there are hostiles inside the palace," one said into his radio.

I growled and pushed myself to my knees. "Well, this is inconvenient," I mumbled.

Jasper stood and got me with a right hook that knocked me back down.

"If we caught you, the queen wanted you brought home. Sadly you put up a fight, and we had to put you down for good," Jasper said slowly. It seemed like his jaw was causing him issues. He put a hand out for one of the guards to give him a gun.

The rest of them never took me out of their sights as Jasper pointed his pistol straight to my forehead.

"Just can't handle being second best, huh?" I asked, laughing at him. The soldiers shifted uncomfortably. My head snapped to the side as he whipped me with the pistol and roared. I spit blood onto the floor and kept laughing. "The serum really bulked you up. It must have had to majorly compensate for something." The guards looked like they though I was crazy. The sun was starting to streak in through the crystal ceiling. My blood painted the marble beneath me.

More footsteps ran toward us. Jasper quickly looked to the door, and the king came rushing in with his guards at his back, their weapons raised. He wasn't a handsom man. The opposite really, I had no idea how the beauty of Esmerleda came from him. His was short and pudgy, and looked to already be sweating.

"Jasper, where have you been?" the king bellowed. Then, his eyes focused on me on my knees, covered in blood on the ground. His beady eyes glittered, and he rubbed his hands together. "Ah, yes, well, I guess that's acceptable." He pulled at his jacket's lapels and ran his hand through his hair. "All of you, spread out and make sure no one enters," he yelled at the guards, and they moved to do as he said, pointing their weapons out instead of at me.

Which was preferable.

"Hey Grandpa." My voice thick with sarcasm as I focused on the king. He bristled at the word.

I smiled, hoping I looked like someone off with a few loose bolts rattling around upstairs. I moved to stand, but the king looked to Jasper who hit me again.

"I have no relation to you. You're a terrorist." He spat the last word. "We're going to make an example of you. The world will see your death," he said as he moved his head close to mine.

246

Made Immortal

I snapped out to try to bite off his bulbous nose. He squeaked and jumped back then glared at me again. "Your daughter might have something to say about that. For some reason, she wants me home. You're just lucky you aren't my job." I sneered at him and enjoyed the confusion on his face.

"What does that mean?" he asked, stamping his foot.

I hated him even more than I expected to. This spineless, evil, little man. I could only wonder how he manged to keep power this entire time.

"You won't be able to make an example out of anyone when we're done with you." I laughed again, turning my head to the sky so the echoes turned the sound into a manic cackle.

There was gunfire in the hallway. The king jumped to look that way. I shot to my feet and went to dashed out the door behind me, needing to lead Jasper away. He was hot on my heels before we could even hear what the king was screaming. The courtyard beyond the door had started to soak up the sun as it rose. I only made it a few paces before the earth rocked so violently I was thrown from my feet.

I covered my head in my hands as some of the windows to the courtyard exploded, sending glass daggers directly at us. The morning rang out with screams, and I couldn't help but grin.

247

38

I swung to my feet, facing Jasper as he pushed himself up. Sweat beaded on his forehead, and a wave of confidence crashed over me. I wasn't even breathing heavily yet. I sped toward him, jumping to bring my punch down from above. He threw up his arm to block just in time and stumbled under the blow. I walked toward him, wiping the back of my hand across my mouth, I saw some blood on it as I pulled it away. Yet, I didn't feel a thing. He started backing up, which just made me increase my speed. His eyes widened with just the smallest amount of fear.

He was so conceited, thinking no one could match him. I didn't think he grasped how much danger he was in right now. I sprinted at him again, launching attack after attack, breaking through his defenses more often than not.

The only problem with his size was that when he connected, it hurt. His next hit to my face was enough to knock me back and make me slide across the slick grass. I let out a scream as I pushed myself to my feet and launched at him. He turned on his heel and raced toward a hole in the wall, back into the building.

Made Immortal

"Don't run from my coward." I felt like I was salivating as I chased him. I was finally the predator and would get my prey. He picked turns seemingly at random, slammed doors closed, and knocked decorations down to try to trip me up. It wasn't enough to lose me; I kept right on his tail.

"Jasper!" I called. "Face me!" I raced past a confused-looking guard before I realized Jasper had taken his gun. I threw myself to the floor as he sprayed behind him, getting the guard in the neck as he did so. The guard grasped at the blood pouring from his throat, nothing but garbles coming from as he shuddered. I shook my head and closed his eyes as his last breath left him before I took off after Jasper again.

When I approached the next intersection, I stopped and listened. I couldn't hear him, so he must have been hiding. I whistled a taunting melody into the air. Still nothing.

"I can't wait to tell tales of how you hid from me. Too scared to face what you wrought?" I called out.

I heard his hands adjust on the gun and the twist of his foot. I pushed the door next to me open. Then, the one across the hall. Hoping to give him a sense of confidence, like I didn't know where he was.

"Come out, come out wherever you are," I sang as I neared the room he actually hid within. I crouched as I walked over and kicked the door open as bullets flew above my head. I launched myself at him like a tiger pouncing on its next meal. I sent him toppling back off balance. I fell on him throwing blow after blow. He yelled as he tried to knock me off. He finally managed to get his feet between us and launched me back with a swift kick. I shifted my arm, keeping me balanced as the other held me up; my boots slipped in the mix of blood on the polished floor.

His screams of fury just stoked the fire in me. The

249

building rocked by another set of explosions, and the floor started to cave in beneath us until we tumbled down.

I cursed, my stomach flipping as I fell. I grasped at a piece of stone, but it tore away from me. I landed and screamed as something crushed me a moment later. I looked over to see Jasper was skewered on some rebar but was still moving. I took a few deep breaths, trying to assess the damage. Two slabs of stone had me pinned been them, but nothing seemed broken. I got my hands under the lip of what was on top of me and worked to push it away. For a few terrifying moments, it didn't budge, but then I heard the grinding of the stones as they moved. I held it for a moment, taking a few more deep breaths now that my chest wasn't crushed, then I screamed as I gave one last push and it went falling away. I dropped my head back against the stone below me and smiled. Small victories.

"Vi!" I heard Atty call out. "Vi, is that you?"

My head snapped to where he stood farther in whatever room we had fallen into. As I crawled over the stone, his face relaxed with relief when he saw my head pop up.

"I'm so sorry. I didn't know you'd be there."

A groan came from Jasper as he pulled himself free of the rebar. He was closer to Atty than he was to me, and terror gripped me. He saw Atty, licked his lips, and started to lumber his way.

"Run, Atty! Run!" I yelled and scrambled to get over the pile of rubble. My footing slipped as the stones moved under me, and I fell. My heart froze as everything seemed to move in slow motion. As soon as I made it to level ground, I raced toward them.

Just a bit more. I was almost there. Atty had barely turned to start running when Jasper grabbed his arm, picked him up, and smashed him into the ground. I heard the gasp

Made Immortal

from Atty as he hit the ground, and I heard the snaps of bones.

I screamed and slammed into Jasper, pushing him back. I scraped at my comms to turn them on. "Help! Gods, help. Find Atty," I yelled and went to clash into Jasper again, trying to get him away from my friend. The comms overlapped, and I couldn't make any of it out.

"Vi?" I managed to catch someone saying.

"Find Atty! We're on a lower level," I begged before Jasper caught me off guard and I went flying across the room, grunting at the impact. I looked to Atty again, and he was gasping. Tears threatened to fall as I heard too much liquid in those breaths. All I could do was keep Jasper away.

Jasper and I locked onto each other again, our hits vicious. We were two alphas evenly matched and unable to gain any ground on the other. As he lifted me up, I clamped my teeth down on his neck, and he screamed when skin came away as he threw me off.

Where was everyone? Atty didn't have much time left. My heart raced with fear for him. This couldn't happen; I could lose him. This wasn't how things were supposed to go. This was my worst fear—not being able to protect my family.

Jasper snarled and managed to get me on my back. He grasped at my neck with his meaty hands. He leaned down with his bulk and squeezed. My eyes bulged as my lungs burned. I slashed out with my nails, scraping them down his face, catching in the cuts already there. There was a singular moment where his concentration flickered, and I slammed my knee into his side, rolling us over. I gasped, finally able to breathe, while I slammed punches into him to give myself the time I needed to recover.

My eyes went to Atty, and he was too still. Finally, I

heard the footsteps of people running this way. I just hoped they were the right people. I roared my rage as I slammed Jasper's head into the floor again and again. He got an arm around my leg and threw me off of him. I looked up quickly and was relieved to see Gwen, some rebels, and Marco. He had made it, so the communications network must be ours.

Jasper's eyes landed on them too, and he smiled as he tried to get to them. I grabbed his ankle, pulled him back then snatched up a piece of nearby rebar and slammed it through his calf. He cried out in pain. I just had to keep him away from them so they could save Atty. I saw one of the rebels who looked to be a medic getting to Atty and leaning over him, starting to do whatever he needed.

I moved between them and Jasper, gasping for breath.

"Gun," I shouted, and one came sliding toward my feet. I grabbed it and turned to Jasper, firing the entire clip. In my stolen guard's uniform, I had another clip, and I swapped them before firing the entire second one too. His chest was riddled with lead, but he still squirmed.

The world stopped as I heard Gwen's guttural scream. As if part of her was being torn away. I stopped in my tracks. Gwen had thrown herself over Atty's chest. She was covered in blood as she shook him. The medic just shook her head, there was nothing more she could do.

My brain couldn't put together what was going on. I felt like I wasn't attached to my body. Turning my attention back to Jasper. I would do something to him he couldn't recover from. He would pay for what he had done.

His leg was still skewered to the floor by the rebar. His chest bleeding from dozens of bullet wounds. One large sword-like blade came to life in my hand. He whimpered as I stood over him. There was no question of how this would end. I saw true fear in his eyes.

252

Made Immortal

"May you never find peace." I told him as I stabbed the sword straight into his chest— into his heart. I twisted the sword as I bared my teeth at him, leaning over so all he could see was me. I pulled the nanobots back, and the blade disappeared, the removal causing blood to spurt from his open chest.

He gasped a last breath, but my attention was so focused on the strange last smirk on face I didn't see his hand release a canister. I heard it roll across the floor before I saw mist releasing from it. My eyes widened as I looked through it to the others.

"Masks!" Marco snapped. He grabbed Gwen's from her vest and held it to her as she still didn't seem to know what was going on, too locked in her grief.

The medic pulled her own out, but she looked down in horror, and I saw it was cracked in her hand. I looked back at Jasper, but his eyes were empty, his soul, if he had one, was gone. I put on my mask and raced through the mist to the others. Marco smiled sadly as he handed his mask to the medic, putting it on her face before she could argue. I grabbed him and tried to tug him with me, but he was already coughing. This mist had no target, everyone was in danger.

"Everyone in the area, mask up. Mist has been released," the medic said into her comm. She tried to pull Gwen away, but she clung to Atty. Marco patted my shoulder before I let him go, and the medic grabbed him and pulled him away.

"Gwen, I've got him," I pleaded. "Come on. We have to go." I pulled her face to look me in the eye, but she wasn't there. She was too lost in her grief. I got her to let go, so I picked him up. Putting her hand on his arm, I led us up through the palace, heading toward where the hover copter

Benson had been talking about waited. "Gwen, I need you to give me directions. Look at your map."

"This way," Marco's voice was barely more than a whipser. He must have known she wouldn't have been able to help.

"We need to get to the helipad," I told him, and he moved his map to find it.

"Left when we get to the top of the stairs."

I paused a few times when I heard footsteps running our way, but every time, it was the rebels. Marco led us past the room where I had left the king, and I saw Naya standing above him, making him look at her by pulling his hair back. She glanced over her shoulder and saw us, her eyes wide when she saw Atty in my arms. When she nodded, I returned it, and then our small group continued to the helipad.

There was a hover copter with its engines already running and Benson flipping switches in the cockpit.

"Gods!" Benson bellowed as I placed Atty onto the floor of the copter. I grabbed Gwen and pushed her inside. She curled up next to him on the floor, her hand in his hair. My heart broke again seeing her. I wished they would have had more time.

I turned to Marco, grabbed him, and hauled him in. He protested softly, still coughing. Blue bruised veins were spreading under his skin. He didn't have long.

"Come with us," I said, and he sat back in the seat, exhausted and barely able to hold himself up.

"Where is Chase?" I yelled at Benson over the noise of the engines.

"I don't know." He was shaking his head.

"If we're not back in five minutes go, without us," I called back and jumped out of the copter. Landing on the

Made Immortal

grass and took off back into the palace. I pulled up my map, trying to locate Chase's beacon. My throat was closing tightly. I couldn't breathe, worry gripping every fiber of my being. I finally saw his ping and realized he was a few corridors away.

I slammed my shoulder into the door, not willing to slow, and went skidding into the king's office. Chase looked up, his hand hovering over a flash device lying on the king's computer. My heart raced seeing him safe.

"Time to go," I told him, and he nodded.

"How's Atty?" Chase asked as we turned to run through the building once more.

I didn't say anything, just pushed our pace to return to the others. We crashed through the door to the courtyard.

I pushed Chase in ahead of me. The copter had already started to rise from the ground when I finally jumped in. Chase's eyes locked onto our friend's lifeless body on the floor. His gaze swung to Marco, who was pale against the blue veins turning to black under his skin.

I pushed myself through the gap in the front to sit next to Benson. His face was haunted, but he looked at me.

"Vi," My father's voice came through my comm.

"Dad?" I asked.

"You all need to get back right now, something's happened." Static came over the comm and then it shut off.

I turned to Benson "Kabria, as fast as we can." I didn't know what else had gone wrong, but I had at least one promise I still could keep today. The job was over, we were going home. We'd check in with everyone once we got there.

We flew away from the palace with the sun shining down, as the morning fully broke upon this day that would change us and Neria forever.

39

The only sound apart from the copter itself was Gwen's sobs. Chase had his head between his knees and his eyes squeezed shut. Marco just watched out the window, peace etched on his features. As we crossed the border to Kabria, I slipped into the back to sit with him, focusing on him to stave off the devastation I would feel when I could grieve.

I took his hands in mine, and he rolled his eyes toward me. He clearly didn't even have the energy to move his head. I kissed his fingers as tears slipped down my cheeks.

"I wanted you to see Kabria," I said softly, my words sticking in my throat. I sat behind him and grabbed his hand. I pointed at things for him to see. "Over there, those mountains are tipped in white in the winter from the snow." I showed him a farm below us. "They raise crops there, and over there, can you see that herd of cattle? They graze on these fields as they grow."

As we flew, a smile crept onto his face.

"It's beautiful." His words were so quiet, his breathing so shallow. Until he fell still in my arms. I closed my hand

256

Made Immortal

around his wrist, trying to feel for a pulse. He was gone, and I locked every muscle down, afraid if I moved, I'd come apart. Eventually, I ran my fingers through his hair, pulling it away from his face and pressing a kiss to his temple.

"Thank you for everything," I whispered to him. I cried silently over him, not wanting to alert the others, but soon my shoulders shook with each breath, and Chase looked up to me. His eyes landed on Marco, and I saw his understanding. I slipped out from behind Marco, leaning him against the seat and placed his arms crossed in his lap. I crawled to Chase and curled up in his arms, and he held me as we cried. I reached an arm out through the gap and grasped Benson's shoulder, so we could all be together in these moments before we had to share our pain with everyone else.

As we flew over the countryside, up on the horizon, we saw smoke from a massive fire rising into the air.

"Gods. What now?" Benson ground out. Chase unwrapped himself from me, moving to the front, and I slid to put my hand on Gwen's back. She startled and looked at me, like an animal unsure if it should fight or flee.

"Vi." She moaned before she broke into sobs again and flung herself to me. I caught her and held her close.

"I'm so sorry," I whispered, and we both shook under the weight of her sobs. I held her tightly, and she gripped me like I was her lifeline. My apologies would never fix this, and they echoed in my mind as I contemplated how I hadn't been able to save Atty. I was there. I had done everything to keep them safe though all we had been through, but I just hadn't been fast enough to save one of the only people I cared about when it mattered.

Chase had worried about me putting myself in danger. We hadn't thought—I hadn't thought—it would be my failure that killed one of our friends. I should have been fast enough; I should have stopped it. I could have taken the punishment of Jasper's blows, but Atty couldn't. I held Gwen as my soul seemed to be sucked into a hole where nothing but blame resided. I had failed again.

"That's the feed factory," Chase said from the front, followed by a curse.

"Isn't that where the new recruits go?" I called to him.

He looked my way and frowned. "Recruits, supplies, info on our underground network... It might even have information on our allies," Chase said in horror. He slammed his fist into the window of the copter. "What in the world happened while we were gone?" Chase started tapping at his comm unit. He grunted in frustration and tried again. "I'm not getting anyone."

"Try David," I pleaded. He nodded, and finally, the call connected.

"David, gods, what is going on?" Chase snapped. I could hear David slightly through the comm.

"What do you mean? We're about to leave with the group to Soland. We just got word that the rebels have the king. They're making the address soon," he replied.

"Nolan called us back to Kabria, we just flew over the feed factory back home, it's destroyed!" Chase almost yelled. "We can't get ahold of anyone." Static started buzzing on the line.

"Just give me a minute. We'll try them," David said.

"David, wait. Wait!" Chase said quickly. "Can you let the others know Marco didn't make it, and..." Chase paused and took a deep breath. "Atty didn't either."

I heard the gasp from both David and Joseph over the line.

"Just make sure the rebels know. We brought Marco

258

Made Immortal

with us; there was just so much going on, but I think he might have liked to be buried in Kabria. We can figure out the plans later," Chase said.

"Yeah, yeah, of course. Okay, I'll call you right back." The line went dead as David hung up.

"I'm going to land," Benson said, and Chase agreed. It didn't take long before the copter made a soft landing. Chase and Benson both hopped out, but I didn't move, afraid to leave the others.

I tried to peek out the windows to see what was around us, the area was thick with black smoke. I didn't hear anything like gunfire, so that was something. Although, I also didn't hear any screams for help or moans of pain. Gwen still held me tightly, and I gripped her back, worried about what the boys would say when they returned.

The time ticked by, and the weight of how quiet it was felt like another crushing blow. I couldn't be sure how long it was before they pulled the doors open and got back in. Both of them were covered in soot and were terribly quiet. They shared a look before Chase glanced back to me, and Benson gripped the controls so hard his knuckles turned white.

"We can't get any calls out or in since we got close. Something must be jamming the area," Chase said. "From some broken clocks, it happened right around when the raid of the palace started." He shook his head. The fact that they came back alone was enough to tell me there was no one to save.

Benson took off without saying a word, and we flew toward the mountains to make sure no one in the area would follow us. We went in wrong directions for hours before rising into some cloud cover and turning back toward headquarters.

259

As we flew, I sunk into my own pit of hell. Eventually, numbness took over, but the negative thoughts in my head were on a constant loop. *I failed. I couldn't save them. I wasn't enough. It's my fault.*

Over and over and over again.

The copter jolted slightly as we landed, which snapped me back to myself as I looked around. The door slid open, and my father stood there, worry etched into the lines of his face. He sighed as soon as he laid his eyes on me but looked on with sadness at the bodies with us.

"You," my father shouted at someone. "Yes, you. Get over here with that." He waved his arm toward us. Two men appeared with a stretcher between them. I slipped out, grabbing Marco's arms first as Gwen was still wrapped around Atty. My father took his feet and helped me move him.

"We need another one," I said, and the men's eyes were grave as they nodded. Before long, another group showed up, coming from the direction the others had gone. I turned to Gwen and took her hands. "Gwen."

Her glossy eyes looked at me.

"Gwen, we have to get him down, okay?"

She whimpered and stretched her hands out again, but I pulled them back.

"Let's just get him out and you can go with him," I said gently.

Two men crawled up and started to take Atty's body out of the copter. Gwen shook with sobs, but she had no tears left, it seemed. Benson got out and held open his hands to her. She fell into them, and he hugged her close.

"Come on, Gwen," he said softly and held her as they followed the stretcher with Atty's body.

I went to hop out, but I almost fell, my limbs numb from sitting in that position for so long. My father caught me as I

260

Made Immortal

stumbled and propped me back on my feet. Chase's father, Ethan, and his sister, Thea, were running our way. As they reached Chase, they threw their arms around him and pulled him close. Thea had tears in her eyes at the sight of her brother home safe.

I looked at my father, too tired to fight, but I had to know. "You knew this wouldn't be in and out. You knew this would happen didn't you?"

"I figured it would turn into more." He shrugged and looked at me sadly. "I'm terribly sorry for what you lost."

"You should have told me. You should have warned us. We deserved better and now my friends are dead." I could feel the tears building. As much as we were trying to move past it, I still had a hard time trusting him, and this was going to stick with me for a long time.

"I know. I'm sorry, but Esmelda knew what you were planning. She launched her attack on us as soon as you raided the palace. We don't have a count of the death toll from the feed factory. We have no idea how much we lost in supplies or information. We can have a service, but then we have work to do." He set an arm on my shoulder, and I could only turn away. I couldn't even look at him.

I wrapped my arms around myself and left him standing there as I went to find my friends.

Loss suffocated me. Rage burned in my veins. This war was just beggining, and I would have my revenge.

261

Neria Civil War - Over Before It Started?

In a shocking turn of events, the rebels who had been launching attacks throughout Cinder City, the capital of Neria, over the last few months, stormed the palace and took King Ravensbone hostage. The king had often downplayed the attacks in the city, touting Neria's military power and resolve, putting it down to some unfavorables prompted to act when the Princess non Grata Genevieve Astor arrived in Neria to cause havoc in the city. Apparently, he was wrong about how much we should worry.

Yesterday, the rebels released a video of the king battered and bruised on his knees before the rebel leader, Jupiter Green, and her second in command, Naya Kahn. They announced they plan to dismantle the monarchy, and instead, they will hold free elections within parts of the city to appoint a council so the entire country can have a voice. Until then, there will be martial law for the next week while they set up elections, hoping to restore the political powerhouse that is Neria as soon as possible.

Made Immortal

They have also announced the execution of the king will come before the day is out. Have your video feeds ready at six o'clock. Watch it here for non-stop commentary and all the grizzly details!

Neria - Free the Press

Yesterday, the rebels ousted King Ravensbone from the throne. At the same time, there had been a coup on the National Media Center. In control of the Nerian National News, they released hundreds of hours of video and reports on what had been happening in the city, which the king had previously censored. Journalists who had been trying to get messages out about the terrible living conditions of the people of Neria are being praised for this achievement. Now, we find ourselves with an open line of communication, not just through Neria but to both of our neighbors, Kabria and Soland, as well.

Please reach out by clicking here with any video you may have of the chaos in the city, as they will finally be shown to the world.

It's only been twenty-four hours, but there seems to be no mention or any sightings of the Kabrian princess, Genevieve Astor. We do have first-person accounts that the princess had been seen in the palace during the rebels' raid. All this reporter would like to

Made Immortal

say is thank you, Princess. From those of us who saw the struggle and saw you fight for our families and friends, you will never be forgotten.

Edit: Use the link here to see the hundreds of videos submitted in the last hours from across Neria, of the real life accounts of what it had been like under King Edgar Ravensbone's rule.

Kabrian Press Release – Office of the Queen

Today, the country mourns. My father, King Ravensbone of Neria, was one of the most loving and caring people I've ever known. I have fond memories of the palace that has been so heinously attacked. He taught me the lessons that make me the matriarch I had to become after the terrible passing of my husband all those years ago. He taught me compassion for my people; he taught me to always keep them in mind first before all others.

What has befallen him at the hands of the terrorists is a tragedy. We have sent our emissaries to try to work on a release and transfer but have been unsuccessful in our attempts, as the terrorists that have usurped the throne have no intention of making this a peaceful transition. My heart bleeds for Nerians, my countrymen. We will continue to provide support as we can for the people of Neria, to help provide them comfort as their lives will be changed for the worse.

In this attack, it has come to our attention that Genevieve Astor was one of the major players in the

Made Immortal

coup. It pains me that these people have twisted her mind against her own family. Although I love my step-daugher we are putting out a warrant for her arrest. We have redoubled our efforts in locating her. Please see the attached for details on the reward for help in finding her as we work to provide an unwavering peace for our people.

Due to the influx of threats to our way of life, the draft has been reinstated. Military police shall be enforcing and bringing in all recruits. Any attempt to refuse military service will be branded a traitor and executed for treason. We will root out this evil and burn it from our lands.

May the gods look brightly upon us. Your Queen, Esemerlda Ravensbone-Astor

Wanted: Dead or Alive

To all Kabrian military, Genevieve Astor is wanted for treason. Body can be provided dead or alive.

She is armed and considered incredibly dangerous.

From Jupiter Green and Naya Kahn — Wide Release

Many of you knew Marco Diaz. He was instrumental in helping create the support network that turned into the movement that ousted the king and worked toward bringing safety back to our citizens. He treated each of us with respect and made sure we treated ourselves the same. We are grieved to announce Mr. Diaz was confirmed to have been killed in the raid on the palace yesterday. He gave his life to save another, knowing the choice he made would result in his death. He was brave, bold, and kind. We will be setting up a foundation in his honor, training youth to make sure the freedoms of Neria are never again ripped away in such a grievous manner as they had been over the past decade and more. Please reach us here if you have an interest in working with the foundation.

A memorial service will happen next month after the elections have been held and the first council has been convened.

Personnel File

Atticus "Atty" Tora
Age: 22
Expertise: Explosives
Location: Redacted
Status: Deceased
Next of Kin: None

To Group Chat "Dream Team" - From Atty

Hey, guys. I thought I'd write this just on the off chance one of these times I didn't make it home. I've edited this a few times, as I wrote the first one over a year ago. It's so strange to write as if I'm already gone. I know this must be hard for you. I know how death has trailed all of us, and I'm heartbroken to add another to the list. I want you all to know that meeting you was the best thing that had ever happened to me. I've never felt love as I have from

Made Immortal

you, as I have for you. I'm just writing this to beg you, please don't blame yourselves. Don't ask what-if or how could I have? It's just the way the dice fall sometimes, and we can't control everything as much as we want to. I'm not a big talker, so I'll just leave you with this... Remember I love you and you can get through this.

Oh, and kill that witch.

To Gwen - From Atty

Gwen, gods, I wish I had spent my time loving you instead of being scared to try. I wish we had more time. Every second I spent with you was more than I could have ever hoped for. You are kind, you are thoughtful, you are also a complete badass. I'm sorry this happened now. I wish we had years together. But even an eternity with you would never be enough. Please don't cut yourself off. Please lean on the others; they need you as much as you need them. Please remember the good times and not the hurt you feel now. I'm happy we got even the short amount of time together that we did. It's going to be just one step in front of the other for now, but you can do that. You can do anything.

I love you with every fiber of my being, and I'll see you when you get here. (Just be super old when you do.)

P.S. Please empty my library. No one needs to see how many romance novels I have.

ABOUT THE AUTHOR

Marissa has been writing for as long as she can remember. She graduated with a bachelors and masters degrees in creative writing from SHNU.

You can connect with me here and subscribe to my newsletter:
marissaallencreations.com

facebook.com/MarissaAllenAuthor
instagram.com/marissaallenauthor